PRAISE FOR A G

"A recipe for success: engaging, heartfelt characters, sumptuous food that awakens your taste buds, and eloquent prose that keeps you turning the pages . . . This one is not to be missed."

—**Jo Piazza, internationally bestselling author of *The Sicilian Inheritance***

"*A Good Indian Girl* is a heartfelt exploration of learning to first survive, then thrive, after finding your life plan turned upside down . . . A deeply honest tale of letting go and starting over."

—**Sonali Dev, *USA TODAY* bestselling author of *The Vibrant Years***

"A layered exploration of identity and living on your own terms."

—**Saumya Dave, author of *Well-Behaved Indian Women***

"A delight to the senses [and] a story as mouth-watering as the recipes found within these pages. This novel needs a companion cookbook!"

—**Kerry Lonsdale, bestselling author of *Find Me in California***

"A brimming story of culture, family, forgiveness, and self-discovery . . . Shah uses the sumptuous flavors as another character, both to tantalize and to teach. [Her] captivating voice is one to be heard."

—**Rochelle B. Weinstein, author of *What You Do to Me***

"A truly sensory experience—you can almost taste the recipes!—that will leave you hungry for more."

—**Namrata Patel, author of *The Candid Life of Meena Dave***

"A lush, sophisticated coming-of-age story centering travel, found family, and delicious food you can almost taste on your tongue!"

—**Paulette Kennedy,**
author of *The Devil and Mrs. Davenport*

"An immersive journey of self-discovery [that] will wrap you up and hold you riveted until the last page."

—**Lyn Liao Butler, author of *The Tiger Mom's Tale***

"A heartfelt portrayal of going against expectations . . . I loved this delicious story!"

—**Jamie Varon, author of *Main Character Energy***

SAVING FACE

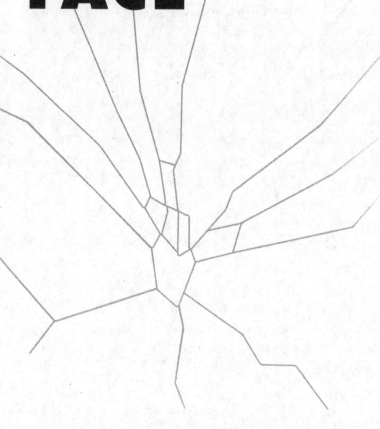

ALSO BY MANSI SHAH

A Good Indian Girl

The Direction of the Wind

The Taste of Ginger

SAVING FACE

A Novel

MANSI SHAH

PARK ROW BOOKS

PARK ROW BOOKS™

Recycling programs for this product may not exist in your area.

ISBN-13: 978-0-7783-6840-3

Saving Face

Copyright © 2025 by Mansi Shah

Title Page Illustration by: Marion Ben Lisa

All rights reserved. No part of this book may be used or reproduced in any manner whatsoever without written permission.

Without limiting the exclusive rights of any author, contributor or the publisher of this publication, any unauthorized use of this publication to train generative artificial intelligence (AI) technologies is expressly prohibited. Harlequin also exercises their rights under Article 4(3) of the Digital Single Market Directive 2019/790 and expressly reserve this publication from the text and data mining exception.

This is a work of fiction. Names, characters, places, and incidents are either the product of the author's imagination or are used fictitiously. Any resemblance to actual persons, living or dead, businesses, companies, events or locales is entirely coincidental.

TM is a trademark of Harlequin Enterprises ULC.

Park Row Books
22 Adelaide St. West, 41st Floor
Toronto, Ontario M5H 4E3, Canada
ParkRowBooks.com

HarperCollins Publishers
Macken House, 39/40 Mayor Street Upper,
Dublin 1, D01 C9W8, Ireland
www.HarperCollins.com

Printed in U.S.A.

For Paulette Kennedy

Every story in life and on the page is made better because of you. Thank you for being one of my root friends.

SAVING FACE

PROLOGUE

January 2002

Ami Shah stood over her maid, Monica Joseph, rifling through a stack of thick envelopes in her hand. "Harvard, Stanford, Melbourne, CEIBS, INSEAD, and LBS. It's hard to choose. Where would you go?"

Monica looked up from the toilet she was scrubbing and barely contained her grimace. Ami remained as oblivious as she'd been since the two had been classmates. Ami was from one of the wealthiest families in Singapore, and despite her mediocre academic record—especially when compared to Monica's perfect grades—it was Ami who had an entire world of possibilities open to her.

"I'm sure life will work out for you regardless of which one you attend," Monica said before turning back to her task.

She checked the underside of the rim to make sure it gleamed a bright white. Whether or not she thought it was fair where her life had ended up, it was ingrained in her to do the best job she could. The Sisters had instilled in all the orphans that they must complete every task to the best of their abilities. Satisfied, she stood and smoothed out the skirt of her gray uniform, knowing it was important to always present herself neatly.

"You're probably right," Ami said, continuing to sift through the glossy leaflets.

Monica would have given anything to attend any of those schools, but she couldn't afford the application fees, let alone the tuition and living expenses, plus what it would cost to leave Singapore. She knew about the hefty fees because she had filled out Ami's applications. Supplying Ami's personal details and life history had been easy because, in addition to working in Ami's home for the past seven years, they had been among the small number of Indian students at the Convent of the Holy Infant Jesus and had spent most of their days together since they were five years old. While Monica had entered the facts of Ami's life precisely, when it came to the essay portions, some of Monica's own ambitions and dreams had spilled onto the page, allowing her to fantasize for just a few moments that the life at the end of that process could be hers.

"It would be nice to say I went to Harvard," Ami mused. "The way people look at you when you casually say you went to school *in Boston* would be so satisfying, don't you think?"

Monica did not occupy the circles in which people said such things, but dutifully peered over Ami's shoulder at the shiny crimson leaflet as if there was nothing else she'd rather be doing right now. Given their long history and shared schooling, Ami sometimes treated Monica as a friend and confidante when they were alone, forgetting or ignoring—Monica was never really sure which it was—how different their lives were. Monica, however, never forgot her place. People at the bottom rarely did.

The pamphlet showed students seated on a lush, verdant

lawn, engaged in deep conversation: an all-American white man with blue eyes and short-cropped blond hair, another white man with brown hair and studious glasses and a crew-neck sweater, a white woman in a twinset, and an East Asian man with suspenders and wired glasses with his attention focused on the others. Monica studied the pamphlet. America had been described as a melting pot, but this photo didn't show it, especially when she was used to seeing Chinese, Malays, and Indians living side by side in Singapore.

Ami stared at her, waiting for a response, so Monica said, "Even maids have heard of Harvard, so you would have the prestige that you like."

"True," Ami said, chewing her bottom lip.

Monica reached for the broom, a signal for Ami to move into the bedroom. She was good about staying out of the way while Monica worked, and hopped onto the bed with her acceptance packets. Monica let out a slow breath as she swept a nearly pristine floor that had only a few loose strands of Ami's hair that had accumulated since Monica had swept it the day before.

"But it's just so far away, and I'm not sure America is a good place to find a husband," Ami said, casting an envelope aside. "CEIBS is the closest to home, but I wonder what kind of men I'd find there. Would they all be Chinese? Or worse, maybe white guys with ethnic fetishes like all the expats around here?"

Monica had no idea what expats were like, beyond what Ami had told her. Ami was the one who went to trendy restaurants in Holland Village and attended events at elitist private clubs like Raffles Town, where foreigners tended to frequent.

"I think the numbers will be on your side no matter where you go," Monica said, as she swept systematically throughout the room.

At Ami's request, Monica had researched the gender makeup,

nightlife scene, restaurant options, and proximity to shopping centers of each of the MBA programs Ami was considering. MBA programs had a far higher ratio of men to women across the board, and with such skewed numbers, at least one of the students was bound to choose Ami, even if for her family wealth rather than her sparkling personality.

Ami looked at Monica and laughed. "I guess it's called an MRS degree for a reason."

If Monica ever had the chance to get her MBA, or even get an undergraduate degree, the last thing on her mind would be marriage. A degree like that would mean a different future. One she could never even dream about. She'd heard stories of people in America and the UK who had been born without money, but had still risen to great heights. Such a move felt impossible in Singapore. But she knew not to linger on such thoughts because the closest she would ever come to America was reading the Harvard pamphlet after Ami was done with it.

Monica watched Ami flipping through the packages, perusing the glossy leaflets that promised futures as captains of industry, quietly seething that Ami's main goal in attending was to find a husband and kill some time before she took over the family business.

When Monica swept near the bed, she paused for a moment to look over Ami's shoulder. "Which one is that?"

"LBS. But I think I can rule that one out. It's far, and if I'm going that far, then I should go for the better rank and name recognition, which is clearly Harvard."

Monica considered how easy Ami's choices in life seemed to be. She supposed hers were the same, in that she had none. If she hadn't been a maid in the Shahs' home, then she'd have been one somewhere else. Choosing between homes in which she would be the help wasn't quite the same as choosing between elite business schools.

"If you want to be close to home, then it seems that CEIBS is the best choice." Monica turned away and continued her sweeping, knowing that was the answer Ami was seeking.

"I guess you're right. I can always transfer to somewhere else if I don't like it." Ami pulled a letter out of the pile with the CEIBS logo on it and checked a box before adding her signature. She jumped off the bed and handed the packet to Monica. "Will you send this out? I need to tell Mum and Dad the news. They'll be so happy. Thanks for helping me decide. You're the best." She pulled Monica in for a hug, not noticing Monica stiffen in her arms.

After letting her go, Ami gestured to the pile of admissions packets on her bed. "Would you also mail back the rejections?"

Ami headed toward the door without waiting for a response. As she was leaving the room, she called over her shoulder, "There are some clothes on the floor in my closet. They are last year's styles, so I don't need them anymore, but you can have them if you want."

That evening, while in her helper's quarters behind the main house, Monica stared at the admissions pamphlet for London Business School. It showed students standing in an archway against a whitewashed building. The covered outdoor areas behind them reminded her of the cloistered walkways at the convent she'd grown up in on Victoria Street. Her eyes lingered on an Indian-looking woman who beamed at the camera, her smile full of possibility and promise.

Monica tried to find similarities between herself and the woman in the photo. Brown skin, dark hair, dark eyes. One of the hardest things about being an orphan was not knowing her heritage. She could be Indian, but she could also be Nepalese,

Pakistani, Burmese, or from any other country in South Asia. The woman in the photo surely knew not only where she was going, but where she had come from.

Monica desperately wished she was about to embark on a journey that would take her far away from her current life. If only the admissions acceptance said her name instead of Ami's. Then, maybe one day she could live in an estate on Goodwood Hill as a resident, rather than the help. Her shoulders slumped and she chastised herself for daring to dream of something that was so far outside of her grasp. Her place was in the servant's quarters where she currently sat, with the twin bed against the wall and the loud thumping noise that happened every time she turned on the hot water in the small bathroom. But she dared not complain about any of it because she knew her circumstances could be worse. There was always someplace lower she could sink.

She flipped through the pages until she found the form to tick the box signifying that Ami would not be attending. Right above it was the box to say that she would. Two entirely different courses a person's life could take separated by mere millimeters on a white page. A couple strokes of a pen that could change a person's life. That could change *her* life if only that letter had been sent to her instead.

Monica's fingers grew clammy around the pen she was holding. An idea was forming in her mind. She had never considered anything like this. Never even entertained the thought because her Catholic upbringing had taught her that God was always watching. Monica embodied the CHIJ motto of *simple in virtue, steadfast in duty*, faithfully living by those beliefs and never questioning the institution in which she'd been raised. But while she knew her place, the Sisters had also convinced her that with a good education, she could excel beyond the circumstances into which she'd been born. She'd held fast to that ideal when she was young and it was rising to the surface now as she stared at the acceptance form, remembering Sister Francis's words that being rich in the mind was far superior to having material goods. "Those can be taken away," she'd said, "but an education will be yours forever."

Monica had held those words close to her heart, but eventually learned that such optimism was a Western attitude Sister Francis had brought over with her from Europe. An orphan in Singapore could never rise above her background. And that meant tending to someone else's home rather than going to university.

But why did it have to be like that? Didn't she deserve more?

She stared at the form in her hand, her pulse quickening. She considered the path ahead that had been paved by the thousands of orphans from CHIJ before her, and decided she wasn't ready to accept her fate without trying to change it. London was a world away, where no one knew Ami Shah or Monica Joseph.

She squeezed the pen and ticked the box.

1

March 2019

Ami Shah built an empire by saving other people's faces. But she did her best to hide her own. As the CEO of an Ayurvedic skin care line, that was no easy feat. She was constantly pressured to be the public image for her brand.

Wearing an aubergine Valentino sheath dress and Prada heels that were described by the designer as "nude" but weren't against her brown skin, Ami looked elegant enough mingling in the backyard pool area of the Viceroy in Santa Monica. Her style and demeanor were demure compared to the influencers, investors, and other guests that her company, Amala, was hosting that evening. She wanted to ensure that the spotlight would always be directed at them, and, most importantly, away from her.

"There's that gorgeous, glowing face," said a milk chocolate–toned beauty influencer named Mira as she leaned in to double air kiss Ami's cheeks.

Mira teetered on her heels, standing far too close to the edge of the swimming pool, her martini sloshing out of her glass. Ami could not fathom why anyone thought the combination of stilettos, alcohol, and water features was a good idea. She flashed her most high wattage smile and took a step back so that Mira would follow and move away from the danger zone. The last thing she needed was a woman with 14.2 million followers falling into the pool while her online frenemies live streamed it.

"You're too kind," Ami said. "We both know you're the beauty people want to see. I'm so thrilled you could join us tonight."

Mira waved her off with false modesty. Her luscious brown skin was the type that never needed a filter, and she always stood as if a camera were trained on her. "I wouldn't have missed it. Some of us who have been with Amala since the beginning were so worried when we heard the announcement."

Ami cocked her head sympathetically. "I know. Hopefully this will put your mind at ease that both Amala and I will be there for our loyal supporters after the merger, just as we have been in the past."

Amala, which meant "clean and most pure" in Sanskrit, had been her baby for the past fifteen years. What had once been a kernel of an idea for a business school assignment had turned into a thriving company. It sometimes still shocked Ami that Los Angeles, the place most synonymous with vanity procedures, enhancements, and superficial quick fixes had become the home of her natural skin care line that focused on healing from the inside out.

Now her baby was in serious merger talks with Propelle, the leading American conglomerate of women's lifestyle brands, which touted a portfolio that ranged from fashion to wellness to fitness and were now looking to round out their portfolio by adding skin care. The only problem was that Walter Johnson, the CEO of Propelle, wanted Amala but not Ami. That part wasn't public yet, in large part because Ami was not about to turn over her inclusive company to a white man in his mid-sixties and was going to do everything in her power to remain exactly where she was. She would never have even considered Propelle's offer if Amala didn't so desperately need the cash. Influencers like Mira had blown them up on social media, but they couldn't fund the inventory to meet the demand, especially with the R&D they'd already invested for a new line. Ami couldn't have anyone knowing that while Amala appeared to be soaring, the company was cash poor.

Mira leaned in conspiratorially to Ami. "I heard a rumor that you have a new line coming out."

Ami tried to hide her surprise that word had gotten out. It wasn't meant to be a secret per se, but she also hadn't been advertising it. In this instance, she didn't see the need to lie. "We do."

The Releaf label that she had poured her heart and soul into—along with Amala's available cash—was Amala's soon-to-be-launched line aimed at helping those with dermatitis-related conditions. It was the crowning glory of her business, because she knew from personal experience how much poor skin health could change the course of an entire life.

Mira's face lit up. "Please tell me you are finally going to put that glowing face of yours on the packages."

Mira was the type that could only see this kind of exposure as something to covet. If only she knew how staunchly Ami had avoided having her face on anything public, and with good reason.

"My face could never compete with yours and those of our other influencers," Ami said.

Mira gave a coy smile. "Well, I can't wait to see the new line and blast it across my socials."

A photographer came closer to them and motioned for Ami and Mira to stand together for a picture, but Ami deftly ducked out of the way before he could take the shot.

She gestured to Mira who was already sticking out her chest and pouting her lips waiting for the flash to go off. "She's the real star."

While the photographer was busy with Mira, Ami made her way through the glammed-up Southern California elite on the lawn. People called out and beckoned for her to join their conversations. She stayed in motion and smiled modestly at the right moments, including when half the attendees called her "Amy" instead of "Ami," and laughed softly when the occasion called for it, like when people offered to set her up. This happened frequently, but she always insisted that she was married to her work. Crowds and schmoozing were a necessary part of life for any successful entrepreneur, and she projected confidence. But it was a facade. She'd never feel like she truly belonged in a group like this.

She saw another photographer approaching and turned her back toward the camera and began chatting with the person behind her.

"Thank you so much for coming," Ami said to Kalisa, another of Amala's influencers.

Kalisa was a Rwandan-born content creator, and with her espresso skin and short natural curls, she was exactly the type of customer Ami had in mind when she came up with the idea for Amala.

She put a hand on Ami's shoulder. "Thank you for recognizing that we can't all use white girl skin products and need something for ourselves."

Ami felt the heat of the flash go off behind her.

Kalisa continued, "I hope that things will stay the same after this merger. I'm sure it's great for you—" Kalisa rubbed her fingers together in the sign for money "—but there is nothing more annoying than finally finding products that work, and then having the manufacturer make some change to the formula. Let's not fix what isn't broken, you know what I mean?"

"I'm doing everything I can to make sure that doesn't happen."

Her company was throwing this party for exactly this purpose: to put their loyal influencers and content creators at ease following the media blitz about Propelle's merger offer with Amala and the frantic messages they'd received in its wake. Amala had come a long way since she'd been hand-packing the products herself from her living room, and she wasn't about to see all that hard work come undone. The brand had grown and developed a loyal following, and she could hardly believe the behemoth that it would become following a merger of this scale. She'd never thought the fabled American Dream was something she could actually achieve.

And while Kalisa was right that Ami had been offered a lot of money to step down, for once, her decision wasn't about the money. It also wasn't about the ego. Although every founder had a healthy one. For her, it was about having a reason to get up every day. Amala was the only thing she knew. She had no family, no friends, no love interests, no real hobbies and no desire to pick up any beyond her sewing. This company was her entire identity, and at forty-two years old, she wasn't ready to start over and reinvent herself. Not again. She had already done that once and knew how high those stakes were. She was Ami Shah, CEO of Amala, today, and she was determined to be that after the deal closed too.

Ami felt a hand on her shoulder and carefully turned to first check if the photographer was still there before locking eyes with Divya, her COO and faithful second in command.

"I'm so sorry to interrupt, Kalisa, but can I steal her away for a moment?" Divya asked.

Kalisa waved them off. "When duty calls, we must answer."

Divya clutched her phone and steered Ami toward a quiet corner of the Viceroy backyard behind a white cabana. Ami and Divya Chandrasekar had known each other since they'd attended London Business School seventeen years ago, and had worked together on Amala since its inception. They were friendly, but not friends in the way that most people would assume given their longstanding history, but that was simply because Ami didn't have close friendships. Not anymore. They were too risky.

Ami tensed at the urgency on Divya's normally calm face, her mind swirling through the various things that could be wrong.

But then Divya smiled, and said in an excited whisper, "You have been nominated for the Global Changemakers Award!"

It took Ami a moment to register the information she'd just heard. The Global Changemakers Award was the most coveted accolade in the entrepreneurial world. It recognized leaders of innovative companies who have had a lasting impact on society. Founded by men in Silicon Valley in 1992, it was created after British inventor Tim Berners-Lee launched the first website in Switzerland and introduced the World Wide Web. Silicon Valley was loathe to be overshadowed by Europeans, so they created their own tribute. Despite having "global" in the title, it mostly had been given to men who looked a lot like the Award's founders, and it had never been given to someone like Ami.

She glanced around to make sure no one else was in earshot. "I didn't apply for anything."

Divya looked like she was about to hug her, but then refrained as if she'd remembered that Ami didn't like to be touched. "There's no application. The industry has recognized your achievements. You were among the first to bring to the Western market an inclusive natural skin care line for people who aren't white, and people are finally starting to pay attention to what we are doing. I know you grew up in Asia where it was normal to have the right products for your skin, but trust me, growing up in the US, that wasn't the case. Amala has helped so many people who are often excluded, and this nomination shows how impactful that work has been." Divya beamed at her.

"They can recognize Amala, but there's no need to make it about me."

Divya looked exasperated. "Why aren't you more excited about this? I never thought we'd see someone like us in the running for something like this. You'd be the first woman and Indian to win the Global Changemakers Award. Think of what it would do for girls who look like us. Actually, you'd be the first ever non-white person to win, so it's even bigger than just our community."

Divya was right that the nomination was groundbreaking, but Ami feared it would be earth-shattering for her. An award at this scale also meant media attention that she could not control. It meant people would start digging into her past. She had worked too hard to get to where she was and was on the brink of saving Amala and launching the dermatitis line that she knew would help so many people who had suffered the way she had as a child. If people learned the truth, she would be stripped of everything, and she could not let that happen.

In a low voice, Ami said, "I don't know if this kind of attention is really a good thing. We have so much to worry about already with the merger."

"This could be exactly what we need. If you win, it could force Propelle to keep you on. The timing couldn't be more perfect to have all eyes on you."

Ami felt like her airways were constricting and her breathing grew shallow and ragged. "I don't want all eyes on me."

"I know you don't like the spotlight," Divya said gently. "Although, I'm not sure why, because if I'd accomplished as much as you have, then I'd be screaming it from the rooftops. But that being said, this is a *good* thing. This kind of visibility could help you keep Amala exactly as you want post-merger. We need to make the most of this opportunity."

Ami glanced at their supporters enjoying the lavish party hosted by Amala. It was a sea of mostly melanin-rich faces. People who were so loyal to what she had built, because every day they were able to use products that they knew were designed for *them*. People that she wanted to continue serving long into the future, because she knew what it felt like to be unseen. She couldn't guarantee Walter Johnson would do that. If anything, she could guarantee that he wouldn't.

Ami clasped her hands tightly at her waist. "This isn't the time for us to shift focus. We are so close to a merger and launching the Releaf line."

"Exactly." Divya's eyes shone. "The winner will be announced two weeks before we are scheduled to close with Propelle. We can use the media attention to our advantage. How would Walter Johnson publicly explain why he is ousting a very capable CEO who is up for one of the most coveted awards of the year, let alone booting you after you win it?"

Ami tensed at the mention of press. She'd done everything she could to avoid the spotlight thus far even though everyone wanted to know "her story." But she'd strategically made the mystery around her part of the allure of the brand. She only did written interviews so she could carefully tailor her answers and ensure her story was always consistent. But she didn't do in-person interviews. Ever.

"The only way to secure Amala's future is to close the deal with Propelle, and we need to be fully committed to that," Ami said.

The upbeat music blaring from the speakers became deafening. A flash of light temporarily made her see spots, and she realized that she'd been so invested in their conversation that she hadn't seen the photographer approach in time to hide her face.

"Please delete that," Ami said brusquely.

The smile washed off the photographer's face and he began to take small steps backward as he fumbled with his camera. "I'm sorry. I hadn't gotten a picture of the woman of the hour."

Ami forced herself to neutralize her tone. "This event is in honor of our clients, so please focus on them. And delete that photo. I don't ever want to see it published."

He nodded and scampered away.

"That poor kid. Was one photo really going to kill you?" Divya asked.

Ami certainly hoped not.

Divya continued, "You are going to have to get past being camera shy really soon. Your face is going to be everywhere once they announce the Global Changemakers nominees."

Ami started to feel an all too familiar itch creeping up her neck and couldn't stop her hand from reaching to touch the area. "This is not what's best for the company."

Divya crossed her arms and looked at Ami sternly. "I don't think this is up to you. They pick who they pick. And even if it were, you're not giving up this award without a fight. This is a big deal for everyone who looks like us, and I'm not letting you throw it away."

Ami didn't bother arguing with her now. They had bigger issues. Besides, CEO trumped COO, so the decision was ultimately hers. She didn't like to play that card often, but she couldn't let the media start poking and prodding into the life she had built without having it crumble around her. She needed to find a way to back out of this award.

2

Ami awoke to a burning sensation on the left side of her neck and gently touched the inflamed skin. The small bumps and dryness were like a familiar, but unwanted, visitor. She removed her silk eye mask, flung back the Egyptian cotton comforter, and made her way to the spacious bathroom adjoining her room. She leaned in close to the mirror to assess the damage. A palm-sized rough leathery patch was glaringly visible along the left side of her neck. She groaned. She hadn't had an issue with her skin in over nine years, and had convinced herself that she'd found the right balance in life that would avoid her having to deal with this again. She should have known that she could never fully expunge her past. The body remembers everything.

She opened a drawer in which Amala products were neatly organized by type. She prided herself on both believing in and using the products she was selling to others. She pulled out Amala's soon-to-be-released Releaf serum. The entire Releaf line was aimed at people suffering from dermatitis, and, while she hoped the products would help with some of her symptoms, the ethos of her company was that true skin health began on the inside and it took time to see results. Nothing could miraculously cure stress-induced eczema, no matter what outlandish proclamations various brands made.

She felt some instant cooling relief from the triphala in the product as she rubbed it in, and applied the serum liberally. She covered that with the Releaf moisturizer that smelled of sandalwood, which was also designed to have a cooling sensation. She hoped it would work as effectively as the R&D testing had suggested, because if she didn't get her eczema under control soon, it would creep up to her jaw and cheeks and eventually her eyelids and forehead—places she couldn't hide with clothing and accessories. She could get by with makeup and styling for day-to-day things, but soon enough people would notice, and it would be hard for her to convince Propelle to buy a skincare company headed by a CEO with unhealthy skin.

She went back to the bedroom to grab her phone and check her schedule for the day, but an endless stream of alerts began as she unsilenced it. She saw emails and texts flooding in from business school classmates and others she had crossed paths with since that time, but with whom she hadn't maintained contact during the years since. The news about the award had gotten out over the weekend and she now had to deal with it.

I saw the nominations, and I am over the moon for you! Becky, a blonde woman from Australia who had been a year behind her at LBS had emailed.

If it can't be me, then I'm glad it's you. Let me know when you're in London next, and we can grab lunch, Alistair, a British LBS classmate had written.

I can't believe your B-school company has come so far. When are you going to have the products available in Asia? Rory, a woman from the Philippines asked.

Never, Ami thought, knowing she would never set foot in Asia again.

Ami couldn't recall having a single meaningful conversation with any of them during her two years at LBS. MBA students were nothing if not opportunistic when it came to making connections, and Ami was now someone worth being connected to. There were more messages of congratulations, many of which felt overly familiar for people whom she hadn't spoken to for fifteen years, and some were even from numbers she didn't recognize. She wondered how those people had even gotten her number. If it was that easy for her former classmates to find her, then there was nothing stopping the media from doing the same thing.

And she was right. The next set of messages were all media requests. *Vanity Fair, Forbes, The New York Times*, the *LA Times, The Washington Post, Entrepreneur*, and so many others. She dropped her phone on the bed as if it were a hot coal.

She panicked at the thought that this media attention could make it all the way across the ocean, and reveal that she had stolen the life of Ami Shah and faked her way into business school. Everything she had done from that point forward hadn't been a lie—it was *her* work that had built Amala. Her brainchild and founded on her ambition. Did it really matter what she'd had to do to get past the gatekeepers in the first place?

As much as she wanted to believe otherwise, she knew that it did. She recalled the day she'd signed the paperwork with the investors to launch Amala. She'd adopted a stoic expression as the lawyer explained the morality clause to her, glossing over it as if it was standard boilerplate and nothing to worry about. It provided that if any of the funding had been obtained under false pretenses, then Ami could be stripped of all her equity in the company that she'd built. It was a standard term in investor agreements. She wasn't worried about the usual things people were protecting against with these clauses: cavorting with sex workers, snorting cocaine, or insider trading. She'd signed the contract believing that she could protect her secrets as long as she stayed on this side of the world and never returned to Singapore.

She began to feel a burning sensation along her midsection, and lifted her shirt to reveal where the skin had already become rough and scaly. She applied the Releaf serum and moisturizer there too. She had to stop thinking about her contract and everything she could lose if she had any hope of bringing down the inflammation that was threatening to take over her body. She would find out who ran the Global Changemakers Award and withdraw from the running. That was the only solution, and she felt her nervous system relax as she realized that she could soon go back to a life where Amala, the Propelle merger, and launching the Releaf line were her top priorities.

She lowered her shirt and stared at her reflection, saddened that she couldn't be excited about something as monumental as being nominated for the Award. She'd watched the parade of white men and occasional white women who'd been nominated for it since its inception, and never thought that she would even have the chance to join that exclusive group. But there was no way she could risk the media attention. Ever since she'd left Singapore, she'd been so careful to keep her face out of the spotlight. She didn't have social media accounts, shied away from photographs, and kept her focus on what mattered most: growing her business. Her chosen name had been a happy coincidence, because there were countless Ami Shahs of all ages in North America ranging from doctors to artists to engineers to landscape architects and everything in between. The only thing she'd ever wanted in life was to avoid standing out, and having one of the most common diasporic Indian names gave her the best possible cover.

She found a high-necked jumpsuit in her closet, and then tied a lavender scarf that matched the Amala logo around her neck as a second layer to hide the problematic areas of her skin. A look in the mirror confirmed that it wasn't good enough, and she removed the scarf.

"Pure love, pure skin," she repeated the Amala slogan that appeared on every label to herself, before applying a healthy amount of department store concealer over her eczema patches. Chemical-ridden makeup would slow down her healing, no doubt, but she didn't have a choice. "There's not always time for pure love, though," she muttered.

She retied the scarf and turned her head to make sure nothing was visible from different angles. Satisfied that between the accessories and makeup no one would notice, she descended the floating staircase in her luxurious modern home along the Venice Canals in Los Angeles. The first floor had initially served as Amala's office when she and Divya had moved to California to launch the company. The home was far nicer than anything they could have afforded, but with the generous help of Leonard Tillman, their first investor, who owned the house, they were able to use it for free. Eventually, Amala became successful enough that they moved operations to a suitable facility in Playa Vista. Divya bought a beachfront condo in a high-rise in Marina del Ray, and Leonard had added the Venice property to Amala's portfolio as a perk for the CEO. "A comfortable entrepreneur makes for a profitable company" had been his exact words.

He wasn't wrong. Without having to worry about any of the big personal expenses like a home or a car that most people had to budget and plan for, Ami's brain was free to focus on Amala's economic growth. Like her home, most of her lavish life was tied to Amala. The high-class travel, restaurants, and glitzy events were paid by the company and she wouldn't have that access without it. People rarely realized that founders had very few assets apart from their companies until there was an event like the Propelle merger that converted the value into cash.

Regardless of whether her lifestyle was supported by the company rather than herself, she was a long way from the orphanage in Singapore where she had grown up. She had exceeded every expectation that anyone on that side of the world could have had for her, and yet she couldn't tell anyone from her old life who she had become. If people learned what she had done to become Ami Shah, then she would lose Amala, and along with it, everything else. Even her visa was tied to the company, and losing that would mean returning to Singapore as the penniless orphan that she'd worked so hard to avoid. She set her jaw. She would not go back. Ever.

3

As soon as Ami got to her office, she began searching for the contact information for the head of the Global Changemakers Committee, but could only find a contact form on the website.

"What happened to actual phone numbers?" she muttered.

There were few things more frustrating than not being able to find a direct number or email address, but she knew that was how organizations operated these days. Amala's website was the same in that a customer would not be able to find any direct access to her. But she couldn't leave a message like this on a random contact form for anyone to find.

After some more searching, she learned the name of the woman who chaired the Committee was Gemma Allen. Now she just had to find a phone number for Ms. Allen, and felt like she could outsource that to her assistant, Pedro. She hit the button that pinged Pedro's desk, and he appeared in the doorway, notepad in hand.

"Yes, boss?"

Pedro had joined Amala four years ago and worked for her

and Divya. He was both a whiz at internet sleuthing and understood the need for discretion. She knew that assistants and helpers were the invisible ears and eyes of a place, and they safeguarded the most sensitive information, which was exactly what she needed right now.

She handed him a sticky note. "Can you please find a phone number for this woman who works at the Global Changemakers Committee?"

His dimples came out as he smiled while reaching for the note. "You know the place is a buzz, buzz, buzz with your good news today."

Pedro had chocolate skin, tiny pores, and high cheekbones, a clear winner of the genetics lottery courtesy of his Black mother and Hispanic father. He made frequent appearances in Amala's social media content that he created, because his bright smile and soulful eyes could sell practically anything.

"Don't get too excited about that," Ami said.

"I don't have to be CEO to know this is a *big* deal. Divya has already had me schedule calls with all the major media outlets. It's going to be like a death match to figure out who gets to tell your story."

Ami's eyes widened. "Don't schedule anything until she and I talk. How long will it take to get that number?" She motioned toward the note in his hand.

He scanned the name. "If I can call the PI, no time at all."

She nodded. "The faster, the better."

True to his word, Pedro returned with a number just a few minutes later. Ami stared at her phone, knowing she had to make the call, but giving herself a moment to feel sad about what she was giving up. She had come so far from CHIJ being the first ever Brown woman nominated for such a prestigious award. Not even any of the paying students from there had ever risen that high. And she *would* be a great example to other women who were coming up behind her. Even though the award and the life that came with it could not be hers, at least she'd always know that she had once risen to that level.

With a heavy heart, she dialed the number Pedro had given her. When Gemma's assistant answered, she gave her name, and was then put through to Gemma.

"Hello, Ms. Shah," said a very perky, quick-talking voice. "It's so nice to hear from you. Congratulations on your historic nomination."

"That's actually what I'm calling about. Thank you for the recognition. It is beyond anything I could have dreamed—"

"It is an extremely prestigious award, and we don't make our choices lightly." Gemma seemed like someone who sustained herself on a diet of caffeine and positive affirmations.

"Yes, I'm sure the process is quite rigorous." Ami spoke more quickly, realizing she needed to match Gemma's pace if she was going to get out what she needed to say. "I'm actually calling to withdraw from the nomination."

"I'm sorry, I think the phone cut out. It sounded like you said *withdraw*." Gemma laughed.

"That's right. I'd like to withdraw."

Gemma chortled. "Withdraw? People are clamoring to get *in*, not trying to get out. I'm not sure I understand."

Ami inhaled sharply. "My company is poised for a significant merger, and we just can't spare the time to deal with what would be needed for this Award."

"We are well aware of the merger, Ms. Shah. It is a big part of why you were nominated."

"Yes, so you'll understand why that has to be a priority."

"Ms. Shah, I don't think you understand what you have at

your fingertips right now. It's recognition for significant contributions to the entrepreneurial world and is something to be proud of. I'm sure a savvy businesswoman like you can parlay this into something beneficial in your merger discussions."

Of course, Ami could do that, if, in fact, she was Ami Shah. But this woman didn't know what was at stake.

"I'm sure you have a long list of people who would be thrilled to take my place," Ami said.

"Naturally, but again, that's not how this works. We announced nominees and you are one of them. That's the protocol. And people are usually thrilled." Ami heard some rustling of papers on the other end of the line. "In fact, I've already emailed with your assistant about the dates for the media outreach. Divya, I believe her name was."

"She's COO, not an assistant. And she was not aware that I'd be pulling out."

"Whatever the case may be, Ms. Shah, as I said before, you can't pull out of the nomination. There's no certainty that you will win, of course. That has yet to be decided. But I would encourage you and your team to keep the press deadlines in mind as I really don't like to chase after people for headshots and things like that. We pride ourselves on presenting polished materials, and I'd hate for anyone to stand in the way of that."

Ami felt a sinking dread knowing this was proceeding with or without her cooperation. Even if she tried to hold back her headshot, it seemed clear this woman was going to ensure that she got something to complete her press materials. The danger had already started because it was the media attention leading up to the announced winner that could expose her, not the winning itself. She wasn't sure how to avoid what was inevitable now, but she had to think of something.

After hanging up with Gemma, Ami asked Pedro to send Divya in.

When Divya came into her office, Ami motioned for her to close the door behind her.

"You emailed Gemma at the Global Changemakers Award?"

"Yeah, why?" Divya said, as she took a seat across from Ami.

"I told you I was going to pull out of the nomination."

Divya looked at her. "I didn't think you were serious. Can you even do that?"

"Apparently not." Ami crossed her arms over her chest.

"You are the only person I know who wouldn't be rubbing this in the faces of everyone we went to school with. It's just some media attention—which is great for Amala. I know you're worried about it taking time away from merger diligence and the Releaf line, but I can handle most of it, and you just have to show up for the photo shoot, do an interview or two, and then you're done."

Ami's mind was swirling as she grasped for solutions. "Why don't you do the interviews? You know as much about Amala as I do."

Divya was excellent at dealing with the press and did most of Ami's written interviews herself, but they both knew the reality was that the media preferred Ami. She had a "better" look for Western society with her socially accepted body size, large eyes, and clear complexion. That is, when she wasn't battling the eczema that currently pocked her skin. Divya's face and figure were round and fleshy, and although she was just as capable, she didn't photograph in the way that people preferred when trying to sell beauty products or news.

Divya laughed. "This isn't an interview about Amala. Sure, you'll talk up our brand as is expected. But this is an interview about *you*. How *you* brought luxurious products that work on skin like ours to the Western Hemisphere. People want to hear your story about growing up in Singapore and taking for granted that these were at your fingertips. Of moving to London and going everywhere from Boots to Fortnum & Mason and realizing no one bothered to carry products that would work with your melanin-rich skin." Ami groaned. "They want to hear how you were baffled when people in London kept telling you how good you looked for your age, and asking what your secret was. And how you realized those expectations were based on white skin, which doesn't age the same as brown skin."

This was why Divya would be perfect at the interviews. She knew Ami's practiced story as well as Ami did. To Ami, it had been a simple concept that the needs of brown skin weren't being met by the skin care industry in the West. The ingredients and application should be different, along with the approach to aging, and her products had filled that void for so many women of color living in the Western Hemisphere who hadn't realized there was another way.

"And look how well it worked." Ami removed her scarf and revealed her red blotches.

Divya grimaced. "That looks painful. Like starting Amala from scratch painful."

"It doesn't feel great."

"I guess that explains the scarf. I had suspected, but was hoping I was wrong."

Ami had learned to use the scarf as a shield when her skin wouldn't cooperate, and Divya knew Ami only wore it when she had something to hide.

"The timing is far from ideal, especially if the Global Changemakers Award expects a big photo shoot."

Ami could see that Divya's wheels were already spinning into crisis control mode.

"Is it merger stress?" she asked.

Ami couldn't tell her the real reason, so she shrugged her shoulders, allowing the words to hang between them. Over the years, she'd learned that people attributed silence to the answer that aligned with their assumption.

Ami's eczema was triggered by stress. She'd had a serious bout of it after she'd turned up at LBS as Ami Shah. She'd blamed it on the weather, but knew that it was from pretending to be Ami. She'd had another when moving to Los Angeles and starting Amala, fearing she'd be caught when she was on the brink of having everything she'd dreamed of. She and Divya had been living under one roof so there was no hiding anything from her during that time. And then during the recession in 2009 when they weren't sure if they could keep Amala afloat, it had reemerged. But since stabilizing the company and pushing it into growth mode, she'd been clear of any issues until now. The uncertainty of the merger and the fear of exposure had clearly tipped her over the edge.

"Let's just keep you hydrated and as free of stress as we can for the time being." Divya picked up her notebook. "We have more pressing issues to deal with before the photo shoot. We've gotten interest from practically every major print and video outlet in the country. We also have some freelance journalists who want to do the interview and then sell it to AP or other publications. LBS is going to do a feature on you for its magazine, but I already took care of that one over the weekend. It was just an alumni article with written questions, so nothing to think twice about."

Ami's eyes narrowed. "If you want me to be free of stress, then getting rid of this whole media piece would be a start."

Divya looked at her sympathetically, but her expression made clear that wasn't possible.

"Why are people so focused on this?" Ami said. "We didn't

get nearly this much interest when the merger with Propelle was announced, and that is a far bigger deal."

"To you, maybe. The first South Asian woman to be nominated for an award that has exclusively gone to white men since its inception twenty-seven years ago? The story practically writes itself."

Ami covered her face with the scarf. "I can see the headlines now: Skin care maven suffers from eczema. Her products are a scam."

"We will make sure your skin is as pristine as possible before setting up anything in person. But we have to let someone take the lead on the interview. An exclusive is the best way to have some influence on the narrative."

Ami sat straighter. "I like having control. Maybe we can make them focus more on the products and less on me. I'm just one person in a much larger team that has worked hard for over a decade to get here."

Divya was jotting notes. "That's a great line. Definitely suggest you use that in the piece. Humility is good. And people especially want to see that from women, so it tracks."

These types of interviews went very differently with men.

Ami met her eyes pleadingly. "Is there any way to skip this part? You know I hate talking about myself and having people pry into my personal life."

Divya lowered her notebook and met Ami's eyes. "Just think of all the good this can do. I'm not sure what you're worried about. This is designed to be a puff piece where people get to congratulate themselves on how far they've come by nominating a Brown woman. That's it. You just have to be yourself, and that's enough. They'll snap some photos, run a story about how progressive the world is becoming, and if we are lucky, you win, and then we get more favorable deal terms, including you staying on and keeping the team intact—including me. Or you have this award on your CV forever and can find some VCs for a new project—and you, of course, take me with you."

It sounded simple, except for the part about being herself. She hadn't been that person for a long time. Staring at Divya's hopeful face, Monica wondered what would happen if she just told her the truth. Divya was the closest thing she had to a friend in this life that she'd built, and carrying her secrets was starting to become lonely. She thought about the merger closing and her team toasting with a glass of champagne and then her feigning mysterious plans she had to dash off to, only to return to her empty house to drink wine alone with her needlework. There had been a time in her life when she'd made genuine connections rather than always keeping people at arm's length, but those days felt like another lifetime, and she began to wonder if that part of herself that she'd buried so deep could ever be unearthed again.

Divya was staring at her notepad, and Monica opened her mouth, not sure what words would come out, but then Divya spoke without looking up.

"This one is interesting. Naira Kaur. Could be nice to have an Indian reporter. You don't see too many of those. She'd appreciate how significant this is."

Monica retreated back to Ami as she felt her earlier moment of weakness slip away. Divya was focused on Amala and that was where she needed to be, too, and, whether or not she liked it, that job belonged to Ami Shah and there was too much at stake to be anyone else right now. So, if that meant there was going to be an article about her, then she wanted to control as much as she could about that narrative.

"No," she said too quickly and too forcefully.

Divya looked surprised by her reaction.

"You know how Indian women can be," Ami rushed to say. "Always competing with each other."

Divya gave her a quizzical look. "We aren't competing with each other."

Because there's no competition. It's my company and you work for me, Ami thought, but would never say aloud.

To Divya, she said, "I don't want to make it about being Indian. This is about my achievements as a human being, right? I'm not being measured by some lower bar because I'm an Indian woman, am I?"

"Of course not, but it doesn't have to be black-and-white. Giving the exclusive to one of our own could help elevate her career on such a big story too. Brown women helping each other out and all of that. We shouldn't squander this opportunity."

Ami chewed her bottom lip. "I think it's better to go with experience. I imagine she has less than the others."

Divya rolled her eyes. "Really? The experience excuse? The white men are going to have more experience because the world is set up to give them that. How many times have we discussed that when looking for our own investors? We had to go with white men because that's where the money was and there was no other choice."

Ami shot her a look, and Divya corrected. "Maybe not the entire world, but definitely the part we live in now."

Ami and Divya had spoken many times about how Ami had needed to adjust to white privilege after moving to the Western Hemisphere because Singapore had a Chinese majority. What they had not discussed, however, was that Ami also had to get used to a patriarchal system as well. Having grown up within the confines of the Town Convent, she had spent her life influenced almost exclusively by strong, capable women, and men hadn't played any role at all.

Divya consulted her notes. "That said, Naira Kaur was at *The New Yorker* right out of journalism school and now has been freelancing for a few years."

"I know you want to lift everyone up and help bridge the inequities, but let's pick one of the older people who will be efficient and get this done quickly. We have a lot to get through for the merger and the Releaf launch. We don't need to spend any more time on this media distraction than is absolutely necessary."

Ami offered a half smile to ease some of the tension in the room. She understood why Divya wanted to pick the Indian reporter. But it was out of the question. Ami hadn't had an Indian childhood or upbringing and other Indians could often sniff that out from miles away. She didn't even know if she *was* Indian. She'd been as thorough as she could when she adopted the ways of a wealthy Gujarati woman, but it was when she was around other Indians that she felt most like an imposter. Indians, especially in the West, seemed to fall into one of two camps: the ones who steadfastly clung to their ancestral heritage and the ones who shed it in order to assimilate into white culture. But even the latter group knew themselves and their backgrounds well enough to know which parts of it needed to be hidden. She didn't need a hungry young reporter from either of these camps pulling at the threads in the delicate tapestry she'd carefully woven.

Divya sighed. "Most of the other people on the list are white guys with names like Harlan Cooper or Robert Montgomery. Do you really want to trust your story to someone like that?"

Ami shrugged.

Divya closed the notebook. "Let me at least have an initial chat with Naira. She's called me every day since the announcement was made practically begging for the opportunity, and I think she'll do a good job. So, let me tease that out and come back to you."

Ami didn't want someone who was that hungry for the job, but she knew there wouldn't be any way to convince Divya now. Divya had always been in the first camp of Indians and did everything she could to maintain and elevate Indian culture. She'd let Divya do whatever due diligence she wanted, and then ultimately pull rank if she had to in order to avoid this. Divya might not understand just how much they could lose, but Ami certainly did.

4

Later that afternoon, Ami was at her desk staring at the Pacific Ocean instead of the cash flow analysis in front of her. But turning away wouldn't change the numbers. Amala's growth in the past eighteen months had been rapid as some big influencers like Kalisa and Mira began to tout the products across their social media channels, but rapid growth also needed rapid investment to satisfy the new orders. And they'd already been positioned to launch the Releaf line and had invested heavily in R&D for that prior to blowing up on social media. It was the perfect storm of increased sales against diminished cash flow and very limited inventory.

Without the deep pockets and widespread distribution arm of a conglomerate like Propelle, Amala would cease operations in the coming months, so the merger was extremely pivotal. If all went according to plan, Propelle would see its investment increase exponentially within the first few years, so it was worth them taking on what might otherwise seem like a risky investment. And given their scale, if they acquired Amala and it failed, it was just a line item loss they could use to offset their gains in another area. It was only the Amala team that would suffer, and Ami was determined to ensure that Amala remained a success.

She was stressed about the numbers but also about the Changemakers Award. She carefully lifted her blouse to reveal the dry, scaly red blotches that were expanding. They were more painful and itchy than the patch on her neck, but at least these were easy to cover up with clothing and didn't need to be further irritated with makeup. She took some deep breaths and tried to convince herself that if they found the right reporter, she could get through a puff piece. She'd been careful about the public information that anyone could dig up about her, so there would be very little that could contradict her carefully constructed story.

She locked the door to her office before opening the bottom drawer of her desk and pulling out her loom with a half-finished piece stretched within it. Her nervous system began to calm as she felt the familiar fabric. The image was of a villa set against a grayish-blue sky and swirling water. She ran her fingers over the bargello stitches she'd used to help show the movement of the water. She'd always been good at embroidery, the needle feeling like an extension of her body as she deftly formed intricate patterns with precision. She loved how delicate thread could be woven into something so strong with the right care and attention. It was a skill the Sisters had impressed upon the girls, because it was one of the few forms of income that could generate additional funds to help keep the orphanage, schools, and convent running. Monica had become quite adept and her work had been highly sought during her time there.

Now she could afford to buy any designer piece of clothing she wanted, but found that when she was alone pushing her needle through cloth and feeling the thread follow until taut, she felt most like herself. Embroidery was the only part of her past that she'd carried into her new life. She had never let anyone catch a glimpse of that side of her, worried it would bring questions that would need more lies, and she was determined to keep one area of her life pure. But she always kept it near, so that if she ever needed to remind herself of who she was, the answer was never far away.

She plucked the needle from the loom and began to work on the thatched roof of the villa, using a blanket stitch so she could give the straw texture and depth. She was deep into her work, her fingers creating the image stitch by stitch, when her cell phone buzzed and a familiar name appeared on the screen. It had been years since they had spoken but curiosity prevented her from letting it go to voicemail.

"Oli," she said hesitantly, as she placed the loom back into its hiding place. "To what do I owe the pleasure?"

Oliver Dalton had been at LBS with her, but given their complicated past, the two had remained only loosely connected in that business-school way of being cordial with potential future contacts.

"I dare say congratulations are in order," he said.

Despite the fact that he had also moved to Los Angeles after LBS, he'd made no attempt to sound more American the way Ami had, and he still maintained his posh, aristocratic British accent. A white guy with a European accent was adored in America, but a Brown girl with an Asian accent definitely wasn't.

"Congratulations for me, or for you?" Ami asked. With Oliver, she never really knew.

He let out a chuckle. "I suppose for us both, really. It seems we shall be in a bit of competition again."

Ami widened her eyes. Of course. She had been so focused on how to get out of this predicament for herself, that she hadn't bothered to check who else had made the list. "You were nominated too."

"Indeed. Anyway, I just called to extend my sincere congratulations. I wasn't surprised to see your name on the list, given the current climate and all. I was a bit gobsmacked to learn I'd made the short list. Never fear though, I suspect you are a far more likely winner than me."

Ami gritted her teeth at his implication.

"Yes, well," she began, her voice laced with a sweetness that they both knew was unnatural to her, "as I understand it, it has historically been quite difficult for men like you to achieve this award." She smiled smugly.

She'd admittedly had very little interaction with white men prior to moving to London, but Singapore's colonialist background combined with CHIJ's European ties meant she knew history was replete with examples of them succeeding at rates that far exceeded what would have been possible from a meritocracy. It seemed clear that an ingrained societal favoritism had been at play, but she couldn't figure out how or why it had started. After living in England and America, she had learned that people like Oliver wanted to downplay their privilege and pretend their whiteness didn't have an outsized value. She would never understand why anyone would want to act like they were from a social position that was lower than what they were.

Oliver cleared his throat. "I didn't call to fight. I genuinely wanted to say that I'm proud of you." He sounded more contrite and quickly said, "And I don't mean that in any patronizing or paternal or any other misogynistic or anti-feminist way. I only meant to say that it's really magnificent to see you turn a school project into the business it is today."

Ami unclenched her jaw, sensing that his sentiment was genuine even if his words could use some finessing. Matching his softer tone, she said, "Does that mean you are no longer holding a grudge that Amala is the one the investors picked?"

Oliver laughed. "Grudge is a bit harsh, now, isn't it? It may have taken some extra years and a tad more legwork, but I eventually managed to get one of my ideas off the ground. Enough to be in your esteemed company today."

Ami smiled wryly. "Your dad must be so proud."

"Pride isn't an emotion he's prone to doling out, especially to me, but I did get a 'well done, chap,' so I suppose that's as good as I can expect."

Oliver came from a wealthy British family and his father was one of the most prominent venture capitalists in England. Oliver had a built-in safety net of knowing that Dalton Holdings Limited would always be able to fund his latest venture, as long as he could convince his father, and that was exactly what happened with the garden seed bed company he had started following the 2009 recession.

"It was never a competition for me. You know that, right?" Ami said. "I just wanted to do well in school and then use that education to do something meaningful. I never expected to get the funding from Leonard after that pitch."

"I know. It almost made it worse. You got it without even trying. But that's all then and this is now."

It was this rare vulnerable side of Oliver that had charmed her during business school. Enough to start dating him after he'd returned from their first winter break newly single, like so many of their classmates.

"Exactly," Ami said. "And UrbanGreen is doing so well. You've really made a difference."

Oliver had kicked around a few ideas after LBS, but couldn't find the right funding or convince his dad to invest in any of them. Entrepreneurship was a delicate balance of the right idea, at the right time, with the right resources to back it. His idea of turning small spaces like the tops of bus stops and other previously wasted areas into gardens that generated herbs and other produce had been innovative at a time when people were interested in urban gardening, eating local, and reducing waste. Finally, he'd had an idea that his dad was willing to support.

"Thanks, Ami. That's very kind of you to say."

Ami had actually used UrbanGreen seed beds to plant herbs in her front garden in Venice, and she mulled over disclosing that to him. It was a true marker of the quality of his product, because she was far from having a green thumb. He'd bought her some plants while at LBS, but they had promptly withered and died. She blamed the lack of sunlight in the UK, and he had blamed her, and while she'd never admit it, she suspected he was correct.

She bit the inside of her cheek, not ready to give him the satisfaction of knowing she was a customer. "I really mean it. It's been too many years, and I dare say it's nice to hear your voice. And congrats on your nomination. It's well deserved."

"I imagine the reporters are banging down your door as they are mine?" he said.

"Fortunately, that's Divya's area to handle."

"This one called Naira has been especially persistent. I imagine for you as well?"

"Divya mentioned her."

"She seems keen on interviewing us both. She loves the fact that we were at LBS together. Are you going to use her?"

"I think Divya is still working out who would be best."

"She's quite the looker." Oliver let out a low whistle.

"Of course, that's how you'd base your decision."

"I can't help that I have eyes," Oliver said in a chagrined tone.

"Pity you can't see me rolling mine."

"You're right. I'd better opt for the video call next time so I can get the full Ami Shah effect."

"Bye, Oli," Ami said, her tone playfully annoyed. "Thanks for the chat."

She hung up and considered the many contradicting sides of Oliver that she'd seen over the years. He was the epitome of privilege, someone who had seen very little hardship in his life. Since getting to Los Angeles, he'd become a cliché who was often seen with twentysomething aspiring models, actors, writers, illustrators, or designers. But with her, he had been genuine and vulnerable on a number of occasions. She doubted that courtesy would have extended to every person in his life, and she wondered if the way she ended things with him so abruptly in B-school had contributed to the way he now treated women. Some scars could never be fully erased.

She shook her head at the coincidence that they'd both been nominated in the same year. He would no doubt be doing everything possible to win, not just for himself, but to prove himself to his father. She'd always thought people with money never worried about acceptance, but through Oliver, she had seen that even a bottomless bank account couldn't erase self-doubt. Seeking his father's approval, but always feeling like he'd fallen short, had been a frequent topic of conversation during their time at LBS. She'd always felt like he put so much undue pressure on himself, and never understood why he needed other people to think he'd achieved everything on his own rather than on the backs of the generations before him. That type of existential crisis felt like a luxury that only those of a certain means could even entertain. To her, it seemed ludicrous to not take advantage of all the resources someone had available. She'd certainly never tried to make life harder than it needed to be just to battle some inner sense of worth. There were enough external reminders that she wasn't worthy, so she never felt the need to manufacture more.

5

As Ami walked from her office to the conference room to meet the Board a couple days later, her phone buzzed in her hand. She saw a text that said: From CHIJ to Global Changemaker. It was from a number that wasn't saved and she didn't recognize the area code. No one had referred to CHIJ around her in a long time, but she'd gotten so many random messages since the Global Changemakers nomination, that she didn't think much of it. She slipped her phone into her pocket—she would figure out who it was later. Right now, she had to put on her founder face and play her part.

She stepped into Amala's nicest conference room and took in the sun setting over the Pacific Ocean outside the panoramic windows. She still marveled over the luxury of seeing this view every single day. Singapore was surrounded by water, but her world there had been so small that she had never seen the ocean. Leonard and their other four board members, all middle-aged or older white men, were already in the room, sipping coffee, while Divya sat with her laptop, ready to take notes, wearing a polite smile. Both of them had perfected the polite smile over their years working with these men.

"There she is," Leonard said as Ami entered the room. "Our shining star. I knew we picked the right horse all those years ago."

After a decade of sidling up to these men who controlled the purse, she had grown accustomed to comments like those.

"It's nothing, really," Ami said, with a courteous smile. "An award can't save our company, but the merger can, so let's not lose focus."

Chad Knight, a man in his mid-fifties who was an investor from their funding round in 2009, stepped forward to give Ami a hug. He was also the most "overly familiar" with female entrepreneurs, and Ami tensed at the physical contact and squirmed away. Men never invaded the personal space of other men. If they wouldn't choose the urinal directly next to someone in a public toilet, then there was no need to embrace a woman in a conference room.

Chad seemed oblivious to Ami's inching away from him and didn't give her more space. "You might be wrong there, Amy. This is the best combination an investor could ask for."

Despite the years they'd known each other and the millions she had earned him, he still hadn't managed to learn the correct pronunciation of her three-letter name. She supposed she shouldn't be too offended though because he also anglicized the name of his current Asian wife, as well as the two before her.

"And the timing. We couldn't have scripted that better ourselves." Steve Radin stood behind his chair and beamed at Ami. Unlike Chad, who served as little more than an ATM, Steve at least was good with stretching their budget, especially during the times when cash flow was very lean. He should be, given that despite often being the wealthiest one at any table, Steve was the last to grab for the check. No one knew better than him how to utilize other resources in order to conserve your own. He narrowed his eyes in a joking manner. "Did you pay someone to make this happen?"

Ami balked. "Of course not." She'd have paid someone to *not* have this attention if she'd had any warning.

Leonard came to her side and guided her toward a chair. "Come now. You know our Ami is too ethical for any of that. Beauty starts from the inside out, and all that stuff we say in our marketing." He gave Ami a wink. "This girl right here, you couldn't pay her to tell a lie. Isn't that right?"

Ami's eyes met Leonard's, and she tried not to think about her morality clause as she gently adjusted her scarf to make sure it was covering as much of the blossoming angry red skin on her neck and chest as possible.

"You know me, Leonard." She cleared her throat. "Can we get back to hammering out the final details of the Propelle deal?"

Kyle Cunningham waved her off. "Chad's right. We need to make sure you win the Award. That is now the main event. Given the timing, we should add a clause in the merger that the value goes up if you do. Every other company whose founder has won it has blown up practically overnight. Propelle shouldn't get that windfall without giving us a piece of it."

He was the newest board member and deepest pocket—old money passed down through generations—but still always wanted more. Leonard had gone to business school with him and vouched for him and especially his contacts, so Ami and Divya had relented to him joining the team. To Leonard's credit, it was Kyle's network and relationship with Walter Johnson that had led them to Propelle in the first place.

John Bradley chimed in. "Excellent point, Kyle. It almost makes me wonder if we want to do the deal at all. We would likely have a lot more suitors after Ami wins that Award, and nothing raises the value more than competition. I can think of some European brands that might be interested if Amala is more recognizable. There's brown skin there, too, right?"

John was a true trust fund baby and bachelor, having been wise enough to never put himself in the position of owing anyone alimony or child support. He had enough money to see any part of the world, but he split his time between Western Europe and America, never deigning other parts worthy to visit, but that meant his contacts in Europe were second to none, and if he thought he could get some interest there, then he probably could.

Ami paused for a moment, thinking about what it would mean if Amala did get enough money just by her nomination and could fund the purchase orders without Propelle. Maybe they wouldn't need the merger and she would be able to keep everything in place, just how she wanted it. But then she shook her head at how unlikely it was that she would win at all, let alone win without her past coming back to haunt her. She and Divya had considered all the options when Kyle proposed the Propelle merger, and both had come to the unfortunate conclusion that the only way to keep the company afloat was to cede some of their control in exchange for money. As much as Ami wished there were another choice, that was still the best solution because the other options were unreliable and would likely not meet the timeline they needed.

"We need to focus on the bird in the hand," Ami said to the group. "It's easy to get starry-eyed at the possibility of more, but let's not forget that Amala doesn't survive without a major influx of cash. We can't throw out our best option in the hopes that I win an award that leads to an overnight increase in sales by a significant multiple, and that the money comes in quickly enough to stay afloat."

Leonard rubbed his chin. "I like Kyle's idea best. We keep

going with Propelle and include a kicker for if Ami wins." He flashed her a bright, fatherly smile. "And I'm sure she will, so we better make it a good kicker."

"Just picture it," Chad said, spreading his hands apart as if seeing her name in lights. "Amy Shaw. The first South Asian woman to win the Global Changemakers Award. That's money in the bank. We can slap Amy's pretty face on every media outlet."

Ami held her tongue as he butchered both her first and last name, as if she were of Irish descent rather than Indian, and then made plans for the use of her body without consulting her. "I really appreciate the enthusiasm, but we don't know if I'm going to win, and we need a strategy that doesn't hinge on that. Propelle was interested in us before anything about the Global Changemakers came up, so let's make sure our deal isn't contingent on that."

"We're not saying it will be contingent," Kyle said. "Just that we get cut in if your value goes up right before we close. A little extra cash never hurt anyone. Am I right?"

Ami looked at these five men who had absolutely no need for more money. It had become sport to them—more for the sake of more. These men would have no change in their lives or spending habits based on whether this deal went through, regardless of the number of zeros on the final amount. She couldn't imagine operating from such an immensely wealthy baseline. And although this deal would be a drop in the bucket to her investors, it would give her and her team more security and freedom than they could ever have dreamed. She didn't know how that type of financial windfall would change her entire outlook on life, but she vowed to do everything possible not to take it for granted like the men around her.

"Speaking of cash, I've looked at the latest financials and we are spending a lot developing this new Releaf line that much of the market doesn't need," Steve said. "Aren't we better suited holding off on more R&D until after the merger to keep our books looking tight? Especially since Kyle mentioned Propelle wants to kill that line anyway."

Ami set her jaw. "I think you'll be surprised by how many people have skin conditions that they are trying to hide. Divya and I have conducted plenty of market research and I'm sure the numbers will convince Walter Johnson that the Releaf line is not only socially necessary but financially sound. The market rate for self-confidence is higher than you might realize." She adopted a breezier tone. "Besides, R&D in India is far cheaper and more efficient than it would be anywhere else given that our Ayurvedic ingredients are local and the developers are familiar with the concepts."

This group had no understanding of the Ayurvedic roots in which all Amala products were based, and that was something she and Divya used to their advantage. Divya's family was from Tamil Nadu and her access to Ayurvedic doctors and herbs was a big part of why she was the perfect second in command for Amala. Her connections helped make things far smoother than if Ami had tried to source ingredients on her own with no knowledge of the culture. It was through Divya that she learned about the three doshas—the fundamental energies that comprise the body's functioning—and which ingredients would work across all of them and suit the majority of the population. She coupled that knowledge with her own skin treatments in Singapore and found the right natural blends. Prior to starting Amala, Ami had never set foot in India, but fortunately white investors looked at her brown face and made assumptions that, in this case, were beneficial to her. They didn't need to know that when she started, she had known as little about India and Ayurveda as they did.

Divya chimed in. "The pricing we negotiated for the larger

orders will help bring down our COGS and increase our margins. So, if our data is correct about the demand for this type of product line, then we should see profitability relatively quickly."

"All that matters is if you can convince Propelle that you're right." Kyle rubbed his thumb against his fingers.

Ami caught Divya's eyes as the men went around the table throwing out more comments about how imperative it was to get the most out of this deal. That had been her goal, too, when she'd started Amala—to profit from recognizing a need in the marketplace. It was the starting place of any good idea. And, in turn, would give her a life that she could never have otherwise had. But over the years, Amala had taken over more and more of her identity. Not just because of the lifestyle that came with it—although, there was no denying that part was nice and she had no desire to give it up—but also because she really did believe in the mission. She deeply understood how it felt to be overlooked. The internal damage it caused was the same, regardless of the reason, which was why she truly believed they were selling more than simply skin care.

She couldn't imagine waking up each day and not serving the needs of people who looked like her, Divya, Mira, or Kalisa. Her life felt like it would be meaningless without that, and she had given up so much of herself to make sure she found a life that was not only profitable, but meaningful. One where she could assume her full potential, and even she had been surprised by just how far she had come, especially given how many secrets she was harboring that had the power to unravel everything she had built.

After the meeting ended, as the rest of the men headed toward their Teslas that would take them to their multi-million-dollar, energy-guzzling homes, Leonard pulled Ami aside.

"Are you sure about this?" he asked.

"What do you mean?"

"Staying on with Propelle. Aren't you better off moving on? When a new parent comes in, they have their own way of doing things. A vision for the mark they intend to leave on their new asset. Your payout will be higher if you get out now rather than go with them and then try to exit after things aren't going well."

"That's exactly why I need to be there," Ami said. "They'll take Amala and strip the products of the saffron and gold because those ingredients are expensive and difficult to source. They'll make the products low-cost and generic so they can sell to Midwestern housewives. And I know they'll shut down production on the dermatitis line because they think it won't have mass appeal."

"Would it be so bad if the products were at a price point that made them accessible to more people?"

Ami clenched her jaw. "Profit margins are much higher for products geared toward the affluent. You know that as well as I do. Getting higher quality ingredients and raising the pricing is what saved us in the past. Skin care is a luxury to the lower classes whose spending is dictated by the prices of necessities like gas, heating, electricity, and groceries. But to the affluent, their skin care routines are a necessity and don't fluctuate with the economy. It was by going up a couple class tiers that we pulled ourselves out of our downward spiral after the 2009 recession. Propelle doesn't have all that history. Why sacrifice those margins with an inferior product to end up back at the same profitability, or maybe even a worse one the next time there is a global event that impacts spending for lower classes? Not to mention, the only way to have a more widespread brand at a lower price point is to make something generic that no longer serves the inclusive market that was the bedrock of this company in the first place."

Leonard sighed. "I'm thinking about you. The personal headache that goes with swimming against the tide after a takeover is never fun."

"It's a merger."

He cocked his head. "It's a takeover. It doesn't matter what people call it, it's always a takeover."

He was right. But he didn't understand that this was about more than money to her. Having grown up poor, she knew that catering to the rich was the only way to be accepted by them. No matter how much money she had in her bank accounts, if she had a product that involved standing in Walmart and offering samples to stay-at-home moms, then she'd never be the person invited to upper-class events like art openings or the symphony. She'd sacrificed a lot of herself to earn these coveted places in society, and she wasn't about to give it all up.

"There's no deal without me staying exactly where I am," Ami said.

Leonard ran a hand over his shiny bald head. "This is the best exit we are going to get, and we have to make it work. You're smart. You'll think of something new if they dig their heels in and want their own management."

She was smart. Smarter than most of her childhood peers had given her credit for. She wasn't meant to amount to anything. No one in her position ever had. She'd exceeded all expectations. But she couldn't start again. She *wouldn't* start again. It had been hard enough to build the life she had now on the foundation of lies she'd created. She wasn't ready to knock it all down and try to start over. Try to go through another vetting process of her background. To go through another thick contract with a morality clause that she knew she had broken even before signing. With Amala, she'd gotten past the difficult part, and was finally able to worry less about whether her past would come out and she'd be stripped of everything she'd earned. And she would be if any of the board members learned the truth before this deal closed. There was no loyalty where money was concerned.

"I'm sorry, Leonard. Maybe you all get a few fewer bucks if I stay on, but I doubt you're even going to notice."

He seemed to capitulate. "I know you grew up with a silver spoon in Singapore, but just remember that there are people who live a different life than you do, and they deserve good products too."

She held back a laugh at his suggestion of her childhood. If only he knew. Thanks to Western media, Americans seemed to think that everyone in Singapore was eating at Michelin-starred hawker stalls, moving through the city in fancy cars helmed by uniformed drivers, and living in palatial estates guarded by former Sikh military. That media bias had made it much easier for people like Leonard to believe her fabricated life in Singapore, but none of this was the real Singapura for the majority of its citizens. When the colonizers segregated Singapore, they focused on the Chinese majority and glossed over the Indian and Malay communities, pushing them to the outskirts. Centuries later, the effects of not being the ethnicity that the British had chosen to elevate could still be felt, and those deeply entrenched systems could not be undone even though much effort had been made to try to undo the segregation imposed by the British, even down to quotas mandating that certain numbers of Chinese, Indians, and Malays worked and lived together. But once a hierarchy was established, it was very difficult to change. Individuals at the top rarely volunteered to demote themselves for a greater good, so while the races integrated, the class differences within the country became more pronounced.

Class, rather than her skin color, was the immutable characteristic that she had been born into and could not transcend beyond. Class was the reason she'd done what she had to leave Singapore. What people failed to realize was that wherever great wealth was visible, great poverty also lurked in the shadows. And most people living in the darkness would do anything to move into the light.

6

The next day, Divya came into her office and handed her a glossy leaflet with the LBS logo on it.

"This is that alumni interview I sent in for you in case you want to read it."

Ami glanced at the photos of her and Oliver on the cover. Hers was the standard professional headshot that Divya always used. Oliver had a more debonair look that seemed like it should be on the cover of *GQ* rather than an alumni leaflet that's sole purpose was likely to encourage donations. Ami slipped it into her recycling bin as she did with all the other press or interviews Divya ever brought to show her.

"Was that all?" Ami asked.

Divya pointed to the scarf around Ami's neck. "How's your skin doing?"

"Better with the Releaf products that everyone wants to kill."

Since the eczema had appeared, she had been using the Releaf line and it had calmed some of the inflamed skin, but as she knew all too well, it was merely a salve because the real problem was the anxiety lying within her.

"The woman from the Global Changemakers Award said she needs your photos for the formal announcement they are going to be making next week. Do you think that's feasible?" Divya asked.

Ami gestured toward the leaflet she had just tossed. "Can't she just use the same headshot you used for this one?"

Divya shook her head. "She's quite insistent that it has to be a recent photo that hasn't been used elsewhere. They also have a specific format and posture they want you to use. It's all quite scripted."

"I guess I shouldn't be surprised." Ami thought back to her brief conversation with Gemma and knew she was a woman who didn't like having her vision altered.

"I thought that we could pair the photo shoot with the interview, so it's all done in one day and then you never have to think about either of them again."

Ami leaned back and crossed her arms over her chest. "So, this was the real purpose for your visit?"

Divya gave her a faux innocent smile.

"Who says we have to do it at all? Is there some rule that nominees need to commit to photo shoots and press coverage?" Ami said.

"There's not, but people like us need to play by their rules if we don't want to be seen as difficult."

Ami knew Divya was right.

"So," Divya cautiously continued, "I've talked to the reporters who have reached out, and most of them are completely clueless about the nuance of race and gender at play with your nomination. We can't in good conscience give someone like that such an important exclusive. I know you said you didn't want to use that Indian reporter who reached out, but I've spoken to her at length, and I'm convinced that she's the best for the job."

Ami crossed her arms, not liking where this was going.

"She offered to do an informal meet and greet, so you can see for yourself that she's the right pick. Everything strictly off the record, and I really think you should do it."

Ami hated to go against Divya, especially when she didn't have a good reason that she could share as an explanation. Their professional partnership had been rooted in trusting the other for their areas of expertise and Divya's judgment regarding media had always been sound. She wanted Amala to succeed as much as Ami did, and she understood that meant Ami succeeding as well.

"If I meet her and I don't want to proceed, then do you promise we won't discuss this again and you'll find someone else?"

"I can live with that." She had more bounce in her step as she made her way to the door. Before leaving, she turned and said, "I think you're going to like her though."

Ami laughed. "I'll make sure I don't, just to spite you."

Her phone buzzed as Divya was closing the door.

No response? That's not very becoming of an IJ girl, is it?

She stared at it, seeing it was from the same number she'd ignored the day before that had referenced CHIJ. She quickly googled the 573 area code and learned it was from rural Eastern Missouri. She couldn't think of anyone she knew who was from that part of the country, but maybe there had been an LBS classmate who had moved to the area for a job. The familiarity of referring to her as an "IJ girl" seemed like something only someone from Singapore would say, but no one from her old life knew anything about her current one. She'd made sure of that. The only person who had even known she'd left Singapore to go to school was Sister Francis, and she hadn't even known which university. Ami had a hollow feeling as she thought about the woman who was the closest thing she'd ever had to a maternal figure. Severing that tie had been the hardest one for her. Sister Francis would be in her eighties now, and it was possible that she wasn't even alive anymore. Maybe Sister Francis would have relayed the story Monica had told her to the other orphans Monica had grown up with, her dear friends whom she had also left behind without a word. But she couldn't picture any of them trying to taunt her with text messages even if they had somehow learned the truth of her life now.

She stared at the words on her phone again, trying to make sense of who could be behind them. She decided to ignore it again, hoping whoever it was would take the hint.

Ami's heels clipped against the cement as she rushed down the sidewalk toward the Venice restaurant where Divya had arranged for her to meet the young journalist, Naira Kaur, that evening after work. The restaurant was packed with people, buzzing with anticipation for the weekend ahead. Ami saw friends gathered around tables and laughing, nervous couples that appeared to be on early dates, and settled-in ones that were eating without the pressure of conversation. For a moment, she imagined that she was one of those people, sauntering into the restaurant to meet friends and chat about her tragic boss or a date gone wrong. That this would have been the part of her day that she was most looking forward to rather than feeling anxious about and dreading the encounter. But that wasn't the life she had chosen.

She glanced around the crowded bar area in the cavernous

space and was grateful that it was dimly lit and loud. It would be easy for Ami to hide her skin and pretend she hadn't heard a question if she needed more time to respond. Divya was always thoughtful and strategic.

Among the sea of mostly white faces, it was easy to spot Naira at a small cocktail table near the bar. She had pristine youthful skin, and long black hair that fell down her back. Her skin was a wheatish complexion and several shades lighter than the rich caramel brown of Ami's. From her frequent trips to India for Amala, Ami had learned that fairer skin typically meant upper caste, although, as Divya always noted, there were exceptions to everything.

Naira stood as Ami approached, and Ami stretched out her hand to shake Naira's, making sure it was clear that she was not receptive to a hug. Naira had a solid handshake with the right amount of firmness without being overbearing. Ami always noticed those things, especially in business meetings, and never trusted people with limp handshakes.

"Thanks for meeting me," Naira said, as they both sat.

"It sounds like you didn't give Divya much of a choice. She said you called her multiple times a day until she relented." Ami's tone was light as she picked up the cocktail menu, but she made sure to surreptitiously study Naira's expression.

Naira looked sheepish. "I would really be honored to take the lead on telling your story, so I might have come across as overzealous. Maybe calling Divya once a day instead of twice begging for the story would have been more appropriate, but it's not often that someone like us gets nominated for such a prestigious award."

Like us. Ami considered how easily Naira assumed their solidarity. Divya had done the same thing when they'd first met in London, and Ami had watched Divya behave similarly with so many Indians who had crossed their paths in the years since.

That shared cultural heritage was enough for Divya to accept someone before any vetting had really occurred. But Ami had always struggled when she was around Indians. She tried to embody the assumptions and the stereotypes that went with her chosen identity, but she still always felt like she was trying on a shirt that wasn't quite the right size for her. Labels were something so many took for granted: American, Indian, British, Gujarati, Sikh. There was so much represented in a single word, and very few people could relate to the void of not knowing which words applied to them.

Ami put down the menu as she saw a server approaching. "I'm sure Divya told you that I prefer to focus on my work rather than the press, especially at this critical juncture in Amala's future."

"Yes, she mentioned that this was the last thing you wanted to spend time on."

They quickly placed their drink orders, and then resumed their conversation.

Naira said, "Why is it that you hate press so much? There's very little public information about someone so successful. Most people at your level are clamoring to get as much attention as possible."

"Most people at my level aren't women or from a collectivist background. I don't need that external validation to feel worthy."

"I know you don't need the attention," Naira said, "but it is such a rare occurrence that someone like us gets to take center stage in this way."

There it was again: *someone like us.*

Naira continued, "I know you have reporters knocking down your door, but I promise that no one else will be as committed to truly understanding your story like I would."

That's what I'm afraid of, Ami thought to herself.

"I don't see a need to get my story out there. You know there is a big merger in the works, and I need to keep that as my main focus. I have very little time for distractions. While I'm honored to be nominated, and I'm humbled if other people who look like me see some new path just by seeing my face, I can't risk the merger for either of those things."

"It doesn't have to be all or nothing," Naira countered. "Don't you think the right story could help you secure the merger and the Award?"

"That is asking a lot of a few thousand words. These media pieces are never the full picture—they simply can't be."

"No, of course it can't deliver your entire life story, but a good writer can drill down to find the essential essence of the message that needs to be shared."

Ami raised her eyebrows as if to check if Naira thought herself such an accomplished writer, and Naira neither amplified nor backed down from what she had just said. Ami had to admire her confidence and ability to quietly stand her ground. She'd called upon those skills many times in her own career.

Naira met Ami's eyes. "I'm not saying I've walked in your shoes. Only you know the path that led you to where you are today, but give me a chance. You were able to navigate a world that is overrun by white men and come out ahead. I'm sure that wasn't easy and there were things you had to do that you wish you hadn't, and I think there are a lot of people who could benefit from hearing what those things were."

"I'm far from ahead. This nomination doesn't change the fact that in North America businesses are still predominantly led by white men. Even our merger would be with a company that stands for an equity and inclusion ideology, but is run by yet another upper-class white man. Ideas need money to thrive. And those purses aren't held by people like . . . me."

She'd almost said *us*, before catching herself. She'd found herself drifting into easy conversation with Naira, but then she remembered that she couldn't get comfortable. That was when she was most likely to make a mistake.

The server dropped off their cocktails before beelining toward the next table, and Ami pushed back her shoulders and reminded herself why she was there. Ami wasn't like the people around them meeting friends and loved ones and sharing trusted confidences. She was here to satisfy Divya, so she could reject this idea and move on. She just had to make it through one drink and then offer a polite excuse and dash back to the safety of her home, where she could then spend the evening embroidering on her couch alone.

Naira held out her glass to clink with Ami's. "Cheers to breaking through barriers." She then launched back in. "Did you use family money to help fund Amala in the beginning? I believe you've said in other interviews that you came from affluent means."

Ami stalled by taking a sip of her herbaceous cucumber cocktail. "No, my parents died when I was young. Amala was an idea for a business school project during my first year that ultimately received investor backing. I was incredibly lucky. For every Amala that gets funded, there are at least a hundred other good ideas that don't."

"Yes, I read what you said about your parents passing. I'm so sorry. But was there no inheritance that helped you or anything like that? Only child from a wealthy family seems like it would all pass to you . . ."

Ami looked at her pointedly, and Naira held up her hands in surrender.

"I'm sorry. I can't stop with the questions even when it's supposed to be a social meeting. My partner says I'm the worst person to bring to a party." Naira took a sip of her cocktail.

"But just remember that anything you say to me is off the record tonight, so you can speak freely."

Ami never spoke freely. People with secrets rarely did. Or, at least, they shouldn't.

She sipped her drink, signifying that the last question would not be answered, and to Naira's credit, she moved on.

"I know it's not the same as what you've had to go through in business, but I do know a little something about swimming upstream and being different. That's why it's so important to me to share our stories. They open people's minds. And I don't mean only white people who see us a certain way, but also other Indians and marginalized communities. We all have biases, whether they are about our own people or others. It's not just white people who need to see us flourish in their worlds. It's our own families that need to see there is more to life than doctor, lawyer, engineer, and marriage and kids. If our communities see someone like you doing well, then it's not so scary if their own children want to live in a way that is beyond their narrow set of expectations." Naira shifted her gaze downward. "I went through a very hard time with my family when I told them I was queer."

Naira paused and then quickly caught Ami's eye. Ami recognized that look. It was one searching for whether it was safe to continue. She used to feel that way whenever she had to tell someone in Singapore that she was an orphan from CHIJ. Of course, Naira also was sharing a deeply personal part of her history in the hopes that Ami would then reciprocate, but Naira was still being vulnerable and Ami did not take that trust lightly. Ami's expression conveyed that her confidence was safe and urged Naira to continue.

"I'm sure you can imagine that a traditional Sikh family isn't overly welcoming to a daughter who wants to bring home a woman. There were several years during which we didn't speak at all. I poured myself into my career because I felt like I needed something to show for that loss." Naira offered a wry smile. "Without a family, you at least need to have a career, right?"

While Ami hadn't experienced being raised in a conservative Indian household or the pain associated with her sexual orientation being accepted, she could relate to pouring herself into her career in order to have something to show for her lack of a family. And she very much understood being born into a life with certain limitations and lack of acceptance.

"I'm sorry you went through that." Ami thought about reaching to touch Naira's hand, but refrained. She didn't want to get too close. "I imagine that must have been really hard."

Naira shrugged. "Hard things are how we grow, right?"

"I suppose so." Ami trailed a finger along the rim of her glass. "Are things better with your family now?"

She rarely asked people about families because she didn't want the question turned on her, but she couldn't help her curiosity. Being abandoned by people you never knew was one thing, but being abandoned after a lifetime of togetherness was entirely another. It was hard to say which was worse, but she suspected it was easier to be without someone you never really had.

Naira's shoulders hunched inward, a telltale sign of defeat. "We try. And I guess that's the most I can hope for. I can't change who I am, and I have to accept that they can't either."

Ami considered Naira's sentiment. It was something people often said, but Ami wondered if Naira's family simply didn't want to put in the work to change their views.

Sitting taller and arranging her features into a sunnier disposition, Naira said, "Enough about me. The world wants to know about you."

Ami leaned back in her chair. "There's really not much to tell."

"What compelled you to leave Singapore?" Naira pressed.

"School."

"There are such good universities in Singapore and throughout Asia, so why London?"

"A perk of colonization." Ami's tone was dry. "Easy passage to England from the Far East."

"But what was it about LBS specifically? I imagine someone with your background could have gone anywhere. Harvard, Stanford, INSEAD, CEIBS—you'd have had so many choices."

Naira wasn't wrong. Ami did have all those choices. Monica, however, did not. And just because Naira had opened up to her didn't mean she was going to be reckless enough to do the same.

"I liked the pamphlet."

Naira raised her eyebrows. "That was how you made your decision?"

Ami shrugged. "Why not? As you said, there were a plethora of good options."

"And that's where you met Oliver Dalton."

"You already know that. I know you've reached out to him." Naira perked. "So, the two of you have stayed in touch?"

"I wouldn't put it that way. We cross paths now and again, but it's been years since LBS and we have our own lives now."

Naira looked disappointed that there wasn't more of a connection with Oliver but pushed ahead. Her tone sympathetic, she asked, "Did your parents have something to do with you choosing to go so far away?"

Ami's story had been that her parents had died in an auto accident the year before she started business school. Being an orphan came naturally to her, so even if she changed the timeline and details around it, she knew she could present that authentically in her new life.

"In hindsight, I suppose it did. We can never fully understand the decisions we make in grief."

"I suppose not." She met Ami's gaze. "Is that something you can tell me more about? Your parents passing and how that impacted you?"

Ami crossed her arms. "I'd rather not. It has nothing to do with Amala or the Global Changemakers Award, so it doesn't seem relevant."

"It's just that our origin stories shape who we are, and parents play such a big role in that, even if they aren't present for all of our lives."

Ami couldn't deny that. The absence of biological parents had profoundly impacted her. But she shook her head. This was not territory she could delve into.

"If there's anything you want to share with me about them, just know I'll handle it delicately. We are off the record. I want to understand who you are and how you got here. That's the essence of every good story."

Ami drained the last of her cocktail. "I understand your passion for the job. I was once a decade younger trying to claw my way up in a white man's world, but the reality is that this is a difficult time for me to stop everything I'm doing to delve into my past. My company needs me now more than ever, and while the Global Changemakers is important, it will never come before Amala. And with that said, I really need to get back to work." She stood, signaling that their evening was over.

Naira rose as well. "I understand, but just think of how liberating it could be for you. I'll be here whenever you are ready to do that."

Ami smiled apologetically before making her way past the tables of people talking and laughing as if they had nothing to hide. If only she could be that carefree for even just one night.

On her walk home, she thought about her life in Singapore, Sister Francis, and her friends from the orphanage. She, Esther, Qi, and Victoria had all grown up under the watchful eyes of the Sisters and had created their own kind of family. It had been so hard for Monica to leave them without an explanation after they had thought they would always be in each other's lives. She'd arrived in London guilt-ridden and heartbroken, experiencing being alone for the first time in her life. She'd known that it wasn't wise to get close to people at school and have to tell her fake story again and again. But somehow Divya had weaseled her way into Ami's life, and then Oliver had made his intentions known, and she thought that maybe she could indulge in a few close connections, as long as she kept her stories straight.

As Ami continued toward her Venice home, she paused on a bridge overlooking the canals. Her neighborhood was quiet, and with no distractions she couldn't stop the memories from flooding through her.

It was during their second semester at LBS that she'd learned that connections meant comfort, and comfort meant she relaxed her focus, and when she did that, she made mistakes. It had been easy to supply the facts of Ami Shah's life because those were so readily available to her, save for the lie about the deceased parents. But Monica had never emotionally put herself in Ami's shoes. So, one day when she and Oliver were walking along the Thames and he asked her what it had felt like to lose her parents, she had forgotten that he was asking Ami, not Monica.

"You can't lose something you never had," she said as she stared out at the water. "And I'm not going to chase after someone who didn't want me."

He turned to her. "What do you mean? I thought you were close before they died?"

His comment jolted her back, and panic flooded through her as she realized she had broken from her rehearsed story that her parents had died in a car accident the year before and that was why she'd come to London for graduate school.

"I was," she said, forcing a lightness in her voice. "You know how it is though. At that age, we're always fighting against our parents. I'd have been kinder to them if I had known how little time we had left."

Her eyes began to shimmer with tears—a tactic she had gotten rather good at. She could tell he wanted to ask her more, but he put his arm around her shoulders as they continued walking.

"I'm sorry for bringing it up. I guess I just want to know everything about you." His lips eased into a chaste smile before his expression turned serious again. "My dad and I are constantly at loggerheads, but I can only imagine what you've been through. As much as we fight, I can't imagine him not being there."

"No one gets to choose the life they are born into," Ami said, and they walked in silence the rest of the way.

She knew that staying together would mean so many more near misses like the one they'd had along the river and she couldn't bring herself to jeopardize her future for a chance at romance, so she ended things with him a week later. Their relationship was likely to fail anyway, as so many young couples did after school ended and they went their separate ways. There was no man who was worth risking her entire future.

7

Divya bounced into Ami's office before Ami had even set down her handbag.

"How was it?" she asked. "Not so terrible, right?"

Ami hit the button to start her computer. "Naira was nice. Young and hungry, as you said. It wasn't miserable, I'll give you that."

"Can we go with her, then?" Divya's pen was poised over her notebook, ready to tick this off her list.

Ami sat in her chair. "I don't know, Div. You saw the emails last night from India about the Releaf line?"

Divya nodded.

They'd been told there had been an issue with the products remaining shelf stable for the number of months they needed. Amala used fresh natural ingredients, and one of the big concerns was keeping them shelf stable long enough for consumers to use the entirety of the products before they expired. Given their price points, it was essential to not have a moisturizer that separated into something that resembled oily curdled milk after a few months. They kept their current stock in a refrigerated storage facility, but could hardly expect home consumers to do that. The products needed to be stable at room temperature for at least six months.

"Div, we need to keep the focus on that. I'm wondering if we increase the amount of vitamin E and lecithin, maybe that would be enough to give it the shelf life we need."

She made a note. "Don't worry, the R&D team in Chennai always find an answer, even if it's not on the timeline we want. I'll suggest those changes to them and see what they say." She sat in the chair opposite Ami. "But we have to decide on our press strategy. Leonard and the others are asking me about it."

Ami glanced out the window at the shimmering Pacific Ocean. "I know, they keep emailing me too."

"And you don't respond to them, so then they reach out to me to get an answer, and you know how much I hate dealing with them directly."

Ami pulled off her neck scarf. "We have more problematic things."

Divya stared at Ami's neck. "That looks worse than before. Is the Releaf line not working like we thought?"

"It's definitely working. It would be worse without the products. I can feel that."

"That's good, I guess. Just hard to explain from a marketing perspective. How are we ever going to get your photos done?"

"I know. I'm sorry."

"You can't control what's popping up on your skin. But maybe we could just do your Global Changemakers interview this weekend to get that out of the way, and then come up with an excuse to push the photo shoot part of it. I can always say we'll do that at the end and then feign an emergency after the interview is over."

Ami's phone dinged and she picked it up. It was the 573 number again.

Was it worth it?

Her hands grew clammy as she realized these messages weren't a fluke. What did the person on the other end know? And how? She'd been careful for so many years and thought her past could no longer haunt her. She had to figure out who was sending these texts.

Without looking up from her phone, she said, "Sorry, Div. I have to deal with something."

"Is everything okay?"

Ami offered a feeble smile. "Sure, yeah. Can you send Pedro in on your way out?"

She nodded and then a moment later Pedro appeared in her doorway.

Ami waved him in. "I need you to do something for me."

Pedro stood with a pen poised over a notepad.

Ami continued, "But I need to keep this between us."

Pedro lowered the pen and nodded.

"I want you to reach out to that PI you know." Ami began scrawling on a small sticky note before handing it to him. "I need to find out who this number belongs to."

Pedro placed it on his notepad. "Company card?"

Ami shook her head. "My personal one."

Without another word, he left, understanding his assignment.

Ami felt a burning and itching sensation around her eye. She brought her finger to rub it and felt the dry, leathery texture of her eyelid. She reached into her purse and pulled out a mirror to confirm what she already knew. Her eczema was spreading and she had to get to the bottom of this before she reached a point of no return.

Walter Johnson wanted to meet Ami. The two had not yet been in the same room, leaving the negotiations to their overpriced legal teams and boards, but it only made sense that they should sit face-to-face if they potentially were going to be working together after the merger. And given that it was one of the largest sticking points holding up the final resolution of the deal, the teams had decided it was time.

With Leonard accompanying her, Ami went to Propelle's offices. Walter had insisted on that, and Ami knew he wanted to establish their relationship on his turf. She'd have done the same if she'd had enough power to swing the balance toward her.

Propelle's offices were housed in a skyscraper in downtown Los Angeles, with the company occupying the top ten floors of the building. Walter's corner office was on the highest floor and had sweeping views from the ocean to the mountains.

Ami had researched Walter online when the merger had been proposed, and, of course, had Pedro use the private investigator to dig up any dirt. The results turned up the usual wealthy white man recriminations: unhappy marriage, a one-off affair, child with a drug habit leading to a couple stints in a bougie rehab center in Wyoming, a couple IRS settlements for aggressive tax-savings behavior. Nothing out of the ordinary for someone at his level.

Despite knowing so much about him and having read so many public articles, it was different being in the room with the pudgy man in his mid-sixties who looked larger than life in the press. For starters, he was much shorter in person. Camera angles really could reshape reality.

She had worn a high-necked dress to hide her eczema, and her hair fell in loose waves around her face to cover up anything that the dress could not. Because of the eczema on her eyelid, she could no longer wear contacts and wore glasses with thick frames that would obscure anyone's direct line of sight to her eyes. She'd also applied makeup for good measure, but the sensitive skin burned and itched beneath it. She presented herself with poise despite the discomfort, knowing confidence was the most important thing she needed to deliver today.

She strode toward him and extended her hand to give him a firm handshake. "It's nice to finally meet you."

"And you." He took her hand and pumped it like it was a battle rope at the gym before gesturing for them to sit down.

He took his place behind his expansive desk, while Ami and Leonard sat in the immovable overstuffed leather chairs across from him.

Walter cleared his throat. "Now, Amy, I know it can be emotional stepping away from a company you created, but we are offering you a very generous package to go and start something new. Isn't that every entrepreneur's dream? To have money in the bank to chase their next passion?"

In professional settings, Ami always had to calculate whether it was worth the dignity of her name being pronounced correctly or whether she had to swallow her pride because the situation was too delicate. She determined this fell into the latter category and held her tongue, both about that and his suggestion that her wanting to stay on was somehow emotional. If she needed to be emotional Amy to stay on, then she would be emotional Amy.

"I do appreciate what you've offered," Ami said with a smile, "but I have to think not only about myself, but also about my team and the future of our brand. I have no doubt that Propelle's global distribution strategy will get Amala placement beyond what we've ever been able to achieve before. As you know, our success has largely been driven by word of mouth and online sales. Major big box retailers haven't been willing to devote shelf space to what they call a *niche* product, but forty percent of people living in America identify as nonwhite. That's over one hundred thirty million people in this country alone, and that number increases with each passing year, and is projected to exceed fifty percent by the year 2045. I'm confident that with us working together, we can change the fallacy of Amala being a niche brand and show how much demand there is for products for people who are outside of the declining white majority."

Walter steepled his fingers. "I see the need and profitability, just as I saw your need to have us fund your purchase orders. That's why we made our offer. But the majority of the population you're talking about isn't wealthy enough to spend $150 on a small tub of cream."

"Mr. Johnson, Amala is priced for the quality. We've done our homework. You'll find we are priced below other luxury brands that are filled with chemicals. Fancy European brands charge $700 for 0.7-ounces of 'gold' eye cream with a list of more than seventy ingredients, most of which are not recognizable to the average person, so our products that are around $150 per unit for two to four ounces is practically a steal for the demographic that we target. We all know catering to the affluent whose habits aren't impacted by economic shifts results in the highest profit margins. People with discretionary income who can pay multiples for a product simply because they care about the brand and status—whether it's clothes, shoes, or skin care—are the ones who have remained loyal to Amala for so many years. Moreover, the products work because they have quality ingredients that are ethically sourced like gold, saffron, and amla, but they are not cheap, especially when committing to the social responsibility component. Our research has shown that our customers are just as interested in that, again, because they are from the social classes that afford them the opportunity to have such principles."

"I can feel your passion, Ms. Shaw, I really can."

Ami clenched her fists at the mispronunciation, but kept a smile on her face as he continued.

"But we are a business. We need to take a long hard look at numbers and work solely from that place. More customers are better, and more customers are possible if we lower the price point. We aren't going to get shelf space in Walmart or Target with these prices. Maybe that means some of the ingredients are different or sourced from another vendor, but it means these products that you stand so firmly behind will be in the hands of so many more people."

She wouldn't stand behind products that were of inferior quality and knew he would not understand the Ayurvedic origins that led to the perfect balance so that their products would be suitable across skin types. In looking at his weathered skin, it was clear he wasn't a consumer of Amala or any other skin care product, low- or high-end. It would be hard to convince someone like him that moisturizers affected people's skin differently, and that when someone noticed a positive change, they would keep buying as long as they had the means.

"It's a consumable good. We have data to back up that our repeat customers increase their spending with each purchase. It's a sign that we are doing something right, and those people will stay with us for as long as the products continue to work for them. Changing the formulas is too big of an alienation risk for our existing demographic. We are better off consistently and continuously servicing the higher end of the market than trying to sell a one-off item to a housewife in Nebraska while she's at a store buying toilet paper and trash bags."

Walter opened his arms as if he were helpless. "My team is telling me differently."

"With respect, your team hasn't built this business from the ground up. They haven't gone through the growing pains and trial and error that led to us developing the successful model we have today. One that you saw value in adding to your portfolio."

Leonard shifted in his chair, a signal to Ami to watch her tone, but it was hard for her to restrain herself when she knew that Propelle would be taking the company in the wrong direction. Amala was a blip in Propelle's massive portfolio, and they'd be able to write off the loss of the entire company without even a thought and maybe even see its failure as a positive to offset some gains. The fallout from such an event would be borne by the team she'd built who had depended on her and wouldn't have the same golden parachute she would if things went awry. She owed them more than that and the only way she could deliver was if she stayed in control.

"You've got gumption," Walter said. "I'll give you that."

Leonard leaned over and clapped her on the back. "That she does, Walt. She's a real asset."

Walter leaned back in this chair. "It's hard to ignore the Global Changemakers nomination. A huge congratulations to you on that. It's a tough thing to get. All these years behind this desk making billions, and I've never had the pleasure, so kudos to you."

Ami sensed that he was insinuating the same thing Oliver had, but she couldn't be as outspoken in this room. Corporate environments meant censoring her words so as not to offend male egos. Holding back her thoughts and opinions had been one of the hardest transitions she'd had to make. It was only after leaving CHIJ that she began to see that outside those cloistered walls, it was women's voices that were often silenced.

Ami sensed she needed to downplay her accomplishment and waved her hand dismissively. "Who even knows how they make these decisions?"

Walter nodded in satisfaction. "However they make them, we can't deny there is visibility around it." He turned his gaze to the high ceiling as if thinking deeply about his next words. He then shifted back to face her. "How about we make a deal? If you win the Global Changemakers Award, then you stay on, and post-merger we try things your way. But if the numbers aren't panning out, then we have to pivot to a new strategy and you have to be on board with that."

Ami swallowed the lump that had formed in her throat. The Award definitely provided visibility, and that was the scariest part about it. She began cycling through the options, but it seemed she was stuck between nothing but difficult choices. She could try to convince the Board not to proceed with Propelle at all, but assuming she could even persuade them to give up their cash-out, there was no guarantee that Amala would survive without the money from Propelle. She could let the merger continue with her stepping down, but this conversation had convinced her that Walter and his team would take Amala in a direction that would run it into the ground, eventually having the company shutter anyway. And finally, she could agree to Walter's deal and do everything in her power to win the Changemakers Award, assuming her past wasn't outed as part of that risky move.

As much as it filled her with dread, it seemed that she needed to win the Award if she had any hope of keeping her company alive and her team intact. Maybe she was being paranoid. Maybe an award like this was only prominent in the Western Hemisphere and no one from her past in Singapore even knew about it. She brushed away the worries she had about the texts she'd been receiving, because she could see that there was only one option that had the potential of the right outcome.

She met Walter's gaze. "You have a deal."

Driving down the I-10 on her way back from Propelle's offices, she thought about how happy Divya would be to learn that Ami was ready to do whatever it took to win the Award. She kept telling herself that she was half a world away from anything that could ruin her, and that so many years had passed. But the truth kept gnawing at her: while America didn't care what was going on in Asia, Asia cared a great deal about what happened in America. Asian media would be very interested in one of their own making it in America and would likely pick up the story. The question was, what were the odds that people from her sheltered Catholic upbringing would even notice such an article, and then piece together what she had done.

Her phone dinged and on the center console of her car, a message popped up: **Confession is the only path toward redemption.** It was the 573 number.

8

Ami's mind was whirring. She couldn't ignore the Catholic connotations in the message. She had abandoned religion along with her old name, but confession was at the heart of the CHIJ values in which she and the other orphans had been raised. The message had come so quickly after she and Leonard had parted ways, that she briefly considered whether it could have been him. He had the resources to uncover most people's secrets, and he had a lot to gain if she was found in violation of her morality clause, but he wouldn't play games. Something about that just didn't feel right, but then again, nothing about these texts did. The only thing she knew for certain was that she couldn't ignore them any longer. Hopefully Pedro had been able to get her some answers.

Before she could get to her office and try to think through her next steps, Divya found her in the hallway.

"How did it go?" Divya asked her.

"It was interesting." Ami motioned for Divya to follow her to her office and then closed the door behind them. "He doesn't seem like he understands our products or clientele."

"No surprise there."

"But he did offer me a deal."

Divya looked at her expectantly.

Ami continued, "If I win the Global Changemakers Award, I can stay on and keep our strategy in place."

"So, all you have to do is win an award that no one like you has ever won before?" Her tone was laced with sarcasm.

"That's right."

Divya leaned forward. "I, for one, am sure you can win. It's time. So, he can bring on that challenge and we will crush it."

Ami loved Divya's optimism. She'd been apprehensive about winning the Award, but after today's meeting, she had to take the risk. And if she was taking the risk, she was going to win. Risks without rewards were worthless.

"Well, to be fair, he seems to think Amy Shaw needs to win, but let's assume that's me."

"Wouldn't that be so much easier," Divya said dryly.

"As much as it pains me, you're right that we need good press coverage if I'm going to win this."

Divya's face broke into a smile, but she had the grace not to flaunt that she'd been right from the start. "Shall I call Naira?"

Ami hesitated. "I get why you want to use her. But given the stakes now, don't you think we need someone more notable to handle it? Someone who already has a big following, and that just isn't Naira."

"Maybe not, but I have checked her social media and she's all about lifting up other Brown women. It's even rumored that she left *The New Yorker* because she was doing an article about a prominent Indian woman and her editors thought that her desire to showcase the woman positively impacted her judgment.

I am trying to get more details, but that is the type of support we want. Even with a smaller following, because of the current climate, I think any article about you will be picked up by a major publication, no matter who writes it."

"Before we get there . . ." Ami pulled off her scarf, revealing the red web taking over her neck. Then she removed her glasses and wiped away the makeup. "There is no way I can do a photo shoot."

Divya flinched. "I can't believe it's on your eyelid now." She picked up her notebook. "I'll see what I can do about pushing that to the absolute last second, but we definitely need to give them what they want if you have any hope of winning."

Ami considered how important winning was now, and raised another idea. "I know it would be tough, and everyone is planning for a launch of the Releaf line in two months, but what if we could get it out before the Global Changemakers? The campaign we have around that with women of various skin tones talking about how much these products have built their confidence is great, and the media attention on them and the line could really show how Amala is not just a for-profit company, but one that has a social responsibility component as well."

Divya paused, considering Ami's suggestion before her face broke into a smile. "I'm not sure if we can actually get the products to market that quickly, especially since we are waiting on samples from the new formula and do really need Propelle to help fund the inventory for it beyond our market samples, but good press is just as effective as products on shelves. And I think moving up our marketing and PR efforts is a great idea. We could start releasing the videos from our influencers who have been trying the samples and have them share their personal stories of how it has helped them. I think that's a brilliant plan."

Ami felt her body tingling as they considered the possibilities and how it could benefit them with the Changemakers Award. It also would make it harder for Walter Johnson to kill the Releaf line if there was already so much buzz about it before he acquired Amala, and they had taken orders that needed to be filled. It was in moments like this when she didn't worry about her name or the way she was supposed to act and felt most like herself: solving problems and coming up with creative strategies for Amala. It gave her such a high to be able to use her brain and skills to their fullest potential.

She held up a hand excitedly. "Why don't we donate a portion of the proceeds from the Releaf line to organizations that support underprivileged people with skin problems? That would not only ratchet up the social component and highlight the company to the Changemakers Committee, but with Propelle's investment, we would finally be in the position to serve the portion of the community that needs our products but can't afford them."

Divya's eyes shone. It was what they had dreamed about in Amala's nascent years when they didn't yet know how difficult the road ahead would be for the company, or that successful and profitable were two entirely separate concepts when growing a business. People so often assumed that brand recognition meant financially viable—but Ami and Divya had learned that projecting success was entirely different from having it.

"I love it." Divya tried to choke down the emotion in her voice. "I have every faith that you will win this Award, but it doesn't hurt to continue to stack the deck in our favor, and I love that we will be able to show the world that everyone deserves Releaf."

Divya agreed to look into whether there was a reporter better than Naira given the reach they needed on this campaign and promised to come back to Ami on that.

Pedro poked his head in as soon as Divya left. "I have an update for you."

Ami motioned for him to close the door, her excitement about the plans she and Divya had just made fading as she felt herself being jolted out of her dreamscapes and back into reality.

"About that number?"

Pedro nodded. "It's not a great update, but this is all there is. The investigator said it was a virtual number. She said it could be coming from anywhere. I suspect that's not much help."

"Not really. Could she narrow it down to a state? Is it even coming from Missouri?"

"Afraid not. She said it's not even necessarily coming from this country. It could be coming from Rwanda or Canada or Argentina or India. With technology these days, it's so easy to fake that kind of stuff."

Or Singapore, Ami thought with a sinking feeling.

"Do you have any other info that I could pass on to her?" Pedro asked.

Ami shook her head. There was no way to share the texts without sharing her true concerns and that was a bridge too far.

She adopted a cheery smile and tone. "It's not a big deal. Just something silly I was curious about. You can tell her there's no need to go further with this." She began writing on a sticky note. "I do, however, need her to look into someone else. This reporter wants to interview me, and I'd like you to ask the PI to do a little digging on her background. She seems to have left her last job under suspicious circumstances."

"Personal card, again?"

She nodded, handing him the sticky note.

"Maybe you should start keeping her on retainer," he said as he left her office.

No sooner had Ami sunk into her chair than her phone alerted her to another message.

Monica, it's time you told the truth. The Global Changemakers Committee deserves to know who you really are.

She exhaled sharply as she stared at the words. She shuddered with dread. The only people in the world who knew her as Monica were in Singapore.

9

She was shaking as she paced around her office trying to think of who could be trying to expose her. The real Ami was the person who would be most angry about what she'd done, but how could she have found out? And she'd never been tech savvy in the way that was needed to fake a phone number, but people could learn new skills. It had been almost twenty years, after all. Sister Francis would never do something malicious, but she did know that Monica planned to attend university in London. The only other people she'd had relationships with were Esther, Qi, and Victoria, who were kindhearted souls who had grown up in the orphanage with her. She couldn't fathom a mean bone in their bodies, but again, people change and perhaps envy arose in them if they'd somehow learned about the life she had built without them. Could it be another classmate at CHIJ that she hadn't thought of? The girls from wealthy families had the means to travel the world and maybe one of them had stumbled upon Amala on one of their trips and somehow pieced it together. Perhaps she hadn't been as invisible in school as she'd always assumed. It all seemed farfetched, but the string of messages on her phone suggested that someone knew more about her than she had ever dared to reveal.

Her phone dinged with another message and she picked it up with an unsteady hand.

How did you even get into America with a fake name?

She inhaled sharply. The person on the other end knew more about her past than she wanted anyone to know, but they didn't know everything. She had legally changed her name to Ami Shah when she'd left Singapore. So, the identity associated with her Singaporean passport and American work visa was legally valid. But her false background would surely prevent her from winning the Global Changemakers Award. And the real problem, as she'd always known, was the morality clause in the agreements with her investors. She'd lose Amala if the truth came out that she had accepted the investments under false pretenses about her academic background, and not with any sort of fancy golden parachute either. Only people like Walter Johnson got those in the face of scandal.

Ami picked up her phone and stared at the messages again, trying to convince herself that they were somehow innocuous. But the words remained unchanged, and she could feel in her bones that the threat was real. Someone knew she was Monica, and that alone was enough to ruin her.

She had to track down who was sending these messages and do whatever it took to make sure they didn't expose her. Her pulse quickened at the thought that they could have only come from someone who knew her in Singapore. Sister Francis was the only person who had even known she was leaving, but Monica had no way of knowing who she could have told or when. So many years had passed. So many years when she'd wondered if she would be exposed. So many years when she'd wondered what would happen to her if she was. So many years when she'd isolated herself out of fear, but also longed to hear the familiar voice she had grown up with. But this was never how she planned it.

She searched for the Convent of the Holy Infant Jesus in Singapore and found a number for the school. If Sister Francis were still alive, she must still be teaching. It was just after nine in the morning there, and with trembling fingers, she dialed.

"Hello. IJ School. How may I direct your call?" a woman said brightly on the other end.

Monica had to force herself to speak. "I'm not sure. I'm looking for a Sister who was a teacher there—Sister Francis—could I speak to her?"

"May I ask who is calling?" the woman's chipper voice had grown cautious.

"Am—" she started to say. "I'm a former student. She will remember me. If I could just speak to her directly . . . it's a personal matter."

"I'm sorry, ma'am. We cannot give out that type of information over the phone. Privacy matters, I'm sure you can understand."

"No, of course." Ami began to change her tact, and sweetened her tone. "What would be the best way to find her? Is there a message or something you can pass to her?"

"You can fill out the information request form and drop it off with the General Office. But we are not at liberty to disclose any personal details about teachers or students over the phone."

"Yes, of course. It's just that I live in North America, and I'm afraid the matter is rather urgent. Is there no list of which Sisters are still in Singapore or anything like that?"

The woman's tone softened. "I'm sorry, ma'am. The rules are quite strict in this regard. But you can come in and fill out the form if you find yourself in the area. Just please bring your identification card, as we need that prior to reviewing any requests. Again, for privacy of the students and faculty."

Monica's heart deflated. America may be a place where smooth words could get someone to bend the rules, but Singapore was not, and she knew it was pointless to keep going.

She glanced around her office, hoping a solution would present itself, but nothing magically appeared. She considered hiring a private investigator to track down Sister Francis, but she worried that she would have to explain too much in order to do that, starting with the name she was using being different from the one Sister Francis would know. At the end of the day, it was a small island where people were inexorably intertwined and she couldn't be giving out that information to a random stranger. She knew the best way for her to figure out who was behind those texts was to retrace her steps in Singapore, starting with finding Sister Francis and determining who else could have learned she was going to London in the first place, but she had promised herself that she'd never set foot in the country again.

The burning sensation from the eczema across her torso, neck, and eyelid reminded her how much she could lose. She couldn't sit idly by in Los Angeles in the hopes that the mysterious person was bluffing and wouldn't tell the world who she really was. She had to save herself, even if protecting her future forced her to reopen her past. And she couldn't trust anyone other than herself to do a job that was this important.

She began to search for the first available flight.

Divya poked her head into Ami's office and motioned that she wanted to talk. Ami's chest constricted at knowing she'd have to run off during this critical time and lie to Divya about why. Lies seemed to build upon one another until that's all there was.

Ami motioned her in and Divya closed the door behind her. "You look like you've seen a ghost. What's going on?"

Ami turned back to the results of her flight search and saw one leaving that evening. She could make it if she hurried.

"I'm sorry, but I have to go out of town for a bit."

"Okay . . ." Divya said slowly. "Seems a bit sudden, no? It's not like we have anything major going on right now." Her tone was measured, clearly trying to assess the situation.

Ami hurriedly grabbed her oversized tote and stealthily opened the drawer with her unfinished needlework and tossed it in before Divya could see what it was. Then she undocked her laptop and threw that in along with her phone.

"It's urgent," Ami said making her way toward the door.

"What's going on?" Divya now seemed panicked. "Did something happen?"

Ami had one foot out the door and wasn't waiting for anyone. "Family emergency," she called over her shoulder.

Divya had a puzzled look on her face, and the last thing Ami heard was Divya saying, "I thought your family died."

Ami went to the back corner of her large walk-in closet and retrieved a manilla envelope from the hidden safe. Inside was her red Singaporean passport, complete with the visa that allowed her to live in the United States. There were also two pink Singapore Identity Cards tucked into the back pages. The first matched her passport with the name of Ami Shah. On the second, the pink color had faded to a dusty blush. She ran her thumb across the worn plastic of the Identity Card bearing the name Monica Joseph and couldn't believe how far she'd come. She set her jaw, determined that no one was going to take away the life she had built. She placed the documents in her handbag and made her way to the black SUV waiting to take her to the airport. She gave one last glance to her home on the Venice Canals and promised herself that she would do whatever it took to keep her life exactly as it was.

10

Monica had never planned to set foot in Singapore again, and certainly never thought she'd be welcome inside the Raffles Hotel. It sat across the street from CHIJ, but the idea of someone like her staying at such an opulent place was inconceivable. Yet, it was the only hotel she knew by name in all of Singapore. As a child, the affluent people inside the beautiful structure had always loomed larger than life, and she'd never dreamed of being a guest there anymore than she'd dreamed she could go to the moon. Yet, here she was now.

She was required to provide her reservation details to the turbaned security guard on Beach Road before she could even walk along the red carpet to enter the lobby. Stepping inside, the white marble floors and walls with the black accents in the reception area reminded her of the Black and Whites in Goodwood Hill, and more specifically, of the last home she'd had in Singapore. Singaporeans heralded classic British colonial architecture rather than seeing it as a blemish on their past the way many other countries interpreted their imperial history. A grand chandelier hung from the high ceiling, crystals dangling and shimmering from every arm of the fixture. Black rafters accented the ceiling, again reinforcing the classic motif, and she couldn't help but be reminded that she was meant to be a maid in buildings as grand as this one, and maybe this place was too far out of her grasp for her even to be that.

The reception area was private, with direct elevators allowing residents to access their rooms without having to walk through the lobby. She was shown to her room without anyone questioning whether she deserved to be there. That was the strangest part. Singapore's classism rivaled America's and England's racism, and she'd assumed the staff would be able to tell that she didn't belong in this regal place. Before today, the closest she'd come to the fine china from Raffles was when washing the dishes after the paying students had eaten off them. People like the real Ami Shah. The orphans ate off steel flatware.

In her suite, Monica felt herself being pulled toward the spacious balcony. She took a deep breath before parting the sheer white curtain and stepping outside, letting the heavy, humid air envelop her. She closed her eyes, her body remembering exactly where she was by the sounds of traffic along Bras Basah and North Bridge Roads. The gears of buses, the revving of car engines, and the cacophony of conversations from pedestrians below her had remained the same. Hearing them again immediately brought her back to her youth. The sound of traffic was the same no matter which side of the street she was on. It was only when she opened her eyes that she remembered she had crossed over.

Across the street, she saw a sign that said **CHIJMES** instead of CHIJ, a play on words, no doubt. She'd known that the Town Convent had been relocated after she'd finished her studies, and that hers was the last class to complete their schooling on Victoria Street, but she'd never had occasion or desire to follow up on what it had become. She peered down North Bridge Road and gaped at the modern new building that stood in place of the two-story orphanage she had grown up in. The Home for Abandoned Babies, and her childhood, appeared to have been eradicated from the city as if they'd never existed at all.

From her room, she looked down onto CHIJMES and saw some familiar structures had survived the renovations: the steeple of the chapel still rose above the white buildings with their red clay–tiled roofs. The exterior of the Sisters' quarters looked the same, but the large Perennial sign suggested that businesses were now housed within those walls. How different it looked when she was no longer at the center of it.

She stared at her former home and felt the pull to return there, but also feared the changes she would see. Even though she'd hidden her background for most of her adult life, she didn't want to see that the place that had shaped her was no longer the same.

It was Tuesday evening in Singapore, and while on the very long flight she had tried to dissect every detail around her leaving and who could have figured out anything about what she had done. The list was short, because her life in Singapore had been very small. Sister Francis was the first person she needed to see, so she would go to the school when it opened in the morning and hopefully find someone chattier than the person who had answered when she had called before, and if all else failed, would fill out the request form and deal with that administrative red tape.

If she couldn't find Sister Francis, then the next place would have to be the Shahs' home in Goodwood Hill. When she'd left there without a word, they might have reached out to Sister Francis for Monica's whereabouts and learned she had gone to London. The real Ami would no doubt have been enraged if she had ever learned the truth, but she wasn't sure if Ami would be living there. If all had gone according to plan, she'd have found her husband at CEIBS and could be anywhere now, but she knew Ami's parents would still be there. A non-Chinese family being able to rent one of those prestigious homes had been no easy feat, and the Shahs would never give up that status symbol. She just hoped that she'd solve this riddle before she had to get to that step because the itching on her neck, eyes, and stomach intensified at the thought of returning to that house.

She knew she should get some sleep given how taxing the following day was likely to be, but she could not stop herself from seeing her old home while it was so close. She exited the hotel on the Bras Basah side and crossed toward the hordes of people rushing in all directions as they exited Raffles City. After crossing North Bridge Road, she descended a few steps and was standing under the familiar cloistered walkway that had once run along the Sisters' quarters. She entered the courtyard, remembering running across the lawn with Esther, Qi, and Victoria. She made a circle in slow motion, now taking in the trendy restaurants and bars around her. People sitting in the courtyard sipping alcohol was a sight she wasn't prepared for. It was now an entertainment destination that was no different from Abbott Kinney back in LA. The place had become an odd mix of familiar and new. Gone was the virtue, having been replaced with vices. But other parts of the area looked exactly as they had when she'd left at age eighteen.

She moved instinctively toward the white Gothic-style chapel, a structure that seemed to be unchanged. The stained-glass windows had cast so many colorful shadows into the church when she'd attended mass there as a young girl. She paused at a stone railing that had not been there during her time, and looked down, stunned to see more bars. There had been no lower level when she'd lived there, and this had been a grassy courtyard where she'd once gathered with classmates or other orphans and sat outside to do schoolwork or play games.

She looked in the direction of where the two-story orphanage once stood, and confirmed that the Baby House was gone without a trace. She felt a pang of sadness at the loss of it. Thousands of little girls had called that building home and formed a community among themselves to look after one another for however long they shared that roof, but there was no trace of that history. She then made her way toward the chapel, only to find that it was closed and now an event space.

She turned around and saw Caldwell House. Lush greenery still surrounded the octagonal reception room. She'd been eighteen years old the last time she'd set foot inside it. She was lined up with the other orphans her age while men paraded through and assessed them for wives. She'd never felt like marriage would be her way out. It was another institution just like the one in which she'd been raised and she desperately wanted to live a life free of institutions. Unlike when parents had come through during her younger years looking for girls to adopt, she'd been relieved when Sister Francis had told her there were no matches. She wasn't surprised. It had been mostly Chinese men looking for Chinese girls. And to ensure she'd never have to face that situation again, she'd swallowed her pride and taken the helper job in the Shahs' home.

As she made her way past influencers posing for the perfect angle, she was pulled toward the gate on Victoria Street near Bras Basah Road, bracing herself for it to have been eradicated like the rest of the cornerstones of her life here. As she looked toward where it should be, she saw a gray door resting higher than ground level with a mail slot and a small round flower design to let someone see who was on the other side. The replica looked similar to the original gate that she remembered but felt like a museum piece now, resting oddly high on the wall compared to when it was a normal gate that she would pass through to get to the street. She touched the wood, warm and damp from the ever-present heat and humidity. The gate where her convent life had begun. The gate where she stopped being somebody's daughter and became a ward. She felt herself slip back into who she'd been growing up here: Monica Joseph, the abandoned orphan, whereas Ami Shah, the successful entrepreneur, seemed very far away.

She removed her hand and took a step back to take in the full picture. To the left was a sepia-toned photo of orphans and a marker calling it the Gate of Hope. She moved closer to the placard, curious about that name that she'd never heard before. The Sisters had always called it the Convent Gate or the Baby Gate, but most often, simply the Gate. Never the Gate of Hope.

Beneath the photo, the text read:

"The Gate of Hope is one of the most historic installations at CHIJMES. From the very beginning in 1954, scores of unwanted baby girls, wrapped in rags or newspapers, were left at the front door. The Infant Jesus Sisters took these babies in and provided each with shelter, education, care, and love. News of these remarkable acts of kindness quickly spread, and in time the front door became known to all as the Gate of Hope."

All, except for those of us who had been left there, Monica thought. It was astounding how easily history could be rewritten and polished to be something else. The facts were mostly true. The Sisters had committed remarkable acts of kindness to little girls who may not have otherwise survived. Baby girls like Monica. She'd been wrapped in rags when Sister Francis had found her crying in the middle of the night, but seeing the details of her early life written so generically made her feel like the specifics of her story did not matter.

The unsettling feeling of going from orphan to tourist marker made Monica feel claustrophobic. She dashed out of the covered area near the gate and into the bustle of Bras Basah Road where she once again felt anonymous among the throngs of people rushing along the sidewalk. She looked back at the Gate of Hope and thought of all the orphans who had come through it just like her, and the only thing she felt certain of was that her decisions had allowed her to achieve more than any of them had. Without taking matters into her own hands, she'd have been another unwanted girl living an unremarkable life, never knowing her full potential. Just being here made her feel worthless again, and she would do whatever it took for her to keep the life she had now.

She made her way back to the sanctuary of the Raffles Hotel and hid beneath the luxurious Egyptian cotton comforter, wishing she hadn't had to come back to Singapore. Nothing good had ever happened to her on this side of the world.

11

Monica's phone rang loudly. She reached for it and saw Leonard's name flash across the screen. She had a Pavlovian response when it came to calls from him or any of Amala's investors, and she always rushed to answer regardless of where she was or what she was doing. After she'd moved to America, she'd learned quickly that catering to white men would be the key to her success.

"I heard you had a family emergency," he said.

"I needed to take care of a few things."

"Where are you?"

She hesitated. "Singapore."

Leonard let out a low whistle. "When Divya said you were dealing with a family emergency, I didn't realize she meant all the way over there. I assumed it was an aunt or uncle in the Valley or Artesia or something like that."

"The timing couldn't be helped."

Leonard had been raised in a sprawling ocean view home in the Pacific Palisades and still lived within walking distance from his elderly parents and his childhood home. He didn't know the lifestyle of so many immigrants who grew up and lived their lives a world away from their families, culture, and support systems. She'd always told herself that he simply didn't know any better, but now that she was back in her birth country—a place he knew nothing about—she began asking herself if there was any acceptable excuse for willful ignorance of how others lived.

"Didn't your parents—"

"Was there something you needed?" Monica cut him off in a sweet tone as if she hadn't heard the start of his last question.

"I'm sure you know this is a really bad time for you to be away."

She clenched her jaw. Of course she knew, and if she'd felt like she'd had a choice, she would never have left.

"I know. I'll get back as soon as I can."

"Divya also said you haven't done your Changemakers photo shoot or interview yet."

"We will get it all done as soon as I'm back."

Her phone dinged with a new message.

"I hope that's soon. The rest of the Board isn't going to be thrilled with the timing. I know I don't need to remind you just how important this Award has now become."

"I understand," she said dutifully, before ending the call.

She opened her messages with some apprehension, afraid that it would be the 573 number, but it was Divya.

> Warning. Leonard wasn't happy when I told him you were gone and might call you

Monica's fingers flew over the letters: Too late.
> You'll be back soon? Divya responded.

Yes.

She considered whether she should call Divya out on letting Leonard know she hadn't completed her Changemakers photo shoot yet. They never shared anything that could make the other look bad with the Board, and Divya preferred not to have direct contact with them, so it was strange for her to even be communicating in the first place. But Monica let it go, knowing she needed to keep Divya happy right now. She placed her phone on the nightstand and sank into the luxurious bedding of her hotel room. The silence felt stifling. It made her uneasy, as if the world had stopped. Especially as she considered what would happen if the world she had so carefully built brick by brick suddenly crumbled around her and she'd have to go back to the life she'd fled. She got up and flung open the balcony doors and let in the echoes of Singapore that she was so accustomed to. The noise felt like a security blanket wrapping itself around her. It gave her far more comfort than the Egyptian cotton sheets.

Leonard's apprehension needled at her, especially because he was rarely riled up. She needed to act as quickly as possible so she could get back home. She began to map out her route. She was native to Singapore, but she didn't know the city at all. She had lived within the walls of the Town Convent. On certain occasions she and the other girls went to the Cathedral of the Good Shepherd across Victoria Street, but that was as far as she had ventured. She'd never gone to the beach or suburbs. Had never seen the ocean here or the iconic Marina Bay Sands Hotel or Supertrees. There had been no need to explore or ingratiate herself to a city that would always remind her of who and what she was. She was a stranger in her native country even more than she was a foreigner in America. But it was one thing to be marginalized in a foreign place, and entirely another to experience that in your birth country. She was already ready to get out of Singapore.

The concierge arranged for a driver to take her to the school in Toa Payoh and she leaned her head against the back seat as they made their way toward the outskirts of the city. The school had moved so far from its longstanding home.

"You're from Singapore originally?" Mr. Tan made eye contact with her through the rearview mirror.

Singaporeans could always identify each other.

She stared out the window at the parts of the city that she was seeing for the first time.

"Yes, Uncle, but I've been gone a long time."

"Lots of people are going now. Australia, America, England . . . they always think it's better than here."

She murmured in agreement, and then they sat in silence for the rest of the twenty-minute drive.

Mr. Tan slowed as he pulled up to a gate with a boom barrier. An elderly woman exited the guardhouse and he rolled down the backseat window so Ami could speak with her. The woman had a clipboard with a list of printed names on it.

"What is your name, ma'am?" She bent to the window.

"Am—" she started to say, but then corrected herself. "Monica."

She noticed the quick quizzical look on Mr. Tan's face when she saw his reflection in the rearview mirror.

"Are you here for the primary school or secondary?" the guard asked.

She hadn't thought that far ahead. This level of security was quite different from the Sister who used to sit in a chair near the Gate on Victoria Street and control the traffic in and out of the Town Convent.

"I'd like to see the principal," Monica said.

"Are you a parent here?" the guard asked.

"No, but I was a former student. From the Town Convent."

The guard smiled widely. "It's always nice to see our alumni. What is your full name? I'll ring the secondary school principal."

"Monica Joseph." The name felt odd on her tongue, not having said it aloud in seventeen years.

Mr. Tan remained unfazed, facing forward as if he weren't paying attention, but Monica had been staff before and knew their eyes and ears were always open. But she also trusted that anyone who was on the roster for the Raffles would be well versed in discretion above all else. Privacy was one of the greatest perks of being affluent.

The security guard went back into the small building and after a few seconds the boom barrier lifted. Mr. Tan parked and said he'd wait for her, and she began walking in the direction the guard had pointed toward. She noticed the spacious three- and four-story buildings that formed a U around a large sports field. This was a far cry from the Town Convent. They'd not had sports fields like this and the buildings had not been as tall. The space was eerily quiet for a Wednesday morning. Perhaps all the girls were in classes. As she walked down the corridor, it opened onto the cafeteria with numerous food stalls representing the multicultural cuisine of the country. It was so different from the mess hall during her time at the Town Convent.

As she continued past the cafeteria, she saw two girls stroll by in their royal blue pinafores with white-collared shirts underneath. Unlike the school itself, the uniforms did not appear to have changed a bit since her time there. The teenagers were clad in the exact shade of royal blue that she recalled wearing herself at that age. There was no mistaking that these girls were paying students. Everyone could tell the difference between the orphans and the paying students. Uniforms were only part of the story. The rest was told in the shoes they wore, the way they styled their hair, jewelry, and the air of confidence with which girls from privileged backgrounds carried themselves. She looked down, as she felt the stench of her past while walking by them in the hall.

In the small waiting area, she sat on the IJ blue bench cushion until a young woman in her early thirties came down the long hallway to greet her. Monica was taken aback by her business casual attire and youthful face but rose to shake her hand. She'd only ever known an elder Sister in a white habit to be principal. This woman was dressed as if she could be working in any modern office building in the city.

"I'm Beatrice Huang, the principal of the secondary school. I'm sorry to keep you waiting. It's a busy time of the year for us, but we always try to make time for our alumni."

"It's not a problem at all. I know I came unannounced. I hadn't expected everything to be so formal," Monica said with a smile, knowing she needed to charm this woman or she'd be back in the purgatory of the dreaded request form.

"You attended the Town Convent on Victoria Street, then?"

Monica nodded. "I was among the last students there before it closed for relocation. I left Singapore shortly after, so I've never seen this property."

"It's quite different from what you were used to, I suppose?"

"Very."

Beatrice smiled and gestured for her to follow. In the hallway were many photographs of students ranging from black-and-whites, to sepia tones, to full color. It looked like they went back to the beginning of CHIJ in 1854. As they neared the middle of the hallway, there were class photos of the girls dressed in their uniforms looking at the camera. She'd glimpsed the one from her final year, but kept walking, not wanting to revisit that part of her past.

In her office Beatrice settled into her desk and typed Monica's name into the computer. Monica regarded her carefully.

At this point, anyone could be a suspect in her mind, but this woman appeared to be truly unaware of her existence before this moment.

"What can I help you with, Monica?"

She shifted before speaking. "I wasn't one of the traditional students at CHIJ."

"Oh?" Beatrice raised an eyebrow.

"I was . . ." Monica knew her face registered the shame she felt—had always felt—about her story, but here, she knew she needed to play up her orphan past to garner some sympathy. "I was left at the Convent Gate . . . when I was a baby."

Beatrice cocked her head and put a hand over her heart. "We don't often hear from the orphans, but it's nice to see you are doing so well."

Monica offered a shy smile. "Yes, I live in Los Angeles now."

Beatrice tried to mask her reaction, but Monica saw the surprise on her face. She knew her story made her an outlier. To be in America signaled to Beatrice that she'd become something other than a maid. Monica also caught Beatrice glancing at her fingers and finding them absent of wedding rings, which suggested that Monica likely hadn't married her way into the Western Hemisphere.

"Do the Sisters still teach here?" Monica asked.

"No, I'm afraid not. After the Town Convent closed, there were very few of them left in Singapore. Some returned to France or Ireland, and others went to IJ schools in other parts of Asia. The few who stayed behind are in Ang Mo Kio where they look after each other and a few of the orphans who were never able to leave and go out on their own."

"Is Sister Francis there?"

Beatrice paused to reflect. "To be honest, I am not too familiar with the Sisters beyond knowing there are a few left."

It was hard for Monica to imagine that the Sisters had been

so easily forgotten, considering how integral they had been to the school.

"Is the new convent open to visitors? Sister Francis was such a big role model for me, and I'm desperate to find her again."

"It's not open to the public, as I understand it. But the location isn't a secret or anything like that, and I'm sure whoever is still there would be better able to help you find the person you are looking for." Beatrice pulled out a notepad and scrawled an address onto it before handing it to Monica. "Is there anything else I can do for you?"

Monica shifted. "I also wanted to inquire as to whether anyone has come to the school asking about me, or maybe even other students from my class year."

Beatrice looked at her curiously. "Is there something we should be worried about?"

"I'm not certain. Has anyone inquired about old student records or anything like that?"

"Not that I'm aware of. But we keep our student information private and wouldn't give out details from a student's time at CHIJ unless it was directly to that student. All student inquiries go through our request form process and are thoroughly vetted."

"That's good to hear. We can never be too cautious in these times." She offered a kind smile. "Is there any information you have about me in your files? I'd love to see anything you still have. Such precious memories from so long ago."

"There is another teacher here who handled all the old files when the school moved from Victoria Street. Will you be in town for a few days? I can ask her to pull anything we might have if you'd like to take it with you. I think it tends to be old schoolwork and things like that in the hard copy folders."

"I expect to be leaving rather soon, but I'll give you my number. I'd like to know what you find."

Monica jotted down her number and wished there were a way she could get Ami's files too. She didn't know what exactly was in them, but she knew she'd feel safer if both were in her possession. Then there'd be nothing beyond the basic digitized dates of attendance and personal details on the computer for anyone else to find, but she didn't know how she could pull that off. She stood and thanked Beatrice for the convent address.

"I hope you find what you're looking for," Beatrice said.

12

Mr. Tan jumped to open her car door as she emerged from the covered walkway near the parking lot. She slid into the back seat and waited for him to return to the driver's side.

"I'd like to go here next." She handed him the address for the IJ House.

"Of course, ma'am." He looked at it and committed it to memory. "Near the St. Nicholas Girls' School. Maybe twenty minutes to get there with the traffic."

The St. Nicholas Girls' School had been the Chinese medium school while she'd been at Victoria Street. She found it hard to believe that the cluster of schools from the Town Convent that were once steps apart were now spread across the city. It couldn't possibly breed the same sense of community she had witnessed within the convent walls.

She continued to take in the parts of Singapore she had never before seen as they made their way further from the city center. As they passed pedestrians on sidewalks and passengers in other cars, she couldn't help but wonder if her parents were among them. Were they still here in Singapore? It was a game she and the other orphans had played as kids. *Could this be my mother*, anytime someone of the same race passed by. The other girls would create entire stories, but she had never allowed herself to linger too long on thoughts like those. She already knew what she needed to about her mother. She'd left Monica at the Convent Gate in the middle of the night when she appeared to be only a few days old. There was no note or birth certificate or any way of knowing who her family was. Sister Francis had found her, and looked in both directions, calling out for the mother, but the street was empty. Sister Francis noticed Monica was covered in red splotches on her yellow-tinged skin. She brought her to the Mother Superior, and they'd had her carefully examined at St. Andrews to make sure her condition was nothing contagious or life-threatening. The red patches were eczema and the yellow tone was jaundice, but they were assured that both would heal in due course.

And so, she was baptized and given the name Monica Joseph because it was fitting both for the Catholic institution in which she would be raised, as well as for the Indian features she had since Malayali Singaporeans often had Catholic names.

As they pulled up to the IJ House, she could see that the St. Nicholas Girls' School loomed large next to the modest two-story building. The convent was minuscule and could house only a small fraction compared to the Sisters' quarters on Victoria Street. Monica just hoped that the one she came to see would still be there.

She walked cautiously down the covered walkway leading to the main door and hesitated before entering the building. The Sisters' quarters had always been off-limits when she'd been growing up, and she felt like she was trespassing.

Taking tentative steps, she entered the foyer, which had

none of the grandeur of Caldwell House, and prepared herself to be scolded for having entered without permission. But no one came to chastise or greet her. She stepped deeper into the building toward the sound of running water that she heard in another room. There, she found a kitchen and a woman filling a tea kettle at the sink.

"Excuse me?" Monica said.

The woman spun around, some of the water spilling down the side of the kettle.

"Oh, dear," she said in a French accent. "You gave me such a fright. Can I help you?"

"I hope so," Monica said, moving closer. The woman appeared to be in her sixties but Monica didn't recognize her as one of the Sisters she'd grown up with. "I'm looking for Sister Francis. I was . . . a student at the Town Convent . . . actually, I was an orphan there. I left Singapore many years ago and haven't seen Sister Francis since then."

A somber smile spread across her face and Monica feared she was too late and she had already lost the only mother figure she'd ever had.

"Is she . . . ?" Monica couldn't finish the question.

The woman's eyes widened. "No, no, *chérie*. She's still here with us. Upstairs, in fact. In body, anyway. Thank the Heavenly Father." She made the sign of the cross.

"Do you work here?" Monica asked, taking in her modest blue paisley dress.

"We are all sent to this planet to work and make a difference, I suppose," she said. "I'm Sister Catherine."

"I'm sorry." Monica's hand flew to her chest. "I thought because of your clothes—"

Sister Catherine waved her off. "Not to worry, *chérie*. We've shifted to a plain clothes life. Most of us anyway. Your Sister

Francis can't seem to give up her white habit no matter how punishing the weather is here. Not that she can get out much anymore, so I suppose it no longer matters."

"Can I see her?"

Sister Catherine looked away for a moment. "I think she would love that. We so rarely get visitors here. What's your name, child?"

"Monica Joseph."

The woman put a hand on Monica's shoulder. "You should know that Sister Francis has good days and bad days."

Monica's eyes widened. "Is she ill?"

"Of a sort. She is in the late stages of Alzheimer's. Some days, she's aware of everything around her, but other days, she's somewhere we can't reach. Lucidity comes and goes, and her body is rather frail, so we have to look after her around the clock."

Monica didn't want to think of the strong woman she had known in so much distress. She felt a bitterness on her tongue. Wasn't a life of devotion meant to give someone a free pass from these evils of the mortal world? There was no one more deserving of peace and ease than a woman who had spent her life selflessly serving others.

"What can I do?" Monica asked.

"Nothing, *chérie*. I just don't want you to be surprised if she doesn't recall you. I came here from France about ten years ago to help with the aging Sisters and the other girls whom we still care for. She loves to spend time with the girls when she's feeling okay. You must remember Qi, Victoria, and Esther, then?"

Monica nodded, relieved that the friends she remembered most fondly from her childhood were still together and being cared for by the Sisters. "I'd love to see them too."

"Qi is at work, but I'll let the others know. First, let me

go see Sister Francis and check her condition. Would you like some tea?"

Monica shook her head and Sister Catherine put down the kettle and walked out of the kitchen, promising to return shortly. Monica took a seat at the table and glanced around her. On the tea towels were intricate hand-sewn designs of local orchids and bougainvillea that looked like Esther's handiwork. On the wall was a cross-stitched pattern of the IJ logo. It seemed sewing and needlework had remained a part of their lives, just as it had for her.

Alone in the room, she processed what Sister Catherine had told her. Sister Francis had always been a thick mass of a woman. Strong and sturdy. And with the quickest wit and ebullient charm. Guilt racked her as she thought about how she had treated this woman who had done everything in her power to help Monica find a life that was better than the one she'd been born into. She knew Sister Francis must have worried about what had happened to her. Why she had taken the money for school and then disappeared without a trace. She'd never reached out again because she didn't know how to explain to a woman who had taken a vow of poverty that she was determined to do anything it took to lift herself out of that fate, even if that meant taking the convent's money to do it.

In a brightly lit room, a frail-looking woman in a loose white gown sat in the chair by the window. She was almost unrecognizable. It was the first time Monica had ever seen her without a white habit covering her hair. She took in her thin and sallow skin, blue veins snaking their way across her thin arms, and swallowed hard at the sight.

"See, Sister Francis? It is one of your old students," Sister Catherine said.

Sister Francis turned toward Monica and her eyes lit up. She patted the bed with her bony hand covered with brown spots, beckoning Monica to come closer. Monica warmed at seeing the smile spread across her face as if no time had passed since they last saw each other.

"I had so many wonderful students. Who has come?" She looked in Monica's direction but appeared to be looking right through her.

Sister Catherine gave Monica a sympathetic glance, before turning her attention back to Sister Francis. "This is your old student, Monica." Sister Catherine motioned for Monica to step closer.

"Who?" Sister Francis looked confused.

Monica felt her throat constrict. There was no way this woman was capable of sending threatening text messages, but what if she had discovered the truth before her decline and shared it with someone else? How would Monica even find out who Sister Francis had told given the state she was now in? She tensed at realizing she might not be able to cover her tracks at all.

Taking another hesitant step forward, Monica squinted in the sun-drenched room, desperate to find some way to tap into the old woman's knowledge.

"Hi, Sister Francis. I'm Monica Joseph. Do you remember me?"

Sister Francis looked at her blankly.

Monica pressed on. "You found me. As a baby. I'd been left outside the Gate."

Sister Francis seemed to have a flicker of knowing cross her face. "There were so many little girls who were left there." She shook her head. "We tried our best to help them all."

Inching closer, Monica kneeled before her. "You saved me. In more ways than I can ever repay you for."

Sister Francis touched her shoulder. "There were not too many Indian girls at the school," she said, looking at Monica and Sister Catherine for confirmation.

"No," Monica said. "There were very few of us. It was mostly Chinese girls."

"Yes, well, that is to be expected," Sister Francis said. "This is Singapore, after all. I taught English there."

"There were some Indian students there too." Monica tried again to refocus her.

Sister Francis clapped her hands together. "Yes, of course."

Monica searched her face for a flicker of recognition.

Sister Francis beamed at her. "There was a girl named Ami. She was part of the last graduation year we had at the Town Convent." She then looked around the room and her face grew quizzical. "This isn't the Town Convent. Where are we?"

"Yes, Ami was there," Monica said. "But so was I. In the same class as Ami during that last year at the Town Convent. Do you remember?"

Sister Francis began to grow more agitated as she glanced around. "Where are we? This isn't my room."

Monica closed her eyes and took in a slow breath as she tried to process how Sister Francis's condition would derail her mission.

Sister Catherine approached Sister Francis and laid a gentle hand on her forearm. "This is your new room, Sister Francis. You moved out of the Town Convent along with everyone else. You're at the IJ House now. Don't worry, you are safe and in God's hands here too."

Sister Francis eyed her, and Monica could almost see the gears in her mind turning as she tried to recall this information that some part of her understood she had known before.

Sister Catherine turned to Monica. "I'm sorry. As I said, some days are better than others. You're welcome to try again tomorrow, but I'm sure it's a comfort to her soul to know you are here even if her mind cannot properly process it."

Monica nodded, even though comfort was far from what she felt. She had lived in the care of Sister Francis for eighteen years and yet the only Indian person Sister Francis remembered seemed to be Ami. Somehow Ami was the more memorable girl. First the buildings, and now Sister Francis. Maybe Monica Joseph was meant to be erased entirely.

13

Monica's thoughts were heavy afterward, seeing how their conversation had strained Sister Francis. It was evident how much her physical and mental health were ailing, and Monica was saddened to think about how difficult it must be for her to live in this diminished state. It must be so lonely to be imprisoned by one's mind, and lonely was one thing Sister Francis had never been. She'd always been surrounded by warmth and love from the girls and Sisters. The isolation was one of the things Monica had found most difficult about the new life she had built for herself. Like Sister Francis, she too had rarely spent a moment alone while growing up at CHIJ. Whether she was sleeping, bathing, doing chores, or in school, she was surrounded by people.

The first time she'd had a room to herself was when she went to work at the Shahs. She'd found it so difficult to sleep in the silence with no one breathing next to her, reminding her that she was not alone. She hadn't known then that it would be good practice for the life she was leading now. She'd chosen financial over emotional security and she'd convinced herself it was worth the tradeoff, especially because she couldn't envision a world in which someone like her could have both.

She was making her way down the hallway, noticing the framed stitched designs along the wall, when she heard a voice behind her.

"Monica?"

She spun at the mention of her name. Standing at the end of the hallway was Victoria Cheng, and Monica's heart skipped a beat at seeing her old friend.

"Monica, is that really you?" Victoria said almost in a whisper as she stepped closer.

Monica stood stiffly as Victoria touched her shoulders as if to get a better look at her. Victoria had always been a surrogate big sister to the girls who had come after her.

"We didn't know what happened to you," Victoria said. "Sister Francis said you went away to school and then we could never find anything about you again. We were worried that . . ."

"I know," Monica said, finally finding her words. "Victoria, I'm so sorry I didn't keep in touch. You're still here. After all this time."

Victoria shrugged. "Where is an orphaned Tiger girl to go?"

She had been in her late twenties when Monica left but would be in her forties now. Her shiny black hair was now streaked with gray. Victoria was among the last of the Chinese girls who had been abandoned due to the superstitions that came with girls being born in the Year of the Tiger. It was feared they'd be rebellious and wild. But Victoria was one of the most mild mannered and kind people Monica had ever met. If only her biological mother had known her daughter's true temperament before casting her aside due to superstition, then maybe Victoria would have grown up with her real family and not in the orphanage. Her parents had returned at various points during her childhood to take her home, but after some time they'd always bring her back, as if they were returning a garment that had fallen out of fashion.

"I'm glad to be here and be able to help Sister Francis," Victoria said. "Qi and Esther are also here with me."

Monica warmed at the thought of the other two orphans who had made up their foursome. "How are they?"

Victoria's tone was cautious, but Monica could not blame her given the way she had left. "They are doing well."

Monica gestured to the walls. "I see you all have kept up your needlework skills."

Victoria offered a half smile. "It's hard not to as a CHIJ girl."

"It was such a big part of our childhood. It's hard to think that from the thousands who passed through the Baby House, you are now down to three."

"It could have been worse," Victoria said.

She had served as a cautionary tale to the other girls, because she'd been married at nineteen. Unlike Monica, she was eager to go to Caldwell House and meet local men who could help her start a new life away from CHIJ. She was excited when a man had chosen her, in the way her parents never had. Victoria left the Town Convent full of hope about the new life she was embarking on, only to return a couple years later, battered and bruised by the abuse she had suffered at his hands. Despite the vetting process that the Sisters always undertook prior to these marriages, some shadows were hard to uncover. After she returned, she had no desire to try again with another man and worked as a maid during the day and returned to the Town Convent each evening to do her chores before waking up and doing it all over again.

"So, you're doing well then? You're happy?"

Victoria paused to consider her answer. "I am. I think we've all found our purpose. It's much quieter outside the city, which took some getting used to, but this is home now. And having air con makes everything more pleasant."

"I'm sure," Monica said, thinking back to those humid nights with her dressing gown sticking to her legs and torso. "How long has Sister Francis been like this?"

Victoria looked up as she considered. "I think it's been about seven or eight years now. Some days, she's the person we know. Others are harder to predict."

"She didn't remember me," Monica said, eyes downcast.

"Don't worry. She spoke of you often in the years before all of this." Victoria stared at Monica as she spoke. "We looked for you. For years, we tried. Sister Francis was worried something had happened to you. We searched all across social media and Google. We never had any luck, so we thought . . ."

"I was never on social media," Monica said, before raising her eyes to meet Victoria's.

Monica studied her friend's face to see if she had any reaction. What if Victoria had been sending the messages? Maybe she had found out what Monica had done while she'd been looking for her and was envious of the life she'd built.

Victoria didn't show any outward reaction to suggest she was behind the messages. Victoria had never been a great liar, but it had been many years and the same could have been said about the Monica that Victoria once knew, so Monica couldn't rule anyone or anything out.

A head poked out of one of the rooms, and Monica smiled at the familiar face.

"Esther," she said, moving closer to the girl she remembered, who was now clearly a woman.

Esther had been seventeen years old when Monica had left. She was autistic and rarely spoke, but her big brown eyes behind her large glasses told so many stories. They'd often played cards or board games in the shade of the chapel or underneath the cloistered walkways on Victoria Street. That's when Monica saw Esther's strategic mind most clearly and knew that Esther noticed everything around them.

Esther's face shifted from confusion to pure elation as she realized who was standing before her. Monica gently squeezed her forearm and Esther patted her hand back. It was their greeting, and Monica was thrilled to see that Esther had remembered it. But she shouldn't have been surprised, because Esther remembered everything.

Victoria joined them. "Look, Esther, your friend is back." To Monica, she said, "What are you doing here after all this time?"

"I needed to see Sister Francis."

"But where have you been?" Victoria pressed.

She cast her gaze away from them, not able to tell these women half-truths while looking into their eyes. "I wanted to thank her for everything she did for me, but it seems I've come too late for that." She then lifted her eyes to meet Victoria's, so she could study her face. "Because of her, I'm doing well. I live in America now. I have a business and a house and all the things we dreamed of and whispered to each other about when we were kids."

She saw surprise flicker across Victoria's face, further making her think that Victoria didn't already know these things about her life, whereas the texter certainly did. Seeing Victoria's expression made Monica's stomach twist into knots. During those many nights of giggling and fantasizing, they'd always planned on moving forward together, but then Monica had run off without them. She'd convinced herself that she couldn't have taken them with her when she left. Even if she could have, they'd have never understood the lies that were necessary to move to a different station in life, and she didn't want to come back down to where they were now. Of the four of them, Monica had been the one most determined to claw her way out of poverty, and the most likely to allow the ends to justify the means.

"You always said you would find your way out of here, and it looks like you did," Victoria said pointedly.

Was that envy in her tone? Maybe Monica had been wrong to dismiss Victoria so quickly. Maybe she was letting her emotions surrounding their shared history cloud her judgment. Institutions were a strange place. It was the only family one knew, but it wasn't family in the way of the loyalty or obligations that came with blood. Everyone within those systems knew the ultimate duty they owed was to themselves to do the best they could. Monica had acted accordingly to obtain her comfortable life, but she'd always been haunted by how she had achieved it, knowing that if somehow their roles had been reversed, the two women standing before her would never have left her behind.

Monica wrung her hands together. "It wasn't easy, but I'm proud of the life I built for myself."

Esther's gaze followed them as they spoke, like she was watching a tennis match.

"I'm happy you got what you wanted," Victoria said, but Monica wasn't completely sure if it was sincere.

"Do you know who else Sister Francis told that I went to school in London?"

"I'm not sure. It's not as if we get a lot of visitors here. Qi is at work, but she also knows. Some of the other Sisters maybe, but they've either moved on or passed away by now. She was so proud of you going to university, and then so confused when you disappeared. I could see how much it affected her."

Monica knew Victoria was ignoring the other part Sister Francis must have told her. That Sister Francis had made sure Monica had the money in order to go to university. Sister Francis's parents in Ireland had passed away and left their modest estate to her. Pursuant to the vow of poverty the Sisters took, her inheritance was turned over to CHIJ. But Sister Francis had asked the Mother Superior to give Monica the amount she needed for school from the inheritance Sister Francis had donated. Sister Francis had assured the Mother Superior that Monica would come back to CHIJ stronger than ever, and help forge a path forward for all of them, so they could help even more girls get educations just like Monica's. In the end, after Monica disappeared with the cash and failed to fulfill her promise to return to CHIJ, everyone at CHIJ must have thought that Monica had lied about university and stolen the money instead.

"I did go to university," Monica said in a small voice, looking to both of them.

Victoria gestured toward Monica's attire. "You dress like the people we work for, so you must have done well there."

Monica felt briefly ashamed that her clothes and handbag cost more than a maid in Singapore would earn in an entire month—likely even several.

She managed a half smile. "I did always like school."

"We always like things we are good at."

Victoria had been one of the orphans who didn't continue her education past primary school and instead began learning the skills she needed to work as a helper at an early age. Monica assumed she still worked as a maid and wondered if she was trying to convey that she didn't look down on herself the way Monica had while she'd had that same position. Monica looked at the doorway, suddenly feeling uncomfortable.

Victoria followed her gaze. "You should try to see Sister Francis again tomorrow. I think she'd really like to see you when she's in a better state."

Monica nodded, knowing that even though she didn't suspect Victoria or Esther as the texter, she still needed to return to see Qi to rule her out. She gave Esther's arm a quick squeeze before rushing out of the IJ House and into the suffocating Singapore sun. So many emotions were coursing through her as she revisited parts of her past that she'd long ago locked away. Seeing people who had once been her chosen family, and she theirs, reminded her of how much she had lost but also how much she had gained. Staying here would have meant no Amala or Divya or London or Los Angeles. But it also would have meant coming home to laughter, and board games, and that she would have had many more good years with Sister Francis. Time was the one thing even money couldn't buy, and she would never get it back.

As she made her way down the path and back to her waiting car, she vowed that this would truly be her last time in Singapore, because if she were successful in covering up her tracks and getting through this merger, then she would never tempt fate again by setting foot in this country. Returning to the past was far too messy, and she had far too much to lose.

14

Monica was spent when she stepped back into Mr. Tan's car. She'd been inside for less than an hour but felt a heavy emotional weight as if she'd returned from a funeral. Before they pulled away, she took in the building that could very well have been her forever home just like it was for Victoria, Esther, and Qi, with the simple life of cleaning up after wealthy Singaporeans as her only profession and found it surreal that, instead, she was being driven to the Raffles Hotel. One decision had changed her fate entirely. As she was dropped off on North Bridge Road at the back of the hotel, she glanced across the street at CHIJMES.

It was the same as yesterday, but with all she had seen today, she couldn't help but look at it differently. As the emotional door to her only mother figure was closing, her thoughts fell to the other door that had closed long ago. She was steps away from the gate she'd been abandoned at. She rarely allowed herself the indulgence of thinking about the woman in whose womb she had grown. Whoever that person was had made her intentions clear.

In her younger years, Monica had often wondered if her birth mother had known her skin condition was eczema and could be treated. In some ways, she hoped not. It was harder to think she was abandoned for a cosmetic defect. A part of her wanted to believe that her mother had thought it was something so grave that only the munificent Sisters could save her, and leaving her had been a maternal act rather than a selfish one. But if that had been true, then why didn't her parents ever come back for her after she was healthy? That was the part that always made it difficult to paint the picture of a saint when it came to her birth mother. Monica didn't know where her parents were, but for eighteen years, she'd been exactly where they had left her.

Monica made her way past the line of tourists waiting to go into The Long Bar, each with their phone ready to snap the social media–worthy photos to prove that they had been to the home of the Singapore Sling. Once she got to her room, she flopped onto the plush bed, enjoying the silence and solitude for once.

She knew she had to go to the Shahs' home now that she had confirmed how unlikely it was that Sister Francis, Victoria, or Esther had any information about who might know her full story. The Shahs could have sought out Sister Francis when she'd left and then maybe the real Ami had pieced it all together. It just seemed odd to her that Ami would have known all this time and not shut her down immediately. Ami would have loved showing up on the LBS campus and confronting her and ensuring she was publicly kicked out. She was deep in her thoughts when she was startled by the sound of her phone and fumbled to find it. Divya's familiar voice was on the line when she answered.

"Hi, Ami. I know you asked for some time, but this couldn't wait."

Monica sat straighter. She'd so seamlessly slipped into Monica upon arriving in Singapore, that it took a moment for her to recalibrate back to Ami.

Taking a breath, Divya continued, "There's been a leak at the storage facility in the Valley. A pipe burst or something, and, apparently, it's a bigger repair job than expected. A lot of the inventory has been soaked and isn't useable." She paused for a moment. "That includes the launch samples for the Releaf line."

Monica rubbed her forehead as if anticipating a headache.

"How much of the dermatitis line was lost?"

"All of what they sent us so far. The team in India is still working on the formula for something with a longer shelf life, but we will need to get something new from them to finish our media blitz around the line. And you know Steve wasn't keen on the cash outlay for that line anyway, so he's riled up the Board into scrapping it completely given the expense to start over. It doesn't help that Propelle isn't interested either."

Monica set her jaw. Her time in Singapore had made her even more determined to change the lives of people who had suffered as she had. Unhealthy skin could change the course of an entire life.

"We are not getting rid of the line."

"I thought that would be your position, so . . ." Her voice trailed off. "I'm not sure what is going on with your emergency, but you need to get back here. Steve has called the Board together for a vote in two days. When he heard you were in Asia, I think he was hoping you'd still be away and he could get people to do what he wants before you came back."

"Does Propelle know about any of this?"

"Not yet. But it wouldn't surprise me if Steve or others are chomping at the bit to share this news with them."

"They'd better not. The company isn't sold yet and their fiduciary duties are still to Amala. What about the other inventory? That's our biggest warehouse."

"We've lost some of that too. We can't cry over that, but we need to find a temperature-controlled facility as soon as possible so we can mitigate the damage. Naturally, this means that shipments will be delayed on top of the lost inventory."

"I'll send them an email reminding them of their fiduciary obligations and letting them know I'll be back in time for the vote. That weasel isn't going to undermine me and take advantage because I happen to be away from the company for a few days for the first time in fifteen years."

Divya breathed a sigh of relief. "I'll ask India to send more Releaf samples and start looking for another spot to store what we can salvage from the rest, and if you have any contacts or think of anyone, let me know. Time is obviously of the essence here."

"Great. I'll message you contact details if I think of anyone." She began going through her mental list of contacts in LA.

In a softer tone, Divya said, "Are you sure everything is okay, Ami? You've been acting strange lately, these flare-ups with your skin and this last-minute trip. I know we don't delve into personal stuff much, but I'm here if you want to talk."

And Monica did. Starting with telling her that she was more comfortable being called Monica. Being back in Singapore reminded her who the real Ami Shah was, and she'd never wanted to be like her. Part of her wanted to divulge all her secrets and rid herself of the pain that came with bearing it alone. But that wasn't fair to Divya, especially since she'd be in the position of having to report Monica to the Board or violate her own employment contract. Monica had always shouldered her own burdens, no matter how heavy they were.

"Thanks, Div, but I'll be fine. I'm lucky I've got you to lean on, and I'll be back at the office as soon as I can."

"Are you able to do the photo shoot for the Global Changemakers when you're back? And the interview with Naira?"

Two things Monica really didn't want to think about. She touched the rough, itchy skin along her neck that was dangerously close to hitting her jawline to confirm it hadn't miraculously disappeared over the course of this call. There was a stinging sensation as she grazed over it, reminding her that nothing had changed. The same as she removed her glasses and ran a finger along her rough eyelid.

"Those seem like smaller problems relative to what else is going on. My skin isn't camera ready anyway, so best to buy as much time as we can for both."

Monica felt the pressure of getting back to LA weighing on her, and while she needed to see Qi to rule her out, she sensed that it was unlikely that Qi was behind the text messages, given that Qi would have said something to Victoria, and Monica felt like Victoria's surprise yesterday had been genuine. So, now her day was starting in the place that she had most wanted to avoid since she'd left Singapore.

She stood at the gate before the large Black and White estate in Goodwood Hill and stared at the familiar house at the end of the long driveway. The lush manicured gardens around the home were well-kept. There were still red terra-cotta pots of tulsi and curry leaves along the covered front verandah. To the right of the main house was a smaller, more modest building.

Inside was the single bed along with the small bathroom where she had lived from the ages of eighteen to twenty-five. Seven years of her life were spent serving the people in this home. She suspected she knew every nook and cranny of the place even better than the Shahs.

"Hello, ma'am," a woman called to her from the garden. "Can I help you?"

Monica startled and turned to her right. There was a young woman in an oversized sun hat who had been tending to the plants along the wall and Monica had not seen her. Monica took a step back as the woman came closer to the gate.

"Is there something I can do for you? Do you have a delivery?" the woman asked in a Filipino accent.

She looked like she was in her early twenties. The same age Monica was when she worked here and suspected she was the Shahs' maid. Monica pictured this woman living in that same small room that she had once been in. Was she also an orphan? It seemed more likely that, like so many other Singaporean maids, she'd come from the Philippines specifically for this work and had left a family behind there. As a local girl, Monica had been a minority among the plethora of imported maids throughout the city.

"I'm sorry to disturb, but are the owners home?"

The woman eyed her suspiciously. "Are you a relative, ma'am?"

Monica wanted to laugh, but held it back. "No, just someone they used to know. Do the Shahs still live here?"

The woman stared at her, seeming unsure of how to respond.

"I'm sorry, let me start again," Monica said, knowing she needed to build rapport with this woman. "My name is Monica, and I used to be a maid here twenty years ago."

The woman took in Monica's polished look with her silk wrap dress, expensive-looking flats, and designer handbag, and narrowed her eyes. Monica knew it was hard for a maid to think of one day looking like she did now when the reality was that most helpers stayed in that role for their entire lives.

Monica pointed to the maid's quarters. "I lived in that little building for seven years. Does the hot water pipe still make that thumping noise as it turns on?"

The woman smiled. Anyone who had lived in those quarters was aware of the noise, and Monica could tell it hadn't been fixed in all these years. There was no need when the Shahs likely didn't even know about it because no helper would ever complain, and the Shahs would never set foot into the space to learn about it themselves.

"Yes, ma'am. Still happens every time." Her tone was warmer now.

"At least there's hot water, right?" Monica said.

The woman nodded. "I'm sorry, ma'am, but the owners are not home right now."

"Is their daughter here? Ami? That's who I'm actually looking for."

"No, ma'am."

Monica's heart leapt. The real Ami had to be married now and living somewhere else. That could be good news. Maybe she could avoid seeing her and only have to deal with her parents. Mrs. Shah had never been a good liar and Monica would easily be able to figure out if the family had learned anything after she left.

"Miss Ami is gone for a few hours, ma'am."

Just as quickly as it rose, her heart sank. Ami still lived here, and was just out on what was no doubt a shopping trip or something like that.

"Can I come back then? I really need to speak with her. We went to school together and were in the same class. So many years ago. It was before I started working here and was how I came to have the job in the first place."

The helper nodded. "I will tell Miss Ami that a Miss Monica stopped by. What is your surname, ma'am?"

"Joseph. Monica Joseph. And what is your name?"

"Grace, ma'am."

"That's such a lovely name."

And was exactly what she hoped the real Ami would have for her once she realized what her old maid Monica had done.

15

Monica didn't have much time to waste if she hoped to make her flight to Los Angeles that evening and get back in time for the vote, so she went back to the IJ House to see Qi while waiting for Ami to return. While she didn't want to be too optimistic—she hadn't received any messages from the 573 number since she'd arrived in Singapore—she needed to be thorough because she had no intention of ever returning here again. Part of her wondered if she'd overreacted in coming all the way here, but her practical side knew it couldn't be a coincidence that the messages stopped as soon as she left LA. Someone was toying with her and likely tracking her movements.

When she arrived at the IJ House, she saw a woman kneeling over a bed of herbs alongside the house, turning soil, and she immediately recognized her. Slowly, she made her way toward Qi.

"It's been a long time," Monica said, squatting next to her.

Qi looked at her shyly before casting her gaze downward and occasionally stealing a glance. She'd always been that way because of her cleft palate. She tried to keep her head pointed down and her hair long and loose to mask the irregularities on her face. She'd never been able to see herself as beautiful or worthy, even though Victoria, Monica, and the other girls had tried to build her confidence. But hers had been shaken early given that she'd been dropped off at the Gate on the day of her birth with hardly a moment of hesitation from her birth mom. She'd never forgotten that her family thought she wasn't even worth taking a chance on.

"They told me you were back," Qi said, using a trowel to smooth out the soil she had just aerated.

Monica knew she shouldn't have expected a warm reunion based on how she had abandoned them. The word stuck with her, because abandonment was the one thing they all had in common. It was the bond that had shaped each of their identities and cemented them together, and it had been an unspoken code that they would never do that to each other. Monica was the only one of them to have broken that promise.

"I'm sorry I was away for so long."

"You always said you wanted a better life." She stole a quick glance at Monica's appearance the way Victoria had. "It looks like you found it."

"I thought about you three. Often."

In a rare showing, Qi looked her squarely in the face. "We were always here. You always knew how to find us, but we had no way of finding you."

Just like their parents. Monica pinched herself to keep the guilt from forming tears in her eyes. Crying was an indulgence she didn't feel she deserved now that she was face-to-face with the people she had left behind.

"I know. After school, things became complicated. It felt like it was better to leave the past where it was."

While using a garden fork to aerate the next plot of dirt on which bright red chilies were growing, Qi said, "I'm sure our mothers thought the same about us."

Monica flinched. "I'm really sorry."

"You have no idea how much we worried. All of us, and especially Sister Francis. We weren't sure if something had happened to you. Sister Francis told us about all the crime and things like that in London. She said it was nothing like here." Qi pressed the earth with a firm but gentle hand around the pepper stalks. "Victoria and I kept searching the internet for you. Sister Francis called every university in London and none had a record of you even applying. Up until the dementia took over, she never gave up on trying to find you."

Monica swallowed the lump that had formed in her throat. "I owe you all so much. Maybe I can make a big donation to the IJ House to help get you anything you might need."

Qi stopped moving but didn't look at her. "We don't need your money. But I'm glad you found what was most important to you." She pointed toward the front door. "Victoria and Esther are inside. Sister Francis seems better today than yesterday if you want to see her."

For the first time in their lives, Qi, whose gentle spirit always had time for her friends, had dismissed Monica.

Monica stood and walked toward the building, knowing she couldn't force Qi to accept her after all that had happened. Her phone vibrated as she neared the entrance and she saw the 573 number.

She deserves to know.

She whipped back to look at Qi, who was busy with the garden and didn't have a phone in her hand. It wasn't her. Monica's heart raced as she began to look around her, hoping to catch someone in the act, but there was no one else around.

When Monica walked into Sister Francis's room that day, she was more prepared. Having ruled out Victoria, Qi, and Esther, that meant her only remaining options were Sister Francis having told someone else or the Shahs having discovered her deception.

Sister Francis looked calmer than when Monica had left her the day before. Sister Catherine had suggested she visit with Sister Francis privately because maybe seeing Monica alone would help jog her memory. Sometimes it was about recreating a scenario from her past she would have been familiar with, like having a private conversation with Monica. She was seated in a chair reading her book and smiled when Monica entered.

"You're back." Sister Francis was sitting by the window and put down her book and regarded her with an air of recognition.

Monica exhaled, hoping they could have a real conversation today. "Yes, I'm so glad you remember me."

Sister Francis patted the bed next to the chair for Monica to have a seat near her. "Of course, you were just here yesterday. Was there something you needed?"

Monica's shoulders slumped. She still didn't fully recognize her.

"Do you recall your old student, Monica?"

Sister Francis furrowed her brow as she thought. "I had a lot of students over the years. It's been such a long time."

"You took care of me from when I was little," she offered.

Sister Francis seemed to study her.

"You helped me go to university," Monica pressed.

Sister Francis's eyes lit up. "We had so many girls go on to the finest universities. We were so proud of them all."

"There were a lot. But there was only one orphan who did. Do you remember that?"

The blank look on Sister Francis's face was the only answer Monica needed. It was going to be impossible for her to figure out who Sister Francis could have shared Monica's story with before her dementia had settled in. If she'd been looking for Monica for all those years, she had likely enlisted others to help track her down, but now there was no way of knowing who knew or what they could have done with that information.

Monica looked at the woman before her, knowing these would be her last moments with her. She considered confessing everything to Sister Francis, but worried that would only confuse and agitate her if she thought Monica was someone else. And what would be the point of that? Would she be doing it for Sister Francis or herself? Apologies were often made so the deliverer could absolve themself rather than to provide comfort to the recipient. Monica swallowed hard knowing she had to accept that she had come too late to learn who Sister Francis could have shared Monica's story with, and for Sister Francis to ever learn the truth and absolve Monica of what she had done.

Sister Francis patted Monica's hand. "It's so nice that you came to check on me. What was your name again?"

Monica squeezed the woman's frail fingers, thinking about how many times Sister Francis's strong hand had held her own when she'd needed it. "I'm sorry I didn't come sooner."

"We all wish we could turn back time. It's the one thing we never have enough of."

Even if Monica wouldn't be able to find out from Sister Francis whom she could have told, she let herself appreciate these final memories that Monica could take with her.

"Do you wish you could turn back time?" Monica asked.

Sister Francis paused to reflect. "I have had such a good life. I never thought I'd leave Ireland, but I've built a home a world away from it. How many people are able to do that?"

"Not very many," Monica said, thinking of her own life a world away from where she was now. "But I've done it too."

Sister Francis raised an eyebrow. "You moved?"

Monica smiled, realizing she'd never understand who Sister Francis thought she was in this moment, but also that it didn't matter. "I live in California now."

"I've never been there," Sister Francis said.

"I think you'd like it. The weather is better than here. No humidity."

"Hard to imagine. Although I've never been cold since I left Europe, so I'm not sure my bones would be happy anywhere else."

Sister Francis laughed and the familiar sound warmed Monica's heart.

"I wish I could show you the life that I built. That you helped me create," Monica said.

"Did you get a job?"

"I started a company."

Sister Francis raised an eyebrow. "That's so nice, dear. We need more girls heading up businesses, don't we now? And who better than a CHIJ girl?"

Monica nodded. "You helped so many little girls through your work, so I wanted to find a way to help people too. I help people who have skin like mine to protect and nurture it with the right ingredients."

"That sounds nice, dear," Sister Francis said. "I'm afraid I've gotten too old for my skin to matter."

Monica put an arm around her shoulders for a side hug. "You'll always have a radiance about you."

"We all do, now, don't we? Our hearts shine through and show people who we are."

Monica couldn't help but notice her words were so similar to Amala's sales slogan. She wondered if she'd subconsciously chosen words that reminded her of Sister Francis. For the past couple weeks, her skin kept reminding her that her authenticity wasn't shining through.

Sister Francis was studying her and then pointed to her neck. "What's that there?"

The scarf Monica had been wearing had shifted to the side, revealing some of her scaly red patches. Monica removed it, not feeling like she needed to hide from this woman who had seen the worst parts of her for so many years and had helped nurse her back to health.

"Don't worry, child. This will go away." Sister Francis was still pointing. "There was a girl in the crèche who had that on her skin from time to time. When I found her, I wasn't sure what it was, but now I know it looks worse than it is."

Monica's spirit lifted as she thought maybe this would be how Sister Francis would remember her.

"Yes, there was." Monica tried not to make her voice sound too eager as she fully removed the scarf. "Do you recall her name?"

Sister Francis closed her eyes as if she were straining to pluck the information from the recesses of her mind. Monica tried not to rush her, but she was desperate to have a normal conversation with her.

When Sister Francis opened her eyes after a few moments, she looked around the room and then her gaze settled on Monica again. She blinked.

"Can I help you with something?" Sister Francis asked, confused.

The moment was lost. She wouldn't get the answers she'd hoped for, and her confession, she decided, would be in spirit only. She had donated back to CHIJ the money Sister Francis had given her. Once Amala was on steady ground and she was able to start taking a salary, she donated the whole amount anonymously every year. She'd hoped that Sister Francis would have recognized the number and known that Monica was okay. And that she was sorry. Not sorry for having strategized a way out of her old social class, but deeply sorry for any emotional pain or worry she had caused the people in Singapore who had cared about her.

Monica turned and looked at the IJ House one last time before getting into the car to take her back to Goodwood Hill. She wouldn't see this place or these people again and she wanted to remember everything about the IJ House when she was alone in her sprawling house in Los Angeles. It wasn't as lavish and luxurious, but it was a home filled with love. And for the first time, she started to question whether she had chosen the right path all those years ago.

Her phone rang and she saw an unfamiliar string of numbers starting with the Singapore country code.

"Miss Joseph, this is Beatrice Huang," the person on the other end said. "I'm calling because I had one of my aides check our hard copy files after you left, and she was able to find some of your old school work and essays. It looks like there was even some needlework and stitching patterns in there. Do you want to come collect those items while you are in town?"

Monica glanced at her watch, knowing she only had time for Ami's house and then had to head to the airport. Going to Toa Payoh would be too risky with the unpredictability of traffic.

In any event, it sounded like it wasn't anything incriminating that she had to worry about. There was very little to be learned from some old schoolwork and stitches.

"Would it be possible for you to mail the items to me at my address in Los Angeles? I'd be happy to cover the shipping charges. I'd pick them up myself but I'm flying out tonight."

"Certainly. Please email me the address."

16

Sweat dripped down Monica's back and her dress clung to her as she neared the gate at the Shahs' house. She wished she could have gussied herself up before seeing Ami even though the afternoon heat would have wiped it all away. There was so much to say, but the underlying feeling of inferiority she'd always had around Ami crept up as she tried to tuck loose hairs into her ponytail and used a tissue to wipe the beads of sweat from her face and neck. Any makeup she'd been wearing was now on the tissues and she was sure that her eczema was fully visible. That was at least one thing she didn't need to hide from Ami. Ami had grown up with her and knew that her skin would succumb to fiery rashes from time to time.

She pushed the intercom button at the gate and heard Grace's voice come through it. She knew she was visible in the internal house monitor.

"Hi, Grace. Is Miss Ami back?"

"Oh, yes, ma'am. I told her about you, and she is very anxious to see you."

The gate groaned open and Monica took in a deep breath to calm herself. If Ami was the one that had discovered the truth, that was the worst-case scenario. Ami was vindictive and would feel no qualms about ruining her. She didn't know if she was walking into a confrontation or if Ami was completely clueless as to why she was here. She prayed for the latter, but then that meant the texter was still out there and she didn't know what her next steps would be in that scenario.

She climbed the long driveway toward the main house, realizing that very little had changed other than the addition of a pool in the back corner of the plot. These Black and Whites were considered landmarks from the colonial era, so that must have been quite the feat to get approved. The homes were owned by the government and families like the Shahs rented them. Even though there were plenty of modern mansions available to purchase in affluent neighborhoods, some Singaporean elite cared more about a status symbol than growing their wealth. The Shahs were exactly that type of family.

They epitomized the five *C*'s of Singapore: cash, car, credit card, country club, and condo, having surpassed the last one by having the freestanding house in the glitzy neighborhood. Had she stayed in Singapore, Monica would never be able to attain even a single of the five *C*'s. People like the Shahs who already had that status weren't looking to lift others into that same position. Status had to be exclusive to have any meaning.

Ami stood on the verandah with her arms crossed. Her dark brown hair fell down her back in natural waves, but Monica could see that she'd aged. Her once lithe figure was now fuller and her posture was more slumped. She'd always disliked exercise and her lavish lifestyle meant that she was never called upon to do chores that would otherwise keep her moving, and Monica had no reason to think that had changed since.

"It's really you," Ami said as Monica approached. "I was sure Grace had made a mistake."

Monica could see Grace in the foyer behind Ami with a smile on her face, likely proud that she was proven right despite Ami's insistence that she must be wrong.

"It's been a long time, Ami. How are you?" Monica said.

Ami exhaled dramatically. "Oh, you know. Same old stuff, different decade, right?"

Monica managed a small smile. "Could we talk?"

"After all this time, you probably have quite a few things to say."

Monica took hesitant steps as she followed Ami through the foyer, past the ornate entry table on which freshly cut flowers were in a vase next to the mail that was sorted by family member, the same way Monica had done when she'd worked there. In the formal living room, she noticed the hand-carved furniture had been reupholstered with new fabric but the bases were the same. Ami's family had gained their wealth by selling custom furniture. The business had been started by Ami's grandparents as Singapore had been emerging into its newfound independence. They'd brought skilled laborers from Tamil Nadu to make hand-carved pieces and sold them to the small but growing wealthy class in Singapore. Soon enough, they had earned their place in the same social circles as their clients and were firmly ensconced there by the time her father had taken over the business.

She lowered herself gingerly onto the edge of the Shahs' hand-crafted sofa. She'd never sat on this furniture. She'd only dusted it. It felt strange to be in this home as a guest. She saw the vase on the coffee table was slightly off-center and had to clasp her hands firmly in her lap to keep from reaching out to fix it. Places held your past no matter how long you were away from them. In this home, she would always feel like the maid.

"Grace," Ami called out. "Can you bring some chaa?"

It was hard for Monica to think about being served tea rather than being the one serving it.

"Yes, ma'am," Grace called as she shuffled across the foyer toward the kitchen in the back of the home.

"I didn't think we'd ever see you again," Ami said, narrowing her eyes. "No letter, no goodbye. We did a thorough sweep to see if anything was stolen. We didn't find anything missing, but I guess only you'd know the truth about that."

"I didn't take anything," Monica said. *At least not in the way Ami was suggesting.* Monica eyed her carefully to see if there was a deeper meaning behind Ami's words.

Did she know?

"What brings you back now?" Ami asked, eyeing Monica's appearance.

There was no denying that she no longer looked like a helper.

"I—" Monica wasn't sure where to start because she didn't know how much Ami knew. She folded and unfolded her hands in her lap, finally saying, "I came to see Sister Francis."

Ami leaned back into the cushion. "Oh?"

"She's not doing well. She's developed Alzheimer's."

"That's a long way to come to see her."

"She was an important part of my life."

"You were always one of her favorites. I suppose that makes sense given you lived at the school."

While technically true, the cavalier manner in which Ami spoke reminded Monica of how it had always been with her. She lived at the school because she had nowhere else to go, not to curry favor.

Ami leaned forward. "So, why have you shown up here now?"

It was a fair question, but not one Monica knew how to answer yet. Part of her wondered if she should confess it all. Relieve herself of the guilt and fear that had followed her since she'd walked out of this house seventeen years ago. Seventeen years. The vast majority of her adult life spent hiding and scheming and retreating into herself.

"After seeing Sister Francis, I realized we can't control how much time we have or the quality of that time. I owe you an apology for leaving the way I left. It wasn't right, and I'm sorry."

Ami seemed surprised by her words, and her posture softened. "I thought we were friends. It hurt to find you gone one day. And then to have to explain to my parents after I had vouched for you and brought you into our home. That was really embarrassing."

"We were," Monica lied, unable to stop herself from falling back into her old deferential helper ways.

Monica believed that Ami had thought they were friends. Ami wasn't aware that she'd always tried to assert her dominance over Monica. That when their mutual classmates at CHIJ had come to the house, Ami would ask Monica to mop the floors in the parts of the home where they would be able to see her. That she wanted to show them that even though Monica had been at the top of their class, this was where she had ended up. It had only been when they were alone that Ami treated Monica as anything resembling a friend. But friendship required two willing participants, so while she'd played along, she never forgot how much control Ami exerted over her life.

Grace returned with the chaa and set down the tray on the coffee table before handing each of them a mug.

Monica delicately held the porcelain that she had often served to others. "You were going off to grad school soon and it didn't make sense for me to stay here."

She kept a careful eye on Ami, looking for any hint that Ami could know her true story and be behind the messages.

"That's not a reason to leave without a word. People say goodbye. They give notice. This was a job, not a hostel."

It was comments like that that ensured they could never truly be friends.

"You're right. I should have done those things." She took a sip before continuing. "What did you do after I left? Did you reach out to Sister Francis?"

"Why would we do that? She wasn't going to work here and my parents were never going to trust an orphan from CHIJ again after that. Since then, we've hired through agencies so there's some accountability."

Monica kept her voice neutral. "So, you haven't seen Sister Francis at all since we graduated?"

"Why would I? I wasn't her favorite."

"I wasn't sure if there were CHIJ events and things like that, and maybe the Sisters and the girls still got together."

"Where exactly have you been that you don't know what goes on in Singapore?" Ami looked her up and down again, lingering on her bare left hand. "Did you find a rich husband or something?"

Monica laughed. "No, that was never a priority. I went to university."

"You never said you wanted to do that."

"I always wanted a degree. Fortunately, I had a head start with it by helping you with your university coursework, so it was pretty easy for me once I got there." Monica couldn't resist the subtle dig now that she knew this woman no longer owned her.

"School did always suit you." Ami crossed her arms.

Monica saw Grace in the foyer dusting the full-length mirror and met her eyes. Ami hadn't changed and was no doubt belittling Grace every second she could. Ami was the type who needed to put others down in order to lift herself up. Monica was older now and understood this stemmed from deep-seated insecurity. But when they'd been younger, it had made her feel so small. She smiled at Grace through the mirror, hoping that somehow Grace's life would present options that meant she would no longer have to work here.

"Hard work does come more easily to some than others," Monica said.

Part of her was disgusted that this was the name she carried now and she longed to change it back, or at least to something else. She hated any part of her success being tied to Ami, even if it was just a name and pedigree. They should have banded together as kids, being among the few South Asian students in their classes. But in Singapore, money mattered more than skin color, so Ami settled in with the wealthy Chinese girls, and Monica was cast off to the side.

"And you?" Monica asked. "Did you find that husband at CEIBS that you were looking for?"

Ami gave a dismissive wave. "CEIBS was okay. I ended up coming home after the first year. It was too hard to be away from Mum and Papa, and none of the men there seemed that interesting anyway. It wasn't as if I needed the degree. I can step into the family business whenever I feel like working."

"Looks like we both managed to survive without husbands."

"Seems so. Guess we are more alike than I ever realized."

She'd never understand that their levels of effort would have been vastly different for Monica to be seated across from her right now. A part of her had always wanted to explain to Ami how her background opened the doors that Monica always knew she was capable of walking through if only she were given the chance. To explain that the world wasn't kind to people who didn't enter it with the accepted family situation of two parents and a home in the right neighborhood. That the top classes throughout the world don't allow people to infiltrate them unless they believed you were already one of them.

Monica opened her mouth, not sure if she should speak her

mind, confess what she'd done, or make a quick exit, when she heard her phone ding.

"Do you need to get that?" Ami asked.

Reaching into her bag, Monica said, "I'll just take a peek to make sure it's nothing important."

The 573 number: It's time to go home.

Monica quickly dropped it back into her purse and stared at Ami, who was sitting across from her with no devices in her hand. Monica almost breathed a sigh of relief as she grasped that it couldn't be her. She wanted to laugh as she realized this trip and apology tour she'd begun had not been necessary.

Hasty to make an exit, she rose and smoothed out her skirt. "I'm sorry to have come unannounced after all this time, but I just came to apologize. I'm glad to see you're doing well."

Ami eyed her skeptically. "Same to you," she said as Monica made her way out of the room. Ami trailed her to the front door. "I'll let my parents know you were here. And that you weren't kidnapped or anything back then."

"Please give them my best," Monica said. "And tell them I'm sorry for running out without a proper notice period. I trust they found someone to replace me before they ever had to clean one of their own toilets."

Back outside and past the gate, Monica gulped for air. She was overcome with relief that Ami wasn't behind the messages. She had often feared what would happen if Ami ever had found out.

As she made her way toward the main road where Mr. Tan was waiting with the car, she thought about the life she would have had if she had stayed. Ami would have returned to the home less than a year after she'd left and never married. She and Monica would have resumed the roles they'd always had with each other, and Monica could have still been living in that room Grace was in now, sweeping up after Ami and serving her friends chaa. Ami was the same person she'd been seventeen years ago, so there was no reason to think that Monica wouldn't be too. She'd have seen Sister Francis and her friends at the IJ House more often, but she'd hardly seen them in the seven years that she'd worked at the Shahs before, so maybe she was wrong to think there would have been so much more time together. But perhaps even small amounts of connection were better than her long stretch with none at all.

As she slipped into the back seat of the car and directed Mr. Tan to take her to the airport, apprehension filled her again as she realized she had not achieved her goal in coming to Singapore. She scrolled through the messages and considered their cryptic nature. Where was home? It was a question she had wrestled with for all of her life, but did the person on the other end mean the IJ House, Singapore, Los Angeles? Maybe even London? So much was unknown.

The only thing that she seemed certain of was that someone had insight into her movements, knew too much about her past, and the threat to expose her was very real. What she didn't know was how to find them and stop them.

17

Monica was overwhelmed with relief when she wheeled her suitcase down the sidewalk and her Venice property came into view. During the flight, she'd slipped back into her Amala CEO role, and had been emailing Divya about the inventory issues. Divya had reached out to a few people and hadn't had any luck yet, and finding storage was going to be their first order of business now that she was back. Fortunately, the team in India was sending them more samples for the Releaf line with the old formula that they could use for promotional purposes, and Monica was more determined than ever to launch it and give people like her a better chance at life.

As she swung open the garden gate and made her way to the door, she paused taking in the heady scents of basil and mint that wafted around her. She looked at the UrbanGreen beds she'd planted and the vibrant herbs growing from them. She remembered the packaging they'd arrived in. She felt a mixture of excitement and dread as she realized that they would have been stored in a temperature-controlled facility. For better or worse, she knew the owner of that company.

She unlocked the door, and, as she made her way to her bedroom, she couldn't help but notice how quiet and impersonal the house was. It could have been a staged home on one of those real estate shows. She'd liked it that way, but it felt stifling now. She opened some windows, but the silence remained. People paid a lot of money to live in a quiet, exclusive neighborhood, and that's exactly where she was.

She returned her passport and other documents to the safe in her closet. Then she pushed aside a swath of long dresses and gowns that hung from a rod and revealed a cardboard tube hidden behind them. From it, she pulled out the piece she had done for her sewing final exam at CHIJ. It was the only sentimental item she had taken with her when she left Singapore all those years ago. Ami and her family had returned from their annual trip to the Maldives, but this time Ami had glossy photos from an underwater camera of all the fish she'd seen while snorkeling. Monica knew she'd never have such an experience, but she stamped into her mind the images of the coral reefs with marine life swimming around them. She closed her eyes and ran her fingers over the threads. She could identify each type of stitch by touch. Blanket stitches to show the swaying green grasses along the brown earth on the bottom. The fish stripes had been created with zigzag stitches, satin stitches for their spots, and fly stitches to show the texture of scales. A feather stitch was used for the coral around the fish.

She opened her eyes and admired her handiwork. When she'd first moved into this home, Divya had lived there too, so she'd tucked away her sole personal possession in her closet and hadn't considered it since. She thought about the overwater villa she'd been working on that was still in her bag, and while she thought it was a random ocean image, she realized that, too, had been from the photos Ami had shown her of one of her family's trips to the Maldives. Seeing the embroidered pieces prominently displayed at the IJ House made her want to bring her own into the light as well. She smoothed out the fabric and carried it to her bedroom. She'd need to get a frame to hang it properly, but for the time being, she fastened it to the top of her dresser mirror with some binder clips.

She then pulled out her phone to make the call she didn't want to make.

"To what do I owe this great honor?" Oliver asked as his face filled her screen.

"Can a friend not call just to say hi?" Monica said sweetly.

"I'm not quite sure that's what we are. Are you calling because of Naira?"

"Why would I be calling about her?"

"We had a lovely time during our interview. She asked a lot of questions about you. I almost felt like I was supporting cast rather than the star."

Monica laughed. "As if you could ever be anything other than the star."

"Preposterous, I know."

"What was she asking about me?"

"The usual. How well we knew each other. How quickly you fell madly in love with me. Why I let you go. How you've pined for me ever since."

Monica rolled her eyes. "Oli, I'm being serious."

"You're no fun today." He ran a hand through his hair. "She just thought it was really interesting that two classmates were up in the same year. Said she's still hoping to do your interview when you came back. Where were you by the way?"

How had she known Monica had been gone? Monica pushed the thought aside, figuring Divya had probably kept her up to speed.

"Singapore."

"Singapore?" His voice was incredulous. In a softer tone, he said, "I thought you said it was too painful for you to ever go back there..."

Back at LBS, she'd said she couldn't face Singapore with the subtle reminders of her dead parents all over the city. How many times had he wrapped his arms around her and she longed to tell him the truth? Lying hadn't come naturally to her. It was a learned skill, like any other. And like sewing or entrepreneurship, she'd gotten better at it the more she practiced. Now she was both touched and annoyed that Oliver remembered things about her so many years after their romance had fizzled.

"It was," Monica said. "But a lot of time has passed, and there was something I needed to take care of."

Gently, Oliver said, "I know we banter back and forth, but I do hope that we are genuinely friends. If you ever need to go back again, I could go with you."

It was a kind gesture, but there was no way Monica would have dragged Oliver into this mess. The potential of her fake background unraveling before him was too much for her to consider.

"Thanks. There are some things I need to do on my own."

"I suppose we all have to put on our big boy pants at some point, don't we? Or, big girl pants, as it were." Oliver's tone was playful again.

"Indeed. Maybe one day, you'll try it too," Monica said, relieved to be back to their usual repartee. She had never felt comfortable leaning on anyone other than herself.

"Perhaps." Oliver laughed. "Now, you called me, and I seem to be doing most of the talking. I can't imagine you called just to hear my sultry voice."

Monica smiled. "No, there was a greater purpose. Where do you store your seed beds?"

"Warehouse near Thousand Oaks."

"Do you have any spare cubic feet for storage?"

"I'd have to check with my COO. Why?"

Monica hesitated with whether she could trust him with this information, especially while they were in competition for this Award. She had a hard time trusting anyone with anything, but she weighed the need to salvage their inventory against whatever Oliver could do with the knowledge. She didn't need to tell him how much product had been lost or how much it could impact the merger, but she did need to stress the urgency.

"We've had a small warehouse issue, and I need to store some inventory as quickly as possible while I source a more permanent setup," she said. "I need temperature regulation and I recalled that your UrbanGreen seed beds arrived in insulated packaging."

"You've bought my UrbanGreen products?"

"I have," she said in a measured tone.

"I wouldn't have taken you as much of a gardener."

"No, of course not, but it's always good to support a fellow LBS alum."

"How do you like the product? Have you killed all the seeds yet?"

"I'll have you know they are doing quite well. I'm not sure why you'd assume that I'd kill them."

"Ami, need I remind you of the great houseplant massacre of LBS days?"

"That was a long time ago, and I can't be blamed for the lack of sunshine in London."

"I reckon that's true. People can change a lot in this amount of time. I'll check on the warehouse and get back to you."

"Thanks, Oli. I really appreciate it."

When Monica went back to Amala's offices the next day, she heard the familiar hum of the place and felt like she had come home. This business was the culmination of everything she had sacrificed and seeing it thriving brought her back to her center. Nothing mattered more than Amala.

Divya bounded into her office within moments of Monica sitting at her desk.

"Thank goodness you're back." She collapsed into the chair across from Monica, and then sat erect. "Was everything okay with your family?"

"I took care of what I needed to."

Her answer was cryptic, but, by her design, Divya didn't ask her more personal details about what had happened. Their communications had always been centered on Amala and that was how Ami had always wanted it. The parts of Monica that had been reignited, however, considered what it would have been like if Divya had known all her secrets from the start and she'd had a partner to strategize with.

Monica cleared her throat. "Back to business. I asked Oliver if he had extra storage capability, and he's going to get back to us."

Divya raised an eyebrow. "Didn't realize you still talked to Oliver."

"I knew his UrbanGreen products were temperature controlled, so I thought it wouldn't hurt to ask him. He also mentioned that he did his Global Changemakers Award interview with Naira, and I suspect that is on the top of the list you have on that notepad of yours."

Divya looked sheepish. "Gemma has been breathing down my neck, and we are running out of time."

Monica stared out the window at the majestic Pacific Ocean, its expanse separating her current life from her old one. "Fine, schedule it. But let's get the questions in advance and make sure she sticks to the script."

"It's an interview, not a rehearsal for a play, so I can't control every word that comes out of her mouth," Divya said. "But she has just as much to gain from this piece doing well as we do, so she will be incentivized not to tank it."

Monica turned toward Divya noticing something different in her tone. Was that frustration? Annoyance? She was normally so even-keeled. Monica's mind began spinning as she wondered if Divya could be behind the text messages. She had the most to gain if Monica was ousted from the company. She'd step into the CEO role and claim Monica's seat on the Board, as well as her buyout payment if she became CEO in advance of the merger. Had she somehow discovered the truth and resented having been lied to for all these years? Was she tired of being in Monica's shadow?

"Can we do the Global Changemakers photo shoot at the same time?" Divya asked.

Monica removed her scarf to show Divya the damaged skin along her neck, and then removed her glasses and closed her eyes to show her scaly eyelid. "Is there a choice?"

"Not really. But we can adjust the lighting and angles, and style you to be wearing a scarf and have your hair loose to cover up as much as we can. Your glasses do a good job of hiding your eyes, but maybe we amp that up and use some tinted glasses. In this city, you can easily get away with sunglasses indoors as if that's a fashion element rather than rude. That's the best we can do. Leonard thinks it's important to tackle this immediately. He even suggested getting some extra photos to use in our own press campaign leading up to the Award announcement."

"You talked to Leonard again?"

Monica had always been the one that communicated directly with Leonard and Divya had always preferred that.

Divya's face blanched before she spoke. "Just briefly. You were gone and he wanted to know more about our strategy."

"He could have just asked me when he called."

Divya shrugged. "I was more available."

It was hard to imagine Divya plotting against her, especially given how much she valued Brown female solidarity, but Divya also seemed to be acting strangely and Monica would need to watch her carefully. If she did know the truth about Monica, she could have fed it to Naira, and that could be why she was pushing her so hard to do the interview. Maybe the photo shoot was about exposing her skin rather than hiding it. Monica shook her head, trying to dislodge the toxic thoughts.

"And what about the Board vote tonight?" Monica asked. "You'd think these people would have a better way to spend their Friday evening than sabotaging us."

Divya's expression grew somber. "Steve's been in everyone's ear about it. You're going to have your work cut out for you, but maybe if we have the inventory situation sorted and aren't going to lose more product, that would put some of their minds at ease. Right now, it's the eve of merger, so it's all about dollars to them."

Monica nodded, wondering if somewhere along the way, their interests had diverged and it was all about dollars to Divya too.

When Oliver's face flashed across her screen an hour later with an incoming video call, she rushed to answer it.

"Tell me you have good news," she said, not able to keep the desperation out of her voice. She wanted to distract the Board with something positive.

"You're looking at your savior. I've secured some warehouse space for you." He held the phone away from him so she could see his exaggerated bow. "At your service, as always."

Her shoulders relaxed. "Thank you for doing that. Seriously."

"My pleasure. We LBS kids need to stick together, right?"

"We're hardly kids anymore. I believe middle-aged is the term actual kids now use to describe us."

Oliver pulled his head back and flinched. "No need to be brutal, Ami. We are in the prime of our lives."

"Just because we didn't mature doesn't mean we didn't age."

"At least you've included yourself in that."

"It was the polite thing to say."

"Very British of you."

"I guess those years in London made an impact."

Oliver rolled his eyes. It was well understood between them that Monica thought the stereotypes about English manners were overhyped. Sister Francis had raised her to believe that politeness needed to be sincere, and what she'd seen in London typically fell somewhere between forced and fake.

Monica caught herself and adopted a more conciliatory tone. "I'll have Divya reach out to you to sort out the logistics of moving our inventory. And I really do appreciate it. It should hopefully just be for a little while until we get something more permanent set up."

Oliver waved his hand. "It's nothing, really. Take all the time you need. I know you've got quite a few other items circling that clever brain of yours."

"Good news," Ami said in an overly chipper voice from the doorway to Divya's office. "Oli said he has some warehouse space we can use for our inventory, so we can use that until the merger closes and then we can move everything to Propelle's storage. I wasn't sure he'd come through, but Oliver Dalton never ceases to surprise, I suppose."

Divya pulled out her notepad and struck a line through something. "Never look a gift horse in the mouth, they say."

Monica had never understood that expression. There were so many Americanisms that made no sense to her, but she'd given up on trying to understand their origins. She'd merely done what any good immigrant would do and learned the proper context in which to use them so she'd be able to blend in more.

"I told him you'd call to sort out logistics," Monica said.

Divya nodded and began scribbling in her notepad. The woman was highly competent, and Monica was grateful for that. Could she really be harboring a nefarious plan to expose Monica under all that efficiency?

"I also have markups for the Releaf products for you to look at. We won't have the actual physical products in hand to photograph given the fact that we now have to play catch-up with the lost inventory, but the marketing team has done a great job with digital images that look like they are real. They've also mapped out the social media strategy leading up to it, and that will start going live next week. The Global Changemakers will know about our commitment to underserved groups and the charitable component well before they announce the winner. You should sign off on the social media campaign today. We have a very compressed timeline as it is. Well, I suppose if Steve gets what he wants tonight, then we won't have to worry about the Releaf line and our schedules will clear up."

Monica gave her a look. "Don't even joke about that. This is still my company and I get to decide our future."

Divya saluted her as if she were a captain. Something she'd never done before. Monica couldn't shake the feeling that something did seem off between them. Monica rarely asserted rank, but it was starting to feel like Divya was upset with her place in the hierarchy.

18

As the sun was setting over the beach, casting soft purple and blue hues across the sky, Monica, Divya, and the members of the Board gathered in the conference room.

"Ami," Leonard said, coming in for a hug.

She acquiesced knowing she only had to put up with this group of investors for a little longer. Then, they could all go their separate ways. And if she didn't win the Global Changemakers and remain at the company, then maybe she could go back to being Monica.

"We weren't sure you'd be able to join us," Steve said.

She flashed him a saccharine smile. "Here I am. I couldn't miss such an important vote about the future of my company."

"What is all the fuss about?" Kyle said. "I had to cancel a poker game for this and I was ready to put those guys in their places after clearing me out last week."

Steve cleared his throat. "We need to vote on whether to continue with the Releaf line, especially given that we need to invest in more inventory now before we know if insurance is going to cover all the loss. It's going to look like double the cost on our books pre-merger, and Propelle has said they don't even want it. It seems ridiculous for us to outlay that cash at this point in time. If Propelle wants it, they can spend whatever they want after the merger. But I say we keep our books as tight as possible leading up to that."

Monica shot him daggers before shifting back into the cool, confident CEO that they expected her to be. She adjusted the scarf draped around her neck and began.

"I want to be clear that we will not be doing that." She met the eyes of each of the men in turn. "You boys will ride off into the sunset when this deal closes, but winning that Award is crucial for me and the rest of the team, and the Releaf line helps me do that. We have a campaign launching next week that will highlight how the products are serving a need in the community, and how our social equity component of donating a portion of the proceeds will help those who cannot afford the retail pricing. Corporate social responsibility is something the Award committee will be looking at, in addition to our consumer base. Amala was founded to serve the needs of the people whom North American skin care companies have disregarded, and that ethos is what led to the profitable company we are today. We can all agree that non-white people with dermatitis-related skin conditions have been wholly ignored, and we have a responsibility to support that demographic. This is not a beauty company. This is a *health* company. We are in the business of nourishing the largest organ on a person's body so that it performs optimally. We have run the numbers, and yes, an inventory setback wasn't on anyone's wish list, but insurance will eventually come through and balance out the books. In the meantime, Divya and I have already secured a location to store our product until the merger closes and we can move it to a Propelle warehouse. I trust everyone is in agreement on that path forward."

She again looked at each of them in turn, daring one of them to speak against her, but they all busied themselves with the ends of their ties or their phones to avoid making eye contact. She caught a glimpse of Divya trying to hide her smile behind her laptop in the silent room. Monica had never spoken to the Board in this way, but she was tired of having to always pander to egos that were inherited at birth.

Monica clapped her hands. "Now, as for the money that you are all so interested in, we know that goes up if I win the Global Changemakers Award, and that is what affects your payout the most right now. So, let's use our precious time to be more productive and work toward that goal. Let's get out there and win that Award so you all get your money, and I get to keep my company."

There were some murmurs of agreement.

"Terrific. I move that we proceed with the Releaf line as scheduled and get back to work. All in favor?"

Leonard raised a timid hand and the rest followed suit. Corporate investors were such sheep.

Monica sauntered back to her office, wanting to kick off her heels and sink into the carpet after that speech, but before she could steal a few minutes to herself, Pedro was in the doorway.

"We got an answer about that name you gave me before you left." He handed her the sheets of paper he was holding and then went back to his desk.

Monica sank onto the carpet and leaned against the sofa as she began to scan the documents. The first pages had Naira's CV, education records, addresses, and vehicles owned. But the last few pages had the PI's notes from interviews and other sources:

- Rising star at *The New Yorker*. Focused on pieces that highlighted people of color.

- During her final year at *The New Yorker*, she interviewed a successful Sikh woman—a lawyer who became a civil rights activist after September 11th because her community was being wrongfully targeted as Muslim, and hate crimes against Brown people were running rampant in America.

- Woman had a brother who became part of the anti-American movement following September 11th and worked with the Taliban.

- Naira completed her article without including the facts about the subject's brother citing that it would unduly influence readers to perceive the subject negatively, even though the subject had cut ties with her brother over a decade ago and had nothing to do with his actions.

- Upon learning of the omission, she was removed from *The New Yorker* pursuant to a settlement agreement that kept most of the details confidential. (Settlement agreement could not be located.)

- Not publicly reported: Naira had begun a sexual relationship with the woman's daughter. During the research portion of her interview, she met with the woman's family members, including the daughter, and the two became romantically involved. Resulted in allegations of inappropriate sexual conduct with a source, romantic involvement compromising her journalistic integrity, and biased reporting. Likely the real reason she left *The New Yorker*.

Monica read that last bullet point again. The general bias in favor of a person's culture was something that could be perceived as subconscious and something that could be corrected over time with targeted work and attention. However, sexual misconduct was a permanent stain that could only fade, but never be completely erased, especially for women. Monica understood why Naira had taken so many years away from her profession, and why she was being so careful about how she approached it now. Monica felt better about the upcoming interview. Not because of their "shared" cultural background like Divya had been touting, but because of their shared need to keep secrets to advance their professional goals. Leverage was power, and she now had some to wield if the interview went poorly and she needed to quash the article.

Divya popped into Monica's office and Monica quickly shoved the pages beneath the sofa behind her before Divya could see them.

Divya smiled. "I don't know what brought that on, but did you see their faces?"

"I think they aren't used to women giving them orders." Monica stretched her legs.

Divya kicked off her shoes and joined her on the rug and it felt like old times. "And we aren't used to feeling comfortable enough to speak up."

"Is it a lack of comfort? Or do you think it's because we know that in order for us to get what we want, we have to make them think that everything was their idea?"

Divya laughed. "Two things can be true at once."

"I'm just glad that silly rebellion has been tamped down and we can go back to the business of running our company." Monica met Divya's gaze. "Did you set up the interview with Naira?"

"It's on Sunday."

"Good. We have an award to win and nothing is going to stand in my way."

19

Monica's lower living room that had once been the fledgling home of Amala felt like a fitting place to do the interview. The sliding glass doors opened out to the garden and provided just the right amount of natural light to keep the space warm but not overly bright. Monica and Divya had spent hours in this room, surrounded by products and stuffing them into boxes themselves for distribution. It was a simpler time before either of them knew what their business would grow into—having to answer to a board, and going through due diligence for mergers.

Today, the room was free of any clutter and Divya had positioned the two loveseats across from one another. On the console table behind where Monica would sit, the Amala product line had been tastefully arranged from their lightest shade of purple to the darkest and served as a nice background. Divya had placed some potted plants around the seating area as well to give it a cozy feeling. She always thought of everything.

Monica's hair fell in soft curls around her tinted glasses and along her face, and she had tied a purple scarf around her neck to ensure her eczema would be hidden. Her makeup looked more natural than the many layers she had caked on, and the lighting in the room would conceal that too.

"You ready?" Divya asked, when the two of them were in a quiet corner to themselves.

Monica glanced around the room at the crew adjusting their screens and tripods for the photographs. She saw Naira shuffling through papers and consulting her notes.

"I guess I have to be."

Divya repositioned one of Monica's curls that was out of place. "Just breathe. You'll do great."

Monica adjusted her scarf one final time before making her way to the couch, where the team was ready to take her photos. Divya directed her from the sidelines as she consulted the pose requirements that had come from the Changemakers. Monica felt silly being staged in this way, but it was what she had to do in order to give them what they wanted. Once they were done, Divya instructed the photographer to begin editing the photos so they could finalize and send them in today. Gemma was already annoyed that they were being turned in on the last day, and they were doing everything possible to ensure it wasn't the last minute of that day.

Once that part was done, Naira took a seat across from her, pen poised over her notepad. "Would you prefer that I call you Ami or Ms. Shah during the interview? Or something else?"

"Ami is fine," Monica said, trying not to taste the lie on her tongue.

"Thank you for agreeing to let me do your story. I love highlighting women who are blazing new paths that open up possibilities for future generations. That model minority myth has done so much to harm our choices."

"I'm not sure that going to business school is bucking any trends."

Naira laughed. "Maybe not. But what you built with that degree is a lot different than just becoming a partner at a management or consulting firm. Building something from scratch is a harder road, especially when you've had so much adversity with the loss of your family at a young age. And when you add the mission-driven component that you have with Amala and trying to solve a need for people of color across North America, well, that's a whole other thing."

"That's very generous of you."

People moved around them readjusting cables and then asked each of them to speak into their mics for a sound check.

"I heard you were in Singapore."

Monica wished Divya hadn't been so loose lipped about her whereabouts. "It was a quick trip."

"I imagine it's a complicated place to visit for you. Do you go back often?"

"No." Monica looked to see if they'd begin soon and could stop the small talk portion of this interview.

"I've never been, but it sounds like an intriguing place." Naira tucked a strand of her long hair behind her ear. "I read Lee Kuan Yew's autobiography and was fascinated by the fact that the British voluntarily left the country when the local people like him wanted them to stay. It's the opposite of the normal colonization story, where the Brits have to be forced out. I'd love to learn more about that. Maybe India and other places should have tried to reverse psychology the Brits out too." Naira chuckled. "Not to mention the progress that has been made in such a short amount of time after the British left. It's such a rich history."

Monica smiled absently. "Not everything is about being rich."

Naira raised an eyebrow, but before she could follow up on Monica's comment the man who had been setting up the audio recording said, "We're ready to roll."

Naira cleared her throat and began. "Hi, Ami. Thank you for the privilege of speaking with you today about your nomination for the Global Changemakers Award. As I'm sure you know, this is an historic time in the entrepreneurial world because a woman of your caliber has never even been nominated in the past, let alone won the prestigious award. How does it feel to be making history?"

Ami settled in as the question was nearly verbatim from the list they'd been given in advance of this interview.

"As they say at the Oscars, it's an honor to even be nominated," Monica said with a small smile. "I've never set out to win any awards or have them validate my work, but I am so proud of what I've built with my team at Amala and any recognition of those efforts is truly an honor. It saddens me that no other women of color have been in the running before because I am far from the first such person to have developed a business that is worthy of this recognition. I can only hope that I'm the first of many women to be lauded for the strides we are making in the entrepreneurial world. It's time for the men to move over, because we aren't seeking a seat at their table anymore. We are building our own tables that are bigger, better, and stronger, and then surrounding ourselves with other women who help lift us up."

She and Divya exchanged a smile. Then she turned back to Naira and saw how pleased Naira was with her answer.

"The world would certainly be different if women were running it," Naira said, with a glint in her eye. "It seems you practice what you preach as well. My understanding is that Amala is led almost entirely by a strong, diverse female team. Is that right?"

"Absolutely," Monica said. "I've been fortunate to have strong female role models in my life and believe there is nothing better than women working together toward a common goal."

"Who are some of the strong females in your past that helped you along your path? Is there anyone from your childhood who really stands out as helping you to get to where you are today?"

Monica paused as she processed this question that wasn't on the script. She didn't want to reveal the names of any of the Sisters, especially not to a hungry reporter.

"As is the case for many women, my mother helped shape who I became," Monica said, while forcing the lump down her throat. Being abandoned as a newborn absolutely had shaped who she was today, but she knew that wasn't the assumption people would make about her statement. They'd believe she had had an idyllic childhood with a supportive family until they tragically passed in an auto accident in her mid-twenties.

Naira looked appropriately touched by Monica's statement. "I know you've said she's no longer with us, and it must have been so hard to lose her, especially so young."

Monica adopted her practiced expression of grief. "Yes, well, it's hard to lose a parent at any age. I try not to dwell on what cannot be changed, but—" her voice caught in her throat "—people rarely lose their parents as early as I did."

"I'm so very sorry for what you've been through."

Monica shot her a glistening doe-eyed look, and Naira moved on to the remainder of her questions.

"What prompted you to start Amala in the first place?"

Monica relaxed into her seat, as these were the types of questions she'd answered countless times. "I had never set foot in the Western Hemisphere before beginning business school and was surprised that, while the market was saturated with products, those products only catered toward one particular demographic."

She and Naira looked at each other knowingly.

"White women," Monica explained.

Naira crossed her legs and leaned forward. "And what was it about those products that made you think they were only for white women?"

"For starters, the frequency of use, viscosity, and sheer number of recommended products. I saw face washes filled with harsh chemicals that suggested being used twice a day. If I washed my face twice a day, it would have been bone-dry. And it would be because of those harsh cleansers that I'd now need to use more gloopy moisturizers that would clog pores, and various serums to put back what had been there naturally before the cleanser had stripped it away. While it might be good for capitalism to sell people more and more, it didn't make sense to me to create a problem with one product that then needed to be solved with more products, especially when dealing with our health."

Naira adjusted in her seat. "Are you saying that the entire skin care industry has been getting it wrong since its inception?"

"That's not for me to say. What I knew was that the products didn't work for my skin type. We often forget that skin is the largest organ in our body, and we need to care for it the same way we would our brain, liver, or any other organ. More than anything, our skin reflects what is wrong internally rather than external forces like weather and sun. Those play a role, obviously, but they have less of an impact if we are healthy overall. When I first arrived from Singapore, between the weather and no adequate products for my melanin-rich skin, I started having issues like breakouts and other things I'd never experienced before. So, my first step was to think about how I could improve my overall health with my diet and lifestyle to keep my organs running at optimum levels so that my skin was less affected by the cold, wet London weather. Then, I started thinking about the natural products I grew up with that would help soothe my skin. Things like amla, bakuchi, sandalwood, and rosemary, which have healing properties through digestion or external application. I believe that loading any organ with chemicals, including skin, cannot lead to lasting positive results."

"Is that what you'd say differentiates Amala and has led to your success? Being chemical-free?" Naira asked.

"The success is based on an entire team of people, and I would never presume that it was down to just me." Monica looked at Divya. "But I do think Amala was developed at a time when people were starting to question the old ways of doing things, especially people with skin that looked like mine. I was raised in a place where the products were designed for Asian skin. While there's still a gap between Chinese and Indian skin, there is an even larger gap between white and brown skin. It seemed like, in the Western Hemisphere, Brown people were told to use products made for white people as if it was their skin that needed to adjust to the products as opposed to the other way around. Putting aside that such an idea isn't even possible, there are lots of different skin types, and there need to be products that address them all. So, Amala helps fill that void."

"If people use your products, are they all going to end up with flawless skin?"

Monica gave a small laugh and readjusted her glasses so they were further up the bridge of her nose. "Our products don't make that claim, and I wouldn't trust any brand that does. It's more about *healthy* skin than flawless skin at Amala. Our motto is 'pure love, pure skin,' because we believe in proper hydration, nourishment through food, and stress-relieving practices as the foundation for having healthy skin. The love we give ourselves on the inside is what leads to pure skin on the outside. Our products are there to help supplement that internal work that is being done. But there is no substitute for living a clean, authentic life that aligns with who you are. That's what your skin will reflect back to you. Unhealthy skin is your body's way of trying to get your attention when something feels wrong."

Naira leaned forward. "Let's talk more about that slogan that we see on every box: pure love, pure skin. In fact, Amala itself is a Sanskrit word for *purity*, isn't that right?"

"Yes, and that was a big part of choosing it for the name of the company." Monica smiled coyly. "Amala is also another name for Lakshmi, the Hindu goddess of wealth, which also seemed to be a fitting aspiration for a budding business, and it didn't hurt that it would be easy to pronounce by a Western consumer base."

"I'm sure every business dreams of wealth, but it's so refreshing to see products that are promoting the pure essence of health rather than sweeping anti-aging or more traditional beauty messaging. We might finally be entering an era where beauty isn't defined as a monolith, sending the harmful messaging to girls—especially ones who look like us—that by not having blond hair, blue eyes, or pale skin on a thin frame, we should feel like we are on the fringes of society. How do you ensure you live an authentic life that aligns with the values of your brand?"

Monica paused for a moment, as this question wasn't on the script.

"Each day I demonstrate my commitment to Amala. This company has been my baby for fifteen years now, and I take my responsibility to my team and customers very seriously. That is the most authentic version of myself, and that is how I try to show up every day."

"We could all do with showing up as our authentic selves, couldn't we? Is living authentically what you attribute your own radiant skin to?"

"As I've said, there are so many factors that go into the health of our skin. Nutrition, environment, stress, genetics, etcetera. I do my best to manage those factors, but as you said, some days are harder than others, and no one can be expected to be perfect for every single moment of their lives."

"You mentioned genetics. Did your parents have good skin?"

Monica froze. She hadn't anticipated the question, and obviously she had no idea about any of her genetic predispositions.

"All that heat and humidity in Singapore generally does wonders for skin."

Her non-answer answer technique was one that had served her well ever since she moved to London. When responding to a question confidently, with the right amount of charm, people rarely reflected on it carefully enough to confirm whether or not it had been directly answered.

Wanting to ensure they moved off this topic, Monica began speaking about the points she really wanted to get out today.

"In fact, at Amala we understand that for some people, lifestyle won't be enough to keep their skin as nourished as it needs to be, and I'm so thrilled to share with you before we've announced publicly to anyone else, that we are launching a new line called Releaf for those impacted by dermatitis, and a portion of the proceeds from this new line will be used to help affected people who may not otherwise have access to the products. We are proud to be working toward saving as many faces as we can, because everyone deserves to feel good in the skin they are in."

The interview continued for the next hour with Naira focusing on the pre-approved questions and Monica providing the answers she'd practiced with Divya. It seemed that they'd get the puff piece they had hoped for, and Monica could put this media attention behind her and move on to the real business of positioning Amala for the merger.

As Naira's assistant was packing up the audio equipment after the interview, Naira, Divya, and Monica were sitting on the sofas.

"Did you get everything you need?" Divya asked.

Naira nodded. "Thank you for setting this up. I'm really excited to sit down and write up your story. I think so many people will find it impactful."

Monica waved her off.

Divya jumped in. "Ami cannot handle praise about herself. She's always been that way. Ever since I've known her."

Naira looked at Monica. "Were you that way as a child as well?"

Monica thought back to her time in the orphanage. There hadn't been much opportunity to know if she was skilled at anything outside of school. She'd been good at academics, understanding the theories quickly and getting good grades. She'd been good at sewing, but that was also part of her schooling, so she'd put the time and attention needed to get a high score in that course as well.

"I'm not sure there was much praise as a child, outside of schoolwork," Monica said.

Divya and Naira nodded knowingly as if both thought she was referring to something akin to their own childhoods where their Indian parents were focused on their grades above all else. Misdirection and false assumptions had been another key social strategy ever since she'd become Ami.

Turning to Naira, Divya said, "It would be helpful to get the piece published as soon as possible. I'm sure you know we are in the midst of a merger on top of the Changemakers and every little bit of positive press helps."

"I understand. I'll do my best, but I want to chase down a few other things. My goal is to provide a comprehensive piece that will get the most eyeballs on it."

"We couldn't agree more," Divya said.

Monica, meanwhile, was already shifting her thoughts back to launching their dermatitis line. With this interview out of the way, and it having gone better than she had expected, she was ready to get back to doing what she loved.

As she walked Divya to the front door after everyone had left, Monica turned to her and said, "You were right. Naira was great. I'm sorry I made you jump through hoops to pick her."

Divya beamed. "You know I'm always right. And we did something good today. We helped a young Indian woman catapult her career. She got the story approved to run as an exclusive in *Forbes*, and just think how hard it would be for her to see her name in there without this."

It was true. Divya was never wrong when it came to her professional judgment, and they both could be proud of the fact that they'd helped Naira's career get back on track. One lapse in judgment should not define anyone.

20

Monica woke up a few days after the interview with Naira and could feel that the red patches along her neck had started to recede. She'd seen the photo that had run with the nominee exclusive that the Global Changemakers had put out and there was nothing visibly wrong with her skin. Having survived that and the interview with Naira was a welcome relief not only to her mind, but to her body. And perhaps most significantly to her overall well-being, she hadn't received any text messages from the 573 number for over a week, and hoped whoever was behind that had moved on to someone else to torment.

She dabbed the Releaf serum onto her neck, relishing how the triphala alleviated discomfort on contact. The eczema on her eyelid had cleared and she no longer needed to worry about that. She went to the office that day with more pep in her step. She could feel the weight of the world receding, and was eager to get back to her routine. She felt so focused and grounded when her work was her top priority.

One of the first emails she saw when she logged onto her

computer was a report from the team in Chennai about the dermatitis line. She called Divya to her office so they could go over it together.

They stood at Monica's computer and pored over the small font with the ingredient list and percentages, along with the graphs detailing the shelf life.

"Am I reading this correctly?" Monica asked. "Did the new percentages of vitamin E and lecithin give us the six-month shelf life we wanted?"

Divya smiled. "It appears so. Steve won't love that we succeeded, but at least we'll be done with him after the merger."

"He can run off and count his money in a cave somewhere." Monica closed the email, while Divya moved around the desk and sat in one of the chairs in front of it. "Not that it's great to lose money or inventory, but at least what we lost wasn't the formula we wanted to sell to consumers."

"That's definitely an optimistic view of the inventory debacle."

Monica shrugged. "Take the wins where we have them, right?" Softening her tone, she said, "Are you worried about the merger at all, Div? I know we've been moving full steam ahead, but you and I haven't really sat and talked about what happens when it's all done."

"You mean, if you don't win the Global Changemakers and aren't here? And then Walter Johnson fires us all and strips the company for parts?"

Monica grimaced, but it was a reality they had to consider. "Yes, and honestly even if I am still here. We will have new bosses, and they probably won't be as hands-off as Leonard has been. Things are bound to change. I certainly hope I'm here to manage the transition, but nothing in life is certain."

"The best thing we can do is focus on our products. Within a big conglomerate like Propelle, the numbers are the only thing that matters. If we can prove out the profits, then I suspect they'll leave us alone. If we can't, then I'm sure they'll demand changes."

"Do you think I'm right? About not altering the quality of the products to make them more accessible at a lower price point?"

Monica had been adamant about that decision from the moment she'd made it and had never consulted Divya or anyone else about it.

"I think we sell high-quality products."

"That isn't what I asked."

"It's hard because we didn't grow up the same way. I know you didn't have to worry about money as a kid, but my family did, and we wouldn't have been able to afford the products we sell. My mom loves them, but she's only using them because she gets them for free. She would never be able to buy them on her own." Divya shifted in her seat. "In this part of the world, there is a disproportionately large percentage of people with brown skin who earn incomes that are too low to buy our products, but they are the people who would benefit most from them."

Monica swallowed the lump in her throat. It would be so much easier if she just told Divya the truth and hadn't rebuffed Divya every time she'd tried to get close to her. Seeing Sister Francis, Esther, Qi, and Victoria had reminded her what it had been like to have a family—or the closest thing she knew to one. But she had built her fortress of solitude many years ago and it was too late to change course. She thought back to Divya's strange behavior since her return and wondered again if Divya was behind the 573 number. If she was, then she already knew the truth and maybe her references to Monica's fabricated past were to see if she would crack. If she wasn't, then Monica was simply burdening Divya by having to decide whether to keep Monica's secret. The lies had started to protect herself. But over the years, a lot of people had come to depend on this fabricated version of her, and she couldn't extricate herself without having widespread consequences for the others.

"It's a hard line to straddle with a for-profit business," Monica said. "You said yourself that what will matter to Propelle are the numbers, and consumable products with higher margins targeted toward higher-income individuals are the most profitable."

"I know," Divya said. "Your decisions have gotten us this far. I'm not questioning it. I can wish for a better world while still accepting the one we live in."

"Trust me, if I could change the world, I would. I don't love the capitalist way in which life operates either. But it's going to take something big like another world war or a global pandemic to get people to start behaving differently. And even then, who knows if they'll value social responsibility above personal gain. It's just as likely that people would use such a tragedy to push their own agendas forward rather than come together for the greater good."

Divya rose from her chair. "You're right. I'll let the team in India know to proceed with the formula and send us new samples. Let's focus on what we can control, and that's getting Releaf up and running while we still can."

Monica was enjoying a glass of Valpolicella Ripasso on her rooftop. She had a shawl thrown over her shoulders to block out the chill that settled in after the sun had set. Blue flames danced along the white stones in her firepit and she found the unpredictable movement both mesmerizing and calming. She shook her head at the thought that she'd be able to drink wine at her former convent home now. She wouldn't need the shawl in

Singapore though. Being back there reminded her how much she missed warm nights.

It had been a good professional week, but she couldn't deny the feeling of loneliness that was starting to settle into her. She was working so hard toward the goal of keeping Amala rather than selling it off, and that meant she was continuing her identity as Ami Shah too. She wished there were a way to reveal her true self and show everyone that she hadn't needed an elitist background to be a successful CEO, while still keeping her company. She wished she could bring her friends from Singapore to Los Angeles and show them her new life. She wished she could stop hiding. But life wasn't that simple, and she had to live with the consequences of the choices she had made.

Monica's phone rang and Oliver's photo came up on her screen.

"Didn't think I'd actually catch you," Oliver said after she answered.

"Then why'd you call?"

"Touché, Ms. Shah."

She was so very tired of being Ms. Shah.

"Did you see the article that came out?" he asked.

"Which one?"

"My piece for the Global Changemakers Award. Harlan Cooper did the interview. Nice old chap. It came out a few days ago and I hadn't heard from you."

"So you called to check? I thought Naira was doing your interview. Didn't you say you already met with her?"

"We did. But she was really dragging her feet on getting the article finished. Said she had more research to do, but honestly, I think she just wanted to focus on you. I figured no harm in lining up a bigger name anyway."

Monica shook her head. She could picture the vast array of things that Oliver and Harlan had in common and it seemed like the right fit of interviewer and interviewee. No doubt Harlan's family could trace their ancestry back to somewhere in jolly old England as well.

She felt her phone vibrate and saw that Oliver had sent her the link. "You must be really proud of this article if you're calling to tell me about it."

He laughed. "I might just have it framed for my wall. It is a rather dashing photo of me."

"Photos of you normally are." Monica pulled the shawl tighter around her shoulders.

"Dare I say, is that a compliment?" When she didn't respond, he cleared his throat. "When is yours coming out? I'd think there would be a lovely multi-page spread of all the good you've achieved in the world. I've seen your social media campaign for your new line. Well-timed, no doubt. And yet you're the only nominee who hasn't had any Changemakers media attention so far."

"I didn't realize you were keeping tabs. I'm sure Naira will be publishing it soon. As you said, she's thorough in her research, unlike some others in her field."

"Are you suggesting someone of Harlan's stature isn't thorough?"

"I'm saying that stature isn't always earned."

"I hardly think that's fair to say of someone you've never met."

What he didn't realize was that she had met him. She had met a million Harlan Coopers and Oliver Daltons since she first set foot in America. It was easy to spot the people who felt entitled to the country they lived in. Just like it was easy to identify the ones who didn't.

Monica sighed. "Oli, it's been a long day. Is that all you called for?"

"While I'd love for you to give the article a gander, I'm

calling because it turns out we are going to need the storage space we're renting to you back sooner than I anticipated. The buzz from the article has already generated a flood of new orders and we are upping our inventory. Have you got something else sorted for yours yet?"

This was the last thing she wanted to think about. "How much longer can you help us out?"

"We've got a load of product coming in a couple weeks, so it would be great if we can have the space back by then . . ."

Monica tensed. That would be around the time they'd be receiving the new inventory from the Releaf line and she was counting on Oliver's storage for that. "I'll talk to Divya and find out where things stand. But I appreciate the favor and we'll be sure to get our stuff out of your warehouse by the time you need it."

"Ta. And you might want to get more than you think you need if our increased orders are any indication. You might be doubling your sales soon with this kind of publicity. I imagine that Propelle could help you out with storage? From the press, it seems as if the deal is as good as inked, and they've got heaps of warehouses."

"They do," she said noncommittally.

"Unless," he countered, "they don't know about the issue. That would, of course, make sense given the delicate situation between you right now. I could ask around if you need another solution."

She couldn't blame him for trying to fish for information. She'd have done the same in his position, but she also detected something in his voice that made her wonder if his intentions were not as pure as she'd hoped.

"That's okay. We'll be fine. I'll sort out how to store the stuff that is housed with you at the moment. Consumers are nothing if not unpredictable. I'll stick to the projections and forecasts from our team before expecting a windfall from an article."

"Fair enough. You've got your own windfall coming soon anyway."

Monica wasn't going to give him anything, especially as she processed how much Oliver had to gain from exposing her. "Nothing is final until it is."

"So, I was thinking that maybe we could go together to the gala in a couple weeks. What do you say? For old time's sake."

"Oh."

"Don't sound too enthused. Some people would actually think I'm quite a fetching date. An old version of you would have said so too."

He wasn't wrong. But after Singapore, she was reminded how dangerous it was to revisit her past. And that included Oliver.

"I have no doubt that you'll have a long line of women wanting to be your date."

"Just not you. Understood, Ms. Shah. Please have Divya reach out to me with the instructions regarding the inventory."

"Sorry, Oli. It's just a busy time with the merger and there's a lot I need to think about."

"No explanation needed. I'll see you there, looking even more dashing than that photo, and you'll wish you'd taken me up on my offer."

Monica laughed. To have the unbridled confidence of a white man.

21

Monica filled in Divya on the need to move their inventory while they were going over the final package markups for the Releaf line. Both agreed that approaching Propelle was not the best idea at this delicate time and they'd find another solution. It was a big city. Everything was available for the right price, so they just had to find a place with space. Oliver had been right that after the merger they would bring everything under Propelle's umbrella, so they just needed something temporary that would buy them time until the closing date.

The two sat on the rug in Monica's office with her laptop between them as they enlarged the images on the screen.

"The leaf pattern is great. Subtle, but hints to the name and natural elements without being distracting," Monica said.

Divya nodded. "The team did a good job. I say we lock these and get the labels onto the samples we have stored at Oliver's warehouse. We can at least take some of that inventory and ship it off to the influencers on our schedule so that there's less we need to store on our own."

"I like that plan. Let's make sure we include an instruction card with this outreach that says to store it in the fridge. The last thing we need is people posting with a gloopy moisturizer rather than the enticing, creamy one. And once we get the new formula in, we can note that it's shelf stable for six months."

Divya pulled out her phone and showed Monica some of the social media posts that had already found large audiences. "People are really excited about the products. There are so many personal stories in the comments about how much people have shied away from opportunities because of their skin." Divya scrolled through the messages. "People afraid to take on certain roles at work, or go on a date, or even go to a gym where they'd have to undress in front of others. You were right that a lot of people were hiding in plain sight when it came to skin problems."

"Let's hope I'm also right about how much they are willing to spend to get their confidence back."

"The good news for the short term is that the Global Changemakers Committee seems to be following the news since the announcement as well. That's exactly what we wanted."

Monica hoped that their plan had been enough to sway the Committee in her favor. Of the candidates, hers was the only company with a corporate social responsibility component and that had to count for something. As long as things continued on this trajectory, she felt like things might actually work out the way she wanted. She just had a little while to go.

Monica felt herself starting to move forward with anticipation rather than dread. She was two weeks away from the Global Changemakers Gala, and the merger would follow two weeks after that. In just a month, so much of her life would change.

For the first time, she indulged in thinking about what it would mean to win the Global Changemakers Award beyond the merger deal she'd made with Walter Johnson. If she could be recognized for her hard work and be that beacon for other girls who looked like her and Divya. Even if she had to do it under a name that didn't feel like hers, it didn't change the fact that *she* was the one who had done all the work to develop and grow this business. What would it have meant if she had seen an orphan at CHIJ before her end up as something other than a maid. What if someone had ended up like her now? Would she have felt like she could have approached the world as Monica and still gotten to where she was today? Most likely. But she reminded herself that was a fictional world. And in this reality, the rags to riches story that people pretended was possible, really wasn't.

Seeing how well the Releaf products had worked on her had sharpened her focus. She thought about all the people with similar afflictions who would be more comfortable and confident because of this new line. Amala's social media outreach had shown that the market was larger than anyone realized, full of stories of people doing anything they could to hide their skin problems, whether it be with clothing, makeup, hairstyles, or avoiding being in public entirely. Visible imperfections like bumpy, red irritations, or flaky, leathery areas of roughness, or white patches from vitiligo depigmentation were not normalized, so the people suffering lived with shame.

And most significantly, their PR campaign was resulting in sales. Preorders for Releaf were higher thus far than any other product launch they'd had in the past, and the numbers were enough to stop the chatter from both the Amala Board and Propelle.

Her phone vibrated and when she saw the 573 number, her pulse quickened.

> You didn't tell the truth, Monica. You have until the
> Global Changemakers Award announcement.

Monica's mouth went dry. She was so close to everything working out for her, but now the threat had returned and with a finite date. She homed in on the link to the Global Changemakers Award. That it was focused on that rather than the closing date of the merger struck her. Someone on the outside would think the merger was a more significant date than the Changemakers Award, and no one outside of the merger insiders knew about the link between the two for her fate specifically. She began to think that Oliver coming back into her life hadn't been a mistake. He would be far more invested in the Changemakers Award, because he wanted to win and prove to his father that he was just as good as the Daltons who had come before him. He certainly had the resources to hire private investigators, and it wouldn't surprise her if he'd done that for all the nominees to try to better his chances. She'd never know what Sister Francis had shared over the years and to whom, but the right amount of money, time, and motivation could uncover nearly anything, and Oliver had all three.

Against her better judgment, she responded.

> Why are you doing this?

The dots appeared almost instantly, showing the message had been read, but then disappeared. She stared at her phone, willing them to come back but the screen remained empty. She hurled her phone at the sofa, chiding herself for having taken the bait. She knew better. One of the first lessons in business that Leonard had taught her was to never ask a question that she didn't already know the answer to, and she rarely made that mistake.

A few minutes later, her phone dinged again and she approached it hesitantly.

You're not in a position to demand information.

Furious, Monica raised her phone as if she were about to hurl it again, but then gripped it tighter, realizing she had taken the wrong approach. Everyone had a price.
Her fingers flew over the letters.

Let's make a deal. There must be a way we can both get what we want.

Her heart raced as she saw the dots appear and stay. Then, the response appeared.

There's only one thing you can give me, and it's not money.

Only someone with immense privilege could make a statement like that. She again thought of how Oliver had everything other than the admiration of his father, and the Global Changemakers Award could give him the one thing he was missing. Did he really need the storage space back, or did he just want to create problems and distract her? And was he so confident that if Monica was out of the running for the Global Changemakers, then he'd win against the remaining three men? To that last question, Monica could unequivocally answer yes. He was exactly that confident. And so was the person who had sent that last message.
  She was furious at the thought that her downfall could be his daddy issues. With her door locked, she made her way to her desk and pulled out her needlework to calm her swirl-

ing thoughts, but even the familiar texture of smooth thread beneath the pads of her fingers couldn't stop her hands from shaking. After pricking herself with a needle and a drop of blood appeared on her index finger, she gave up and locked her embroidery in her desk again.

Could it really be Oliver? Her heart and brain were not aligned at the thought that he could be willing to expose her. Did Oliver really care so much about lifting himself that he'd bury her to do it? Or maybe it was more personal than that. He'd been hurt by their short dalliance ending after a few months, but could he really be harboring such resentment twenty years later? She supposed anything was possible when emotions were involved. That's why she'd done her best to rid herself of them so many years ago. But what if it wasn't him? In the life she'd built, she'd surrounded herself almost exclusively with people who didn't need money, so that didn't exactly narrow down the suspects. She wanted so desperately to believe that it wasn't Oliver, but she had to find out.

Through the haze, only one thought was clear: she had to protect her company. She had come too far to let someone who was so cowardly as to send anonymous messages be her downfall. No matter who it was. She set her jaw. She was stronger than that.

As she lay in bed, she felt the telltale itch creeping up her neck again. She had been so close to having her normal skin back, but the last message had undone any of the progress she had made. Her skin was rough and leathery beneath her fingertips. She'd ruled out the people she knew in Singapore as the anonymous texter. But there was still the great unknown of who Sister Francis could have told in the past and what such a person could have done with the information. Divya had been acting strange and seemed to still be an option, but Monica couldn't imagine her making the comment about not needing money. Walter Johnson at Propelle would love to see her removed, but would someone like him really deign to come off his high horse enough to play these games with her? She'd think someone like him would just expose her quickly and put an end to this. Same with the board members. Steve was far from happy that the early data was starting to show that she'd been right about the Releaf line, but she was poised to make him a lot of money and she doubted his ego overshadowed his faith in numbers. The gamesmanship element felt personal. And her sphere of people who knew her intimately enough to be emotionally impacted by her past was incredibly limited.

Oliver stood out to her as the one who had both a personal and professional reason to expose her. How could she find out if it was him? If he was playing these games with her, then she had to find a way to best him because he certainly wasn't going to just confess to her. But that's assuming, of course, that it was him. She reminded herself that she couldn't rule anyone out at this point.

She considered her options. If she exposed herself, then whoever was texting her would have nothing to lord over her. But in that scenario, she would still lose everything because of the morality clause.

A plan started to formulate, and she sat up in bed. What if there was a way in which she didn't have to lose everything? Her idea was far from what she wanted, but at least it would give her some semblance of a chance. And it would certainly lessen the impact of whatever the texter was planning, because it was something no one would ever expect her to do.

22

Monica agonized over the decision, but she'd looked at the problem from every angle over the weekend and this option seemed like it would have the least amount of fallout. There was too much to risk if she just proceeded as is and simply hoped the 573 number would go away. It hadn't thus far, and the person on the other end was clearly toying with her. Her lies were her burden to bear, and she could deal with the aftermath as long as Amala survived and her team was taken care of.

She rushed into work Monday morning and went straight to Divya's office.

"We need to assemble the Board for an emergency meeting."

Divya rose. "Well, hello, to you too. Care to explain why?"

Monica waved her off. "We need to get this deal closed on a faster timetable. Get everyone together."

"Slow down, Ami." Divya gestured toward a chair. "Have a seat. You aren't making any sense."

"I don't have time to discuss it. I need you to do your job and call the meeting."

Divya looked wounded and Monica tried not to crumble. Soon enough, Divya would see that Monica was doing this for her.

Monica spent the remainder of the day in her office with the door closed. Divya did not attempt to see her as she normally would have, canceling their daily touch-base meeting. She did, however, send out the calendar invite for the special meeting of the Board that afternoon. Even Pedro seemed to intuit that he should stay away and didn't ask her if she wanted him to order anything in for lunch. That, or Divya had told him to leave her alone. Either way, she appreciated the solitude. If this wasn't going to be her home much longer, she wanted to savor every last moment while she still belonged here.

When it was time for the meeting, she carefully tied her neck scarf. The eczema had reappeared with a fiery urgency over the weekend, but soon enough, her skin would no longer matter. She took a deep, slow breath before heading to the conference room.

She intentionally arrived several minutes late to ensure that everyone else would already be assembled. She had no desire to make small talk. Divya was seated with her laptop ready to take the minutes and the men were chatting while staring at their phones. They raised their heads when she entered. She saw a tablet with Chad's face on it because he couldn't fly in on such short notice.

"To what do we owe this honor?" Kyle said.

John nodded in agreement. "We have been having quite a few urgent meetings. You do realize it's difficult for people like us to clear calendars at the drop of a hat."

Monica took her seat at the head of the table.

For the last time, she thought to herself.

To John, she said, "You'll be glad you cleared it for this one."

He raised an eyebrow and leaned back waiting for her to continue.

"Is everything okay?" Leonard's expression showed concern.

She took a deep breath, but it didn't stop her throat from constricting. "We all know Propelle doesn't want me to stay on as CEO. I know they want to market the brand at a lower price point to make it more accessible and get rid of the Releaf line, and I've been staunchly against those things." She paused and closed her eyes before uttering her next words. "If we can get the deal closed immediately, then I will agree to step down."

The men around the room exchanged glances with each other. Divya's mouth fell agape and her hands froze over the keyboard as if she couldn't possibly type what she had just heard.

"My one condition is that the Amala team stays intact." Monica glanced at Divya. "Anyone who wants to stay, gets to stay on for at least two years. That has to be written into the agreement. And I mean from Pedro to Divya and everyone in between, without exception. If anyone wants to take a package and move on, then that's their prerogative, but the choice has to be theirs. And, assuming Divya doesn't want a package, it makes sense for her to be the new CEO, and the direct point of contact for working with their team." Monica gestured to Divya. "Divya knows Amala from the ground up and supports their mission to lower the pricing and make the products more accessible for the working class. A transition as large as this one needs to be built on a solid foundation to be successful and Divya is the best person to lay that groundwork."

Divya gave her a wistful smile as she took in everything Monica was saying. The men around the room, however, seemed to be considering how much thicker their wallets could get, which was the exact reaction Monica had expected and wanted. Greed was one of the most reliable motivators.

"Just to be clear," Kyle said. "You're willing to step down and let them have it? No strings? You just get your payout and walk away on closing? No consultancy or any of that? You'll just run off and sit on a beach in Bali or something?"

Monica looked at Divya. "Divya doesn't need me to consult. She's got this all by herself, and I don't want to step on her toes. But, as you know, my visa is tied to Amala, so I'll need an on-paper consultant position for three years, so I have time to figure out what comes next. But I won't be otherwise involved with the company, and I won't step on your toes, Div." She turned her back to the men and said sweetly, "So, if we're giving them the biggest thing they want, then I'd like to think this brain trust can get that deal closed a few weeks early. Am I right, Leonard?"

Leonard shrugged in a gesture of false modesty. "If you're sure that's what you want, then I will take it to them."

"Just make sure they know there is a clock on this deal. If they want me gone, then they need to close within a week."

She stood poised and confident and just hoped that one week wouldn't be too late.

"Why the rush?" Chad said from the screen. "And why now?"

She had rehearsed this answer. "As some of you know, I've been dealing with a . . . situation . . . back in Singapore and I really need to shift my focus to some personal matters in the short run. But this is a one-time offer to Propelle, so if Walter Johnson wants me out, then this is his chance. I'm ready to move on, and I'm sure the rest of you are too."

"This is generous of you," Leonard said, "But we need to discuss this."

"Right," Steve said. "We need to figure out if the offer would be better with you stepping down now versus you winning the Global Changemakers and then stepping down."

"As I said, this offer is only valid if we close by next Tuesday. Otherwise, I will win the Global Changemakers Award and they are stuck with me."

She couldn't reveal her hand. She needed them to believe that she was serious about the timeline without going into details about why.

"Ami, why don't you give us a few minutes to chat among ourselves," Leonard said.

She could not wait to get out of that room and went back to her office on shaky legs.

Divya burst in after the meeting.

"What was that about? Don't you think something as big as this should have been discussed with me?"

"I know you're upset, but the less you know about my reasons, the better."

Divya threw up her hands. "What is that supposed to mean? We have always made Amala decisions together. Always. And then you just ambushed me in there in front of the Board."

"I thought you'd be happy. I'm stepping down and Amala is yours."

Divya looked exasperated. "But why? You are days away from winning the Global Changemakers Award. And I know you think you are doing me a favor, but I deserved to be consulted."

Monica pulled off her scarf, revealing the eczema that had worked its way back. "This skin can't maintain this brand."

Divya took in Monica's skin. "What happened so suddenly? It looks really bad again."

"It's just eczema." Monica retied her scarf. "I'll be fine. But no one wants to buy skin care products from someone who looks like I do right now. Besides, it's time for me to go deal with other parts of my life."

"Is it the stress of the merger that's causing it? That will be over soon, and your skin will go back to normal. It always does. Or is it something else? Was there more with your family?"

"To be honest, it's all of it. Life can be exhausting sometimes. But if I know you and the team are taken care of, then I'll be fine. Don't you want to run Amala?"

Divya slumped into a seat. "I've always pictured us running it together. That's the way it's always been."

"I know. But things change. You are the only person I would ever trust to run this business without me."

Divya managed a half smile.

Monica wrung her hands. "What did they say after I left?"

"Leonard is going to approach Walter with a soft offer and see how he receives it. At the end of the day, they want to pursue whichever path gets them the most money."

Monica shifted angrily. "Does a single one of them need more money? Money is sport to them. Not sustenance like it is for the rest of us. The point is to make sure we secure enough for you and the rest of our team."

"I really wish you would tell me what's going on. I appreciate what you are doing, but to be honest, I think the company is better off with you in it. I think the customers we help are better off with you at the helm. Our team is so cohesive and you haven't given me a good reason as to why you'd step down. I know Amala is your baby, and I know how much you have always wanted to stay on, so I don't really understand this . . . rash . . . decision." Divya met her gaze. "What are you so worried about? I know you don't want to go, especially with the Releaf line about to launch. I've seen how much that means to you."

"I'm trying to do what is best for the company. Just like I always have. And that means closing this deal as quickly as possible. And if that means the company goes on without me, then so be it."

"Even if that were true, it's not that easy. The investors think you will win the Award because it's such a political thing to have nominated a Brown woman after all these years, so it's not easy to convince them to give up the kicker Kyle negotiated when we are so close to achieving that." Divya took a step closer. "You need to tell me what's going on. First the eczema flareups after years of not having an issue and now this. Ami, you can trust me. Whatever it is, we can work through it together."

Monica wished she could unload on Divya, but there were two problems. The first was that she didn't trust anyone, especially without knowing the identity of the texter. And the second was that it would put Divya in the difficult position of having knowledge that her contract required her to report to the Board. The timing of Monica's plan hinged on the sale being completed before the Global Changemaker's announcement so that the papers would be signed, the money would have traded hands, and she'd no longer be CEO if the anonymous texter decided to expose her. If the assets of the company had already been transferred, then any stain would stick only to her. She'd take whatever money she had from the sale and go live a quiet life somewhere far away from where anyone knew her, and in a country from which it would be difficult for anyone to seize the payment she'd received. She'd likely not need to work again, so maybe she could finally go to one of those remote islands in the Maldives that she'd only ever seen in the real Ami's photos. Wherever she went, she knew she wanted to be around water.

"Thanks, Div. But it just feels like it's time for me to move on from this part of my life. Maybe I'll do some charity work. Give back to the community in some way."

Divya scoffed. "As if you'd be happy doing that. You're one of the most ambitious people I know. And a workaholic, so I'm not sure leisure time will be as easy as you think it will be."

She wasn't wrong. "You let me worry about those things. And, Div, I'm sorry about how I spoke to you earlier. I was stressed and it wasn't okay."

"That's one of the things I worry about when it comes to stepping into your role. I don't want to be a complete workaholic like you. I want room in my life for something other than Amala. I know I could run the company, but I'd have liked some time to figure out the best way for me to do that."

Monica hadn't considered that because she was approaching the problem solely from her perspective. "Divya, I'm sorry about the way it happened, but please trust me when I say that without this, there might not be an Amala for either of us to run. We need this merger to go through and pinning Amala's future on the Global Changemakers is too risky."

That evening, Monica was moving through her fancy Venice home thinking about what her life would look like after the deal closed. She ran her hand along the smooth dark gray fabric of the oversized custom sofas and stared at the designer appliances in the kitchen that she hardly used. It was an overindulgent amount of space for one person. It would have been so even for eight people.

She thought of her time at the orphanage so differently now. How could she not? She wondered how many others were born into circumstances in which they'd never know their full potential. She'd only learned hers because she passed herself off as someone who had been born into privilege. She poured herself a glass of Aglianico and made her way to the roof deck, passing so many pieces of furniture and artwork that were worth more than many people around the world earned in a lifetime. People like her were the parts of Singapore that were buried along with so much of its history. The country only showed its glossy finishes to the world, just like she had. Maybe she was truly Singaporean after all.

23

Divya walked into Monica's office with a solemn expression on her face.

"What's wrong?"

She sat in the chair across from Monica. "Propelle accepted your proposal."

"Why the long face? You just got promoted."

Divya sighed. "I still don't feel right about this."

"You've earned this."

"I know. It's not that. It's just that we started this together. It feels strange to do it without you, especially when it was your idea."

"Don't worry about me. It's time to pass the reins."

"You say not to worry, but I also know there's something you're not telling me."

"Nothing that affects you."

"Obviously whatever it is does affect me since it's causing you to step down." The two stared at each other but Monica didn't offer more, so Divya continued. "They agreed in principle to your deal. It shouldn't be an issue, but they need a few extra days to close."

"I said they had to close by Tuesday."

"I know, but it's a lot of money and paperwork and they need a bit more time."

Monica had intentionally selected Tuesday because the Changemakers Gala was on Saturday and she needed this wrapped up before then. Her plan was to be on a flight overseas before the Gala weekend.

"Don't they have fancy lawyers and bankers who can pull this together sooner? People get deals done overnight all the time."

Divya shrugged. "I'm just the messenger. The Board wants to approve it. It's just a few days and it's a good deal for all of us."

"A few days meaning it would still be done by Friday? Before the weekend starts?"

Checking her calendar, Divya nodded. "It would be a busy couple days between closing and the Changemakers Gala the next day. But what a splash if you sold your company and won that Award within a twenty-four-hour period."

Monica swallowed hard and nodded. It was just three more days. She'd come this far and she was so close that she could taste it. Ten days from now, her life as CEO of Amala would be over, and she would have to reinvent herself again. She just didn't know as who. But the one thing she knew for certain was that when she started over this time, she'd have money in the bank and money made everything easier.

When Pedro dropped off her mail she noticed a thick, padded manilla envelope with the CHIJ crest on it. She'd forgotten that Beatrice was going to mail her school file to her and was curious to see what had been saved. She slit open the package and pulled out the contents. There were some thin workbooks from various classes in which she'd handwritten notes. She smiled at her teenage scrawl. Neat and precise, but she'd always pushed too hard on the paper with the pencil, indenting it with each letter. There were some mathematics exams with perfect grades on them. And some essays. She began rifling through those, pausing when she got to one that was titled "After CHIJ." She recalled the assignment. During her final year of school, Sister Francis had tasked the girls with writing about what they expected their lives to look like after graduation. Monica began reading:

> CHIJ is the only home I have ever known and it is hard to picture a life outside of these four walls. I know I cannot stay in the comfort of the Sisters' bosoms forever, but I also know my future is different from that of my peers. While they are busy with O-levels and thinking about universities and which doors the world will open up to them, I am disheartened that my doors are closing. As a student, I had a purpose in furthering my education. When that is completed, however, I will follow in the footsteps of the other girls like me and work as a helper. My education was not a stepping stone toward something greater, but was instead the culmination of the most hopeful years of my life. Sister Francis said she will do her best to find me a good husband. Someone mild-mannered with confidence who will not be afraid that I am educated. It is the best I can do. And I will be grateful, because it could have been worse. Not all the babies from the Gate lived long enough to get to this place. And even the ones who did began working as helpers much earlier than me. I have pushed off my

fate for as long as I can, and I will now accept that I won't see the world like my classmates. I won't go to the Maldives after graduation like Ami. I won't continue to university. I won't have family members at my wedding, whenever that will be. I may not have the same things as those girls, but I have the values and integrity of a CHIJ girl and will accept the life I am being given with honor and grace. I will not complain. There is no purpose in complaining about something that is already written in stone.

She stared at the words, tears pricking her eyes. *I have the values and integrity of a CHIJ girl and will accept the life I am being given with honor and grace.* She hadn't done that. She'd known the place she was meant to have in Singaporean society, but she'd traded her values to circumvent it. Even now, she was constructing a way for her to depart with as much material wealth as she could, rather than confessing the truth and accepting the consequences.

She touched her neck, knowing that was what her eczema was telling her, and wondering if all those years ago, she had made the right decision. But even if she hadn't, what could she do now? How could Monica redeem herself after having been Ami for so long?

She saw some pieces of linen behind the essays and pulled one out. It was a sewn image of Caldwell House with the Gate lurking in the background. She ran her fingers over the satin stitches used to make the flowers framing the octagonal front room, the bargello stitches that gave texture to the roof, and lastly, the butterfly chain stitches she had used to create the Gate. In addition to calming her when stressed in this new life, sewing had always been such a point of pride for her.

As she pulled out the second one, she felt something drop

onto her lap. She saw a very small woven green, orange, and white necklace with a stitched Hindu Swastik pendant in gold thread. Of course she was familiar with the symbol, but she had never seen this necklace before. She picked it up gingerly and ran her fingers along the threads. On one end of it was a faded tag with handwriting that she could identify anywhere: *May 25, 1977–Newborn girl, covered in red rashes with yellow skin. No identification.*

The date and description Sister Francis had written were of the way she'd found Monica at the Gate, but she had never mentioned this necklace. She had so many questions, but based on what she had seen during her last visit, she doubted that there would be much useful information that Sister Francis could give her now. She could sense that this small token was important, and lamented that her window of opportunity to learn more had closed. Sometimes girls had been abandoned with a token from their mothers, but no one had ever told her about anyone leaving anything with her. The Catholic Sisters would surely not have made a Hindu necklace for her. There was only one person who would have.

She brought it closer to her face, suspecting she'd been holding this very necklace in her hand forty-two years ago. It might have been the only thing she had ever held that had also been held by her birth mother. It was a simple trinket, with stitching that wasn't as neat as her own. Something that she would never have given a passing glance to had she not suspected its origin.

A tear slid down her cheek as she felt an overwhelming connection to the way her infant self must have grasped it. Had she been crying that day? Did she know what was about to happen? She wondered if as a baby she could have known this was the last thing her mother would ever give her.

Such a small and simple token but it held such significance.

For starters, it meant that she *was* Indian. She'd spent her life assuming that, and playing the part of an Indian woman via Ami Shah, but there was a vast difference between assuming and knowing one's heritage. Without the explicit tie to the Hindu symbol and colors of the Indian flag, she could have been from one of the many South Asian nations or religions, and that was why she had always felt like an imposter around Divya and others who confidently could claim India as their own. She clutched the necklace as she realized that on all those trips with Divya when she had felt like an outsider in India, it was her country as much as it was Divya's.

She stared at the necklace like it could somehow save her. Like it could absolve her of every wrong she'd ever committed. For the first time in her life, she allowed herself the indulgence of thinking that it was possible that the mother who had abandoned her may have actually loved her. It had been easier to vilify her as someone too irresponsible to have children. Monica had gone through her life never feeling like she owed any love to this person who had brought her into the world, and she was comfortable with that. Love was the necessary precursor to heartbreak, and she did not need any more loss in her life. But this necklace was forcing her to consider other possibilities that she'd rather avoid.

She swiped the tears from her cheeks and put the necklace and papers back into the manilla envelope and shoved it into her handbag. She couldn't second-guess any parts of her life right now. She had created her fate and that was all that mattered.

24

Despite her attempts to put it out of her mind, Monica kept mulling over the words in her essay. She wondered what would happen if she told the truth and tried to honor the girl she once was, and still couldn't come up with a solution that would save Amala and the team from her sinking ship, so she trudged forward. Whatever happened to her after she was bought out would be her problem and not theirs, and she could revisit things then. Propelle only wanted Amala and its assets so they would not care about the actions of a former Amala employee. It was really Leonard and the Board who would be up in arms about it, because they would have split her share of the buyout if she was no longer a part of it. But they would never do anything to risk their larger cash-out that came with the merger. For them, splitting the amount that would go to Monica was a drop in the bucket that wasn't worth the legal fees to try to recoup.

For the time being, she just had to focus on the due diligence that Propelle wanted for the earlier close of the deal. She and

Divya had practically been living at the office, but they had gathered the necessary paperwork and submitted it to the legal team a few days ago. Monica had hoped that if they delivered everything early, then maybe the deal could still close before Friday, like she wanted, but it was now Thursday morning and there had been no such luck.

Her phone rang and she saw it was Naira.

After exchanging some pleasantries, Naira said, "I wanted to touch base as I'm finishing up my article. I know you want it out before the Gala on Saturday."

She startled a bit, having completely forgotten about the interview and its significance to the Global Changemakers Award. Winning that Award no longer carried the same weight it once had. No one outside of Amala knew that the new merger terms involved closing earlier and her stepping down in advance of the Gala.

"Right," Monica said noncommittally.

"Could we meet? I wanted to go over a few last points with you, and I think it would be better to do it in person."

Monica looked at her calendar and saw she had a call with the merger lawyers. "Could you just tell me over the phone? It's going to be difficult for me to get out of the office today."

"I think it's going to be worth you making the time," Naira said evenly.

Suddenly, Monica wondered if Naira was the texter. It seemed like an unorthodox way for a journalist to behave, but she was in the business of uncovering secrets and researching other people. And Monica's own investigator had found that Naira didn't always play by the rules. Something in her gut told her she needed to meet Naira.

"I could sneak away for a few minutes after my next call."

They set a plan to meet at a café near the 3rd Street Promenade.

Monica was exasperated by these lawyers. Amala was paying $1,500 an hour to Freedman, Lerner & Foster, one of the best law firms in California, and they still couldn't manage to get things done on time.

"What do you mean, your database was lost?" Monica's tone was laced with ice.

"It's not that the database was lost," Indika, the mid-level associate on the team, said.

"We still have all the documents you delivered to us," Kent, the junior associate jumped in with a helpful tone.

Monica would not have stood for a junior member of her team interrupting her while she was delivering bad news to a client, and imagined Indika was giving him some sort of stern look right now.

"We have the documents," Indika said, "so we don't need you to do anything further on your end, but Kent and the other junior attorneys were reviewing, categorizing, and coding the documents according to each request made by Propelle. It's that tagging and sorting that somehow wasn't saved in our system and needs to be redone."

Divya was seated across from Monica in her office while they both listened to the call on speaker.

"So, are you calling to tell us it's going to cost us twice as much?" Divya asked.

"No, no," Indika said quickly. "It's our mistake, so the firm won't charge you for us having to redo this."

Monica and Divya gave each other a look as if they weren't sure of the point of this call.

In a hesitant voice, Indika said, "Given the—um, issue—we are going to have to push tomorrow's closing to Monday."

Monica's eyes widened as she realized what that meant. The deal was supposed to be done before the Global Changemakers Gala.

"But don't worry." Indika's tone was a couple registers higher than her normal pitch. "We have already talked to Propelle and explained the situation and they are fine with waiting until Monday. No change in terms."

Monica leaned forward so that her face was very close to the speaker. "You already called Propelle and changed our closing date to Monday without consulting me?"

Her tone was frigid, and it was so silent on the other end that she'd have thought they had been disconnected but for the red light next to the line showing the call was still going.

"Doesn't that seem like something you should consult the client on?" Monica continued.

"Gerald didn't want to worry you, so we wanted to make sure we had a plan in place . . ." Indika's voice trailed off.

"And why isn't Gerald on this call?" Monica barked so loudly that even Divya flinched.

Divya hit the mute button. "Ami, it's just a weekend. It's not a big deal. There's no reason to take this out on Indika."

Gerald was the senior partner running point on the deal and Monica couldn't believe he'd sent his young Sri Lankan associate to deliver this news without him being there to take responsibility. She'd never have done that to a member of her team. In this moment, she regretted Divya insisting that they include non-white attorneys, because the person they thought they'd be helping by getting good experience was now bearing the brunt of a mistake that likely wasn't even hers.

"I'm s-sorry," Indika stammered. "He had another meeting, but we can set a time with him. It was only one business day, so he thought this would be a good solution for everyone."

Monica hadn't heard anything from the 573 number since

the last message, but she had no reason to think that the threat of exposure before the Global Changemakers Award announcement had been rescinded. This timing was far from a good solution for *her*.

Monica unmuted their end of the call. "We really need it closed on Friday rather than Monday. You must have more bodies you can throw at this to get it done, especially since it's your mistake. We already had to push it to Friday to accommodate Propelle's lawyers, which was later than I wanted, and now you're saying it's going to be even later because of the lawyers that *I'm* paying?"

Silence on the other end. She imagined these baby lawyers had no clue how to deal with a client in this situation. That's why Gerald should not have farmed this out to them unsupervised.

"Deals close overnight all the time, and you're telling me you can't make this happen by tomorrow?" Monica said in a marginally less hostile tone.

She knew she was angry at the wrong people. The two on the phone had no authority to give her what she wanted, but like when being exasperated by a customer service person who cannot help after you've been on hold for an hour, she couldn't stop herself from lashing out.

In a meek voice, Indika said, "I'm so sorry, Ms. Shah. I understand your frustration with the situation, but there's nothing we can do at this point."

Before Monica could lay into her again, Divya jumped in. "Let us discuss internally, and we'll get back to you. And please make sure Gerald is available for the next call."

The associates were all too eager to hang up.

"This is so ridiculous," Monica said, crossing her arms.

"It's not ideal, but it's just a weekend. One where you'll be busy with the Global Changemaker's Award anyway. Who cares if it's Monday morning instead of Friday afternoon as long as the numbers are all the same?"

Obviously, Divya couldn't understand because Monica had never given her the information that would allow her to do so. And Monica feared that this was now outside of her control.

Should she plead with the anonymous texter to get her past Monday? The person on the other end surely could not know about the intimate details of the merger timeline. No one outside Amala knew about those dates. But reaching out again after the last exchange was a huge sign of weakness, and she knew that she needed to act from a position of strength. Her entire identity had been founded on her ability to manipulate outcomes in the way that worked best for her. She studied people as only an outsider could, communicating in the manner that put them most at ease and heightened their ability to trust her. She had to come up with something. But before any inspiration struck her, her calendar dinged with a notification that she was due to meet Naira.

25

Naira was already seated at a corner table with two coffee cups before. She pushed one toward Monica as she sat down.

"It's decaf given the hour. Hope that's okay."

"Fine," Monica said, her tone still sour because she had stewed about the lawyers on her drive over. "What's so urgent that it had to be done in person?"

Naira shifted uncomfortably. "I wanted to give you an opportunity to comment."

"On what?" Monica took a sip.

Naira stared at her. "I know your name isn't Ami Shah. And that you were an orphan at CHIJ who used a classmate's name to pass yourself off as her when you moved to London."

Monica froze, as if she were now seated across from a venomous snake who would strike at any wrong move she made. She studied Naira's face, and could see that Naira wasn't bluffing, and she had evidence to back up her statement.

Naira continued to stare at her. "I wanted to give you a

chance to comment before the article is published. If you want to tell your side of the story, I would include it."

Monica didn't know just how much Naira knew, so she had to proceed cautiously.

"I'm not denying that I changed my name, but that's not a crime."

From the look on Naira's face, Monica could tell that, just like the texter, she didn't know about Monica's legal name change, which meant she didn't know every part of the story. That gave Monica some small sliver of hope that Naira might not have enough information to take her down when she was so close to having a clean exit, and that she finally had the identity of the person who'd been coming after her. She just couldn't figure out why Naira would stoop to such a level when she already had access to Monica.

Monica met Naira's gaze and did not look away.

Finally, Naira said, "Why did you do that? What was wrong with being yourself?"

"Sometimes people need a fresh start."

"Stealing someone's identity isn't a fresh start. It's a very calculated one."

The two were engaged in a high-stakes battle of wits, each of them hoping to best the other. Monica knew she needed to shift her approach to appeal to Naira's humanity. She had seen that in their previous interactions, and she had to assume that the reason Naira asked to meet her in person was because she didn't want to strip Monica of everything and was looking for other options.

"Off the record?" Monica asked.

"If that's the only way you'll share, then yes."

Monica nodded. "It was the best chance I had to give myself a better life. And it didn't seem like I was harming anyone. Ami

Shah is a completely generic name, and my choices on this side of the world didn't alter the course of her life in Asia. We both ended up where we were supposed to."

"So, you admit that you stole the identity of your classmate Ami Shah in Singapore?"

"Not exactly. Yes, I used the same name as her—legally— and said I had the same pedigree as her, but all the work I've done with that name has been my own. Amala's success is because of me, not her. I just gave myself the opportunity to have an Amala in the first place rather than have a life spent cleaning up after other people."

Monica could see that Naira was wrestling with her sympathy for Monica, and she tried to capitalize on it by sharing some details about herself as if she and Naira could work together on this.

"My name from before was Monica Joseph."

"I already know that."

"I worked for Ami's family in Singapore, and I took her LBS admissions letter but only after she had already discarded it and decided not to go there."

"I know that too."

Monica was frustrated by how much Naira already knew. But Monica was certain that she could not know about the morality clause and how much she could lose because of it. But she couldn't volunteer the information that would bury her in the hopes of currying favor.

"What I'd really like to understand is why you did it," Naira said.

There was no answer that would absolve her of the lashing she would take from the press. Monica surmised that these answers were simply to bolster Naira's story and she wasn't sure if she should do that, even if they were off the record.

"How did you find out?" Monica asked, thinking that if she

knew who the information had come from, then she'd be better able to figure out what story she should tell.

Naira inhaled. "I can't reveal a source."

"Journalistic integrity, and all that?"

Naira nodded.

Monica didn't believe there was any story about her that Naira could make public that would not invoke a breach of the morality clause, so she tried the last option she had.

"I know why you left *The New Yorker*."

"It's not a secret," Naira said.

"I imagine no one will ever accuse you of favoritism toward Indians again after this piece."

"I am just doing my job."

"And trying to salvage your career."

"I'd think you of all people would understand how important it is to protect one's career. You have gone to great lengths to do that with your own."

"Was this always your goal? From the start? I'm just wondering if any of what you said to me was genuine or if it was all for the story."

"When I first reached out to Divya, I had already researched you enough to learn that you weren't who you said you were. But after meeting you, I knew there had to be a reason, and I wanted to learn what that was. I wanted your true story. All of it. I wanted to believe you had done the things you did because there was no other choice. I wanted to write about the systemic issues that led to you having to make those choices in the first place. I believed you were a decent person who had done what you needed to survive."

"You're right about that part. I have always done what I needed to survive." Monica sat straighter and stared squarely at Naira. "I know that you had a sexual relationship with your subject's daughter and that is the real reason you left *The New Yorker*, rather than this amorphous bias thing that you allowed to be shared publicly."

Naira's face went from shock to anger. "So, your plan is what then? If I report the truth about you, you'll report the truth about me?"

Monica shrugged. "Seems fair."

"Maybe I was giving you too much credit, and you really are just a selfish, conniving con artist," Naira spat.

She began to rise from her chair as if she were about to storm off, but Monica put a hand on her arm and coaxed her to sit back down.

In a gentle tone, Monica said, "I just want you to see that we both have something to lose with this news coming out. We both need to ask ourselves if it's really worth it."

"An eye for an eye is one of the oldest adages in the world, I suppose."

Monica didn't get the sense that Naira would back off the article entirely, so she tried a new tack.

"Not completely. How about if we make a deal and you can publish whatever you want about me, but just do it two weeks from now. If you wait until then, then your secrets are safe with me forever. And I'll even give you an on the record exclusive to make sure that you are the only reporter who has access to my side of the story, and you can quote anything you want from me."

Two weeks would give Monica enough time to close her deal and get herself out of the country just in case her analysis of the Board not pursuing a claim after the deal concluded was incorrect. She could decide then if she wanted to live up to her interview promise to Naira from afar or if she wanted to remain off the grid.

Naira seemed to be mulling over the prospect, so Monica delivered her best sales pitch.

"It will still be widely read and help you get your career back on track, because there is a very good chance that I'm going to win the Global Changemakers Award this weekend. Think how much better it will be if you expose the Global Changemakers *Winner* as opposed to just a nominee."

"Why does the timing matter so much for you?"

Monica was not about to leave all her cards on the table when it seemed like Naira might be considering her proposal. "It gives me a fighting chance to start over again. I'd think you, of all people, would understand that. Do we have a deal?"

Naira crossed her arms over her chest. "Blackmailing reporters isn't generally the best way to get what you want."

"I wouldn't do it unless I felt like I had to."

Monica could see that some part of Naira understood that Monica felt like she was grasping for any possible purchase. But she wasn't sure if she had been convincing enough, and there was one last thing she needed to know. She quickly pulled her phone out of her bag and placed it on her lap before surreptitiously texting the 573 number: You win.

"What are you doing?" Naira asked.

Naira's phone was face up on the table between them and did not move as Monica's message was sent. There were no dings, vibration, or pop-up notifications. She glanced down and saw the three dots appear to signify that the recipient was reading it, but Naira had not moved an inch. She had hoped the 573 number was Naira, because then she knew exactly who she was dealing with. Instead, she had confirmed that there was another person out there who was poised to expose her.

Monica parted from Naira without any confirmation that Naira would not publish the story tomorrow as planned. She had played her only card, and now she had to hope that it was enough. She thought of how tomorrow should have been the day that Amala merged with Propelle and her bank account grew larger than she had ever fathomed. Instead, it looked like tomorrow could be the most humiliating day of her life, and everything was controlled by a young reporter trying to build back her career and a faceless person with a mobile phone and the desire to taunt her.

Monica needed to clear her head and found herself meandering along the streets in Santa Monica. She headed away from the ocean to avoid the throngs of tourists along the Promenade and beach. She had tried everything in her power to get a clean exit for herself that still allowed Amala and her team to have a bright future, but she feared she was going to fall short.

She felt her neck and eyelid start to burn and itch more than in any of the past episodes she'd had. She rummaged in her bag in search of a mirror to assess the damage. As she was pulling it out, she looked up and saw a teenager on a skateboard wearing oversized headphones who appeared like he was about to collide with her. Startled, she sidestepped to avoid him and dropped her mirror in the process. She looked down just in time to see him ride over it. Without even stopping, he tossed an apologetic wave in her direction as he continued down the street.

Grumbling, she picked up the now cracked mirror. She saw multiple versions of her face in the shattered reflection, and in all of them she could see that her eyelid and brow were redder, scalier, and more inflamed than they'd ever been before. She searched the faces staring back at her, hoping one might have the answer she needed, but even a broken mirror couldn't show her something that wasn't there. She tossed it into a nearby garbage bin, placed sunglasses on her face to keep people from staring, and continued ahead.

The chill from the ocean breeze formed goose bumps along her arms. She couldn't recall if she had ever felt so despondent in her life, but she doubted it. Before Amala, she'd never had anything worth losing. Sister Francis would have told her to have faith. In a higher power, in a shared humanity, in who she was at her core. But she hadn't relied on that kind of faith for a very long time. It was only after she'd started making her own destiny that things started working out for her. She felt sick that she couldn't think of a way to do that now.

She looked up as she crossed the street and saw a large church before her that she had never noticed before. The white stone building was larger than the CHIJ church she'd grown up with, and had a far more modern look and less ornate stained-glass windows, but she felt herself drawn there. She'd not set foot in a church—or any religious establishment—since she had left Singapore. A part of her didn't feel she'd earned the right to be in those places of worship given how she'd been living her life, so it was easier to stay away and lock up that part of her past. She was raised knowing the significance such walls held, and she felt duty bound to respect the beliefs held by others even if they were no longer held by her.

She glanced at the sign and her face broke into a wry smile. Saint Monica Catholic Church. She could hardly call this place her namesake, but the irony of its name was not lost on her.

She stared at the doors. Out of options, she felt she had to try one last thing. Maybe it wouldn't change anything, or maybe it would turn out that Sister Francis had always known what was best.

She slipped into an empty pew and removed her sunglasses so she could study the stained-glass windows. They'd been her favorite part of the Town Convent too. All those colors dancing against the sunlight seemed hopeful and hope was what she needed most right now.

She had brought the tiny necklace with her and clasped her hands around it, bowing her head. Her entire life would change tomorrow. There was a chance that Naira would take her deal and wait a couple weeks to jumpstart her career. But even if that happened, she had the person behind the 573 number to contend with. She couldn't game theory the outcomes of an unknown opponent, so anything was possible. Maybe if she were exposed people wouldn't care as much as she'd feared. But that was wishful thinking. People with a financial interest would certainly care, and there was at least a whole boardroom of people with that.

She felt the weight of this being the last day of the life she had built. She would be reborn. Not for the first time. She'd first been born to a mother whom she had never known, who had left her with nothing more than the trinket in her hand. What would her Hindu mother think of her finding solace in a Catholic Church? This was the inevitable consequence of being abandoned at one, so she hardly had room to complain. Her first life lasted mere days. Then, she was reborn in the arms of Sister Francis as Monica Joseph. In hindsight, that had been a good life for twenty-five years. She'd felt love, protection, and connection, even if she'd longed for so much more than that. She'd felt like society had held her back from her truest potential, and that had left a void within her. Her third life had been as Ami Shah. It had been the one where she had honored her ambition and drive and felt the taste of true success. One where she hadn't felt inferior to people around her, and had become accustomed to the material life she thought would make her feel secure and accepted. But it also had been the loneliest. The voids may have changed in each iteration of her life, but one always remained. Her fourth life was a mystery that was yet to unfold, and she wondered what she'd be missing in that one, and if there would ever be a point at which she could accept what she had and not always be searching for more.

With all that remained to be seen, today, she prayed. Not with an agenda for what should happen next. But finally with the acceptance that it was beyond her control. She wasn't quite at the point of believing whatever would happen tomorrow would happen for a reason or some greater purpose, but she also wasn't dismissing that possibility entirely. She had fought back against the shackles that were meant to keep her confined so many times before, and she would find a way to do it again.

Most importantly, she believed that no matter what happened from this point forward, Amala would live on without her. She took solace in knowing she had made a difference with this version of herself. The life she built had mattered and people who looked like her would be better off because of what she had brought to them. Monica wondered if she should reveal the truth to Divya before the fallout tomorrow, but then decided against it. The less Divya knew about everything, the safer she and Amala would be when Monica was gone. Plausible deniability was the final gift Monica could give her.

The church organist began to play and a bold, majestic sound filled the space. Monica closed her eyes and basked in the ethereal melody. So much about her had changed, but the things that brought her comfort in her youth, like stained-glass windows and the sound of an organ, had remained with her for all these years.

26

Monica awoke with a sinking feeling in her stomach and picked up her phone with dread. She anticipated a flood of messages like she'd received after her Global Changemakers nomination, except this time they wouldn't be congratulatory or opportunistic, they'd be scathing and venomous. But there was nothing. She sat straighter and refreshed her emails, making sure the onslaught was not just caught in the ethers. It updated and her inbox still showed nothing out of the ordinary.

She searched for her name but the results were flooded with other Ami Shahs. She added Amala to the search alongside her name and still nothing unusual. Just the usual press interviews or marketing things. There was nothing from today. She tried a few more searches, just to be sure, but she dared herself to believe that maybe she had been convincing enough with Naira, and that her text to the 573 number saying they had won had bought her some time if the person thought she was going to reveal herself and was waiting for that happen.

As she got ready for work, she checked her phone repeatedly for an alert, waiting for the bomb to drop. She examined the rough patches on her eyelid and neck in the mirror. As the ex-CEO of Amala, maybe the eczema would go away completely after this part of her life was over. She loved her work, and never begrudged the long hours—they gave her a sense of purpose—but she was beginning to see that maybe her body didn't love her work as much as her heart and mind did.

By the time she got to lunch, she was less anxious. News this big would have dropped already. Whether it was for journalistic reasons or vengeful ones, a person wanting to expose her would be sure to make the most of a news cycle and that meant publishing it earlier in the day so that outlets across the country would still be able to highlight the story in their respective time zones.

When Divya came into her office, she braced for impact, worrying the news had broken and Divya had seen it first.

"Why are you so jumpy?" Divya asked.

"No reason. Did you need something?" Monica glanced at her phone, but didn't see any alerts.

"Did you check your email?"

With a sinking feeling, Monica navigated over to the screen, expecting the worst to be there. All she saw was an email from the team in India, and she turned back to Divya with a questioning expression.

"India is expediting production on Releaf," Divya said with a smile. "We can go live with it in a couple weeks. I thought you'd want to know, since you aren't going to be here then, and this was really your baby more than mine. And because you have been so invested in it, I wanted to show you the final website photos for it." Divya handed over her tablet that had the images for the Releaf line elegantly displayed against the signature Amala purple backdrop.

Monica smiled, knowing that she had built a brand that would outlive her in the right hands, and she had no doubt that those hands were Divya's.

"Thanks for getting this all done, Div. Even if I'm not running the company, I'll be an Amala customer for life."

"Maybe you can join the influencer ranks. No one could do a better job selling this line than you."

"You won't see me in front of the camera. Not in this lifetime."

Divya laughed. "I guess some things will never change."

Monica knew a lot was about to change, but for the moment, she just wanted to take in her last day as CEO of Amala.

"I put together the statement you asked me to give you about my stepping down from the company. There's a public version for the press and an internal version for the team."

"You don't want to address the team yourself?" Divya asked.

Monica didn't think she had the strength to do it. "Sometimes a clean break is what is best for everyone involved. Besides, it should be seamless for them since you'll be the one running the company and they are already familiar with you."

"I think you're underestimating how much this business and team are invested in you, just as you are invested in them."

"Let's hope that's not the case, because I want you to have the smoothest transition possible."

Alone in her home, Monica tried to figure out how she had managed to survive the day unscathed. The anxiety every time her phone buzzed was maddening, but she knew it would all be over soon. She wondered if she should send Naira a thank-you, but decided that she didn't want to do anything that might tip the delicate balance she had orchestrated. If things had gone according to her original plan, she'd have been on her way to the Maldives today, with people waking up tomorrow and realizing she was gone when she didn't appear at the Global Changemakers Gala. Instead, she would be showing up to keep up appearances until the Propelle deal closed on Monday, but she had to admit that there was something validating about her being able to be a part of this historic award.

In that private moment, she smiled to herself as she thought about just how far little orphan Monica had come. She had achieved something that very few before her ever had, and no one who even remotely resembled her. It seemed Divya had been rubbing off on her and she began to appreciate the magnitude of someone who looked like her achieving such success in America. She had proven to herself that she was just as capable as she'd always thought when she was a little girl in a convent school surrounded by privileged girls. She wished she could share her success with someone, but as she glanced around her, she was met with the emptiness and silence that defined the world in which she had achieved so much.

27

On the day of the Changemakers Gala, she again picked up her phone with dread, but again saw nothing out of the ordinary. She exhaled, finally convinced that Naira had decided to accept her deal to wait to release the story for two weeks. Now she had to give her final big performance as Ami Shah, and then she'd be able to discard that persona completely after the Propelle deal closed on Monday. She went to her closet and pulled out an amethyst gown with a high collar that would cover her neck and began to get ready for the Gala. She looked at herself in the mirror wearing her formal attire, sparkly jewels, trendy eyeglasses, and designer heels, with her hair cascading in soft curls around her face and had a hard time reconciling the life she was born into with the one she had now. She'd worked so hard for the money, the affluence, the material gains . . . but did any of it matter? She was going to this Gala alone. She had no family or close friends to celebrate her successes with. No one to talk to about what the next stage of her life would hold or the stress she was currently facing. After the deal closed, she could finally afford the Maldives trip she'd always been envious of, but she'd be there alone with her needlework and some books. Maybe that wasn't the worst thing. It was uncomplicated, because if she'd learned anything in life, it was that people complicated things. She had no control over them like she did the formulas for her products or the stitches on linen, which produced the same results every time as long as they remained in the same conditions. People, however, could not be counted on for consistency.

Before she could delve further down those spiraling thoughts, she received a text. Dread filled her as it had every time she picked up her phone for the last couple days. It was merely a message that her car service had arrived.

She gathered the hem of her dress and made her way carefully down the stairs and into the black sedan with tinted windows. She leaned her head back and closed her eyes as the chauffeur drove them to the Fairmont Hotel in Santa Monica. She was almost there. So close that she could picture the fish swirling around her feet in the clear waters like she had seen in the real Ami's photos so many years ago. She could taste the salt in the air on her tongue and feel the sun against her skin. In two days, she'd be on that plane to the other side of the world where no one knew Monica Joseph or Ami Shah, and she could be whoever she wanted to be. She just had to get through today.

As the sedan pulled into the long driveway to the entrance of the Fairmont, her phone began vibrating.

Oliver: We need to talk.

Divya: THIS is why you agreed to step down?

Leonard: I don't even know what to say.

There were a flood of other messages from people she'd known at LBS or former employees of Amala. And finally, one that disheartened her, but also made it all make sense.

Naira: I had no choice.

Of course, Naira would know that publishing the article right before the Gala would have the biggest splash and humiliation factor for Monica. But given how much she claimed to want to lift up other Indian women, Monica thought the offer she had made to keep her past a secret and do an exclusive interview would have been enticing enough to wait. But Naira had always been a variable that was outside of her control, and she should never have underestimated how much people would do to lift themselves. There was no clearer way to prove to her industry that she wasn't biased toward Indians than by very publicly destroying one. Hadn't Monica done far more to advance her own professional goals? They were certainly more alike than Monica had given her credit for.

Monica stepped out of the car in the circular driveway that went around the majestic fig tree at the Fairmont and saw a crestfallen Divya standing at the top of the stairs with her phone in hand. Leonard and some of the other investors stood near her, but Monica made eye contact with Divya first.

Divya flew down the stairs toward her. "Is this true?"

"I'm assuming Naira published her piece. I haven't read it yet."

Divya's eyes were wide. "There is a lot in there. No wonder she wouldn't give me a sneak peek."

Divya thrust her phone at Monica, which was open to the

article in *Forbes*. Monica could see by the size of the scroll bar at the right that it was long. The only way the piece could be that long was if Naira had included the whole sordid tale. Monica scrolled through and saw her history laid out in black-and-white.

Abandoned at the Gate of Hope.

Raised by Catholic nuns.

Worked as a maid for the family of a former classmate from CHIJ, Ami Shah.

Stole the identity of that former classmate to get an MBA at LBS.

Used funds taken from one of the Sisters to get herself to London.

Founded Amala using that fake name and background.

Monica felt her knees go weak as she looked around and realized that all the well-dressed, mostly white, attendees of the Gala were staring at her with a look of disgust. The car that had dropped her off had already made its way down the driveway so she couldn't duck back into it and make a quick getaway. She was stuck having to face these people and their judging eyes, knowing that they were not only judging her actions, but forming further biases against all people who looked like her. That was one of the great burdens of being a minority in America. People now would look at any Indian skeptically and think that all of them were capable of doing the things she had individually done. She felt someone take her elbow and start to steer her toward the door and saw Leonard by her side.

"Let's find somewhere private." He walked with urgency through the crowd and led her toward the Starlight Ballroom.

Divya strode next to them, her face still stricken.

When the three of them found a quiet corner near a potted dracaena plant, Leonard turned Monica to face him. "Ami, is this all true? Or has this reporter gone rogue for some fame?

I can have my lawyers issue a cease and desist on her so fast it will make her head spin. She'll never write another word for a media outlet again."

Monica looked from Leonard to Divya and back again. Did she double down on her efforts? Say it was all a lie? She had no doubt that Leonard and his team of lawyers could squash Naira like an ant, especially with the information she already had about Naira's unethical past behavior. She could walk away from this if she really wanted to. Money made the rules. But in that moment as she looked from Leonard to Divya, she was tired of playing the game.

"I've only skimmed it, but the gist of it looks true," Monica said.

"You changed your name to Ami before you got to LBS?" Divya asked.

Monica nodded.

"Your parents didn't die the year before you got there?" Divya's voice was soft.

Monica shook her head.

Leonard's jaw fell slack. "You didn't go to college and just went straight to LBS? But that's preposterous. You need a college degree to go to business school."

"Why? A college degree is necessary for business school only because someone deemed that a requirement, not because it actually helps with the coursework or career that comes after."

"But those requirements are put in place for a reason. Without them, it would be anarchy." Leonard looked flustered as if he couldn't understand this shift in the natural order of things that he was familiar with.

He was of the generation that truly believed that, and of a class for which all doors were always open and waiting for him to walk through them. He was genetically equipped to have burdens lifted rather than borne. If he'd been born into circumstances like Monica's, she doubted he could have achieved anywhere near as much as she had.

"Haven't I proven that pedigree doesn't matter?" Monica said. "If someone is smart and willing to work hard, then why shouldn't she achieve all that I have. All that *we* have together?"

"We've known each other for seventeen years," Divya said. "You knew I was only able to afford LBS because my consulting firm was paying for it. I wasn't a rich kid. You could have told me the truth."

"I'm sorry, Div. I really am, but that's not the same as where I came from. I wasn't ever in a position to have a fancy job that would reimburse me for business school tuition. I worked as a maid in Singapore. I didn't get to go to university. Some people's lives are limited from the moment they are born. Do they deserve less because of the circumstances in which they were raised?"

"Well, no, but this. . . ." Divya raked a hand through her hair as shock and confusion settled onto her face. But then it shifted to anger. "I asked you if I had anything to worry about, and you lied straight to my face. You've put everything we've worked for at risk."

The lights in the ballroom behind them dimmed and then went back to full brightness, signifying that the event was about to begin and guests should enter. The well-coifed and well-dressed who's who of the entrepreneurial world started filing into the space and Monica had no idea what she should do. She saw a thin, white woman in a hunter green pencil dress with an earpiece and small mic making her way toward them with an urgent look on her face.

"Are you Ami Shah?"

Monica nodded.

"I'm Gemma Allen, the president of the Global Changemakers Award Foundation. Can you please come with me?"

Monica knew there was no choice and did as she was told, with Leonard and Divya following her. As she walked past some other people, she caught a glimpse of Oliver, who wore a stoic expression. She couldn't deal with him right now, so she turned back to Gemma who was moving as if she were a professional speed walker toward a room in the back. After she closed the door, she turned to Monica.

"It's come to our attention that there is an article about you that was released today that has some rather serious allegations in it."

Monica met her gaze to confirm she was aware of what Gemma was speaking about.

"I'm afraid I have to ask if the allegations are true."

Leonard and Divya stared at her.

"Some of them are," Monica said. "I still need to read the entire article."

"The part about you lying about going to college and stealing another person's identity to get into LBS is true?"

Monica cast her eyes toward the floor. She knew how it sounded. "Yes."

"No wonder you called to remove yourself after we announced," she mumbled more to herself than the group. Turning back to them, she said, "I'm not really in a position to do a deep dive here. We are moments away from presenting you with this Award. It would have been helpful if you'd said there was no truth to it, but that's not what you're saying, so now we have to figure out what to do."

"I won the Global Changemakers Award?"

She had told herself this entire time that the Award didn't matter as long as Amala was okay, but there was something about the confirmation of how far she'd actually been able to go. An abandoned orphan became the first ever woman and South Asian to win the Global Changemakers Award. Regardless of how she got there, she couldn't help but take some satisfaction in it.

"Well, yes. You would have learned that in a few moments in the ballroom, but this is simply unprecedented and I have no idea what to do now." Gemma paused to listen to something coming through her earpiece. She tapped a button and hissed into her mic, "I don't know how we missed this." Back to Monica, she said, "So the stuff about you lying about your background and engaging in identity theft is true, correct? I want to make sure I'm not missing anything here." Gemma's face seemed to be begging her to say that she'd misspoken before, that everything in the article was a lie, and she was exactly who everyone at this event thought she was.

"Yes, but everything having to do with Amala was fully me. It was my idea. I'd been born with eczema as a child and was abandoned by my birth family. I had wonderful Sisters at the convent who took care of me and gave me an education. I was at the top of my class at LBS despite not having an undergraduate degree, and I put my blood, sweat, and tears into making sure Amala was a success. And by all accounts, Amala is exactly that, and I've been at the helm of the company since its inception."

Gemma looked exasperated. "An orphan who then goes on to become a multi-millionaire entrepreneur by combatting the skin condition she was born with? Why didn't you just say that from the start? That story is media gold." She shook her head, and before Monica could say another word, Gemma turned and rushed toward the door. "I need to speak with the others and see how we're going to resolve this. You head to the ballroom. And act surprised if it's somehow still you."

Monica stole glances at Divya and Leonard who looked so disappointed in her. She had never had someone look at her that way and wondered if that was the intense guilt a child felt when disappointing a parent. She'd been so close to all of this being over, but nothing in her life had been easy thus far, so she really shouldn't have thought this would work out like she'd hoped.

The threesome somberly made their way into the ballroom, unsure of what else to do. Divya fell into step beside Monica and whispered, "If you'd just told me, I could have helped you. I've always taken a back seat to you, accepting that you were more accomplished than me so it made sense. But everything about you has been a lie."

Monica continued walking because what could she say. She knew no words could undo the actions she had taken when she left Singapore, and there was no point in telling Divya that by keeping her in the dark she'd been trying to protect her.

Inside the ballroom, it was impossible not to notice the murmuring while people stared at their phones in shock. As they entered, the focus shifted to the three of them and the guests' eyes on her felt like lasers burning her skin. The nominees' seats were at the front tables before the stage, so they had to walk through the center of the ballroom to get there. Monica saw looks ranging from pity, to disappointment, to smugness, and finally to utter disgust as she took a seat. She felt Oliver's gaze from the table next to hers, but she couldn't look at him. She also couldn't look at the unsympathetic faces of Chad, Kyle, John, and Steve at her own table, so she kept her eyes cast to the floor.

Gemma walked to the podium on the stage, her heels clipping against the wood and punctuating each step. She tapped the mic to gather everyone's attention. She stood with shoulders back and looked rather poised for the amount of stress she was under.

"Good afternoon, everyone."

The murmuring continued and she looked annoyed.

In a louder, more authoritative voice, Gemma repeated, "Good afternoon, everyone."

The crowd began to quiet and turned toward the stage.

"Now, I know we have had some unusual events leading up to this year's Gala, but let's not forget that we are here to celebrate the people who are changing the world through their entrepreneurial endeavors and making it a better place. Let's not shift our focus away from this very important honor and recognition." She used the tone of a stern parent cajoling her children.

Monica saw people ping-ponging their gaze from Gemma to her. She'd never felt so naked in a room before. She dared to steal a glance at the tables behind her and the well-clad group that oozed affluence. Those who had once been her peers now looked at her as if she were an interloper. They felt most comfortable around those who were like them. And in this mostly white arena, she couldn't fit in by the way she looked, so she'd had to do it with the places she supposedly went to school, liked to "summer," and the expensive restaurants that always "held a table" for her. She had to belong based on the clothing she wore, the bags she carried, and the shoes on her feet.

Today, she looked the part, just as she always had, but knowing her true background, she saw what people really thought of her, and it made her fume. She was the same person they'd known hours earlier, but they looked at her like she was vermin now. They'd proven to her that she was right that the only way to have been a part of this group had been to lie her way into it.

Gemma continued from the stage, "Today, I have the honor and privilege of making history by presenting this Award for the first time to—" She fumbled with her notecards and then muttered to herself but the mic still picked it up, "I guess that's not quite right anymore." Gemma seemed to be scanning her prepared remarks for what she could salvage from her speech.

People around the room cleared their throats and exchanged glances, because her introduction made clear that Ami Shah was the intended recipient. Or, at least, she had been. Monica tried not to bristle at being stripped of an award she'd never wanted in the first place, but it was always different to lose something you knew you had compared to hoping to gain something that wasn't yet yours.

Before she could stop herself, she was on her feet. The crowd turned to stare, their eyes following her as she made her way to the stage. Divya's and Leonard's expressions urged her to sit back down. When she stepped onto the stage, Gemma finally noticed her and looked taken aback. She held her notecards in hand, frozen, unsure what was about to happen.

"I'm still finishing my opening remarks," Gemma said, trying to sound breezy, as she gestured for Monica to leave the stage.

Monica reached the podium and was now next to Gemma. "I know. I just felt like before continuing, I should address the elephant in the room."

"Well, well, this is unprecedented." Gemma was visibly flustered. "Perhaps it's best you sit until after the announcement is made, and you can address the group later if there's time."

Monica put her hand on the mic and moved it closer to her, mouthing the word *please* to Gemma, who then acquiesced and stepped to the side so Monica could stand behind the podium.

"I'm Ami Shah, and I know many of you have read an article about me that reveals some things about my past, including that my name was previously Monica Joseph."

She inhaled deeply and took in that all eyes were fixed on her. People were leaning forward in their seats, waiting for her to continue. No one was on their phone, a rarity for this group of self-important individuals.

"You may be wondering why I lied about my background, and I owe at least some of you an answer to that." She felt Oliver's eyes bearing into her, but she refused to look in his direction, making eye contact with Divya and Leonard. "It is true that I was abandoned at a convent in Singapore as an infant. I'd been born with severe eczema and jaundice. I was raised by the Sisters of the Convent of the Holy Infant Jesus, who helped me learn how to care for my skin. By virtue of being their ward, I was able to get an education, which is something not every child gets, so I can only look back on my life and be grateful for the choices made by others—no matter how painful—that led to me being able to be on this stage.

"One thing I realized growing up penniless in Singapore was how much class plays a role in society. I was able to excel in school compared to many of my peers. But life is not a meritocracy and that is true no matter what country you live in. So many of you only know the glamourous, glitzy version of Singapore that you've seen on your screens, but wherever there is great wealth, there is also great poverty. That was the side of Singapore that I knew. But by working as a maid in an affluent home, I got to see how the upper class lives. People like the majority of you in this room. And I wanted to do something other than clean your homes. I didn't want to achieve less simply because that's what people like you expected of someone with my history."

She noticed the mostly Brown servers who had been milling around the room filling drinks pause their work and look at her, welcoming her remarks, even if the rest of the room was horrified.

"So, I did take someone else's place at LBS, and from that point forward, everything I did was on my own merit. I proved that fancy universities and private schools aren't necessary to get to the highest levels of business. Those barriers to entry are in place to keep people like me out. So, the only way in was to pretend to have your background. Corporate America is run by wealthy white men and it is their standards that dictate who gets to participate. Do I wish I could have been my authentic self and gotten to the same place?"

She saw the wealthy white men squirming in their seats.

"Of course, I do. But we all know you wouldn't have let me. I wouldn't have been taken seriously unless you thought I was already one of you. Success isn't based entirely on work ethic or ability. A lot of it is about access. And that access is reserved for people who have had similar upbringings, which perpetuates the cycle of inequity generation after generation. I doubt anyone in this room has spent even a single day of their lives worrying that they might not have enough food to eat or that they won't be able to afford the medical care they need. You probably don't even have friends who have had those experiences. This is a very privileged group, and it is by surrounding yourselves with similarly privileged people that your high-class problems can feel normal and worthy of empathy."

A look of pride flashed across the face of a Hispanic server who appeared to be in her fifties, willing Monica to continue even if the people connecting with her message were not the ones who needed to hear it.

"I ask you all to imagine for just a moment, how different the world would be if it were truly a meritocracy. Would each of you be where you are today? Or would it be possible that you'd be serving the drinks to the people who are currently serving you?"

The affluent people seated at the tables looked disturbed by the thought, while the service staff bit their lips to keep from smiling.

"Would we have more innovation in the world than we have now if there were more varied types of education and backgrounds in positions of leadership? Would it have taken so long for a company like Amala to exist and be recognized, or would the need for products for all skin types have been developed decades earlier because people beyond the white majority would have been *seen* so much earlier? Would the past winners of the Global Changemakers Award actually look *global*, rather than a who's who of white men lifting each other up? I admit that I made mistakes and am far from perfect, but I'd ask each of you to look at how you contribute to a world in which someone like me has to pretend to be like you in order to have my voice heard."

Gemma looked like she was about to have an aneurism, but Monica put her out of her misery and took a small step back to signal that she was done. The room was silent. She wasn't sure if she'd expected a smattering of applause, followed by a standing ovation as if this were a movie, but there was none of that. Because this was real life. And in real life, when you threaten someone's identity and the very core of who they are, they don't have an instantaneous epiphany and see the flaws in themselves. In real life, those people hunker down and make sure the interloper is excised in a way that ensures no one else would dare threaten the established order again. Monica began to walk off the stage with her head held high because those were the most honest words she had ever uttered.

Gemma cleared her throat and pasted on a smile. "Now, that was an unexpected part of our program today, and I apologize for that. I think it's best that we get on with the ceremony and put all of that unpleasantness behind us. Now, without more fanfare, the Global Changemakers Award goes to Oliver Dalton of UrbanGreen."

Monica saw Oliver awkwardly stand. His eyes met hers but then scanned the room as if he wasn't sure what he was supposed to do next. Someone at his table gave him a soft push and he made his way to the stage, having to cross by Monica as she was walking toward the exit.

"Congratulations. You won," she mouthed to him as she passed. He stared at her, wide-eyed.

As she was exiting the ballroom, she heard Oliver begin to speak.

"I reckon I'm not sure what to say, other than to give my thanks for such prestigious recognition of my work . . ."

As she walked out of the Fairmont, she couldn't help but think that the award went to exactly who it should have: someone utterly familiar and relatable to everyone seated in that ballroom. Someone who didn't challenge them. Someone who was the opposite of her.

28

Monica was not surprised when she had an urgent message from Leonard saying to meet at the Amala offices a few hours later. She knew her actions would have consequences, but at least in the last few moments in which she'd had a platform that could garner any attention, she'd spoken up for the people who rarely had their voices heard. Even if it had fallen on deaf ears beyond the Brown waitstaff, for the first time in her adult life, she'd spoken up as herself and on behalf of people like her. There was something empowering about that even if she was about to be stripped of any power she'd ever had in entrepreneurial America.

She walked into the conference room and found all the members of the Board and Divya.

"Nothing better to do on a Saturday night?" She tried to joke, knowing none of them wanted to be where they were right now.

"Have a seat," Leonard said solemnly.

"I prefer to stand." Monica stood just inside the door, making sure she had a clear exit once this was over.

"This is some stunt you pulled." John slapped his palm on the table.

"What exactly was the stunt, John? Building a legitimate business that has made you a ton of money?" Monica said.

He glared at her. "I've got other VCs asking me how I could have let this slip. What kind of diligence teams I have in place that something like this could have happened. It's embarrassing."

Leonard held up a hand to signal John to calm down. Turning to Monica, he said, "We are all disappointed by this. We've known you a long time. Me longer than anyone, and I know your work ethic and what you did to build this business. But I'm sure you can imagine that Propelle is up in arms about this, and we've got to do everything in our power to make sure this deal still closes on Monday."

"The thought of giving you a big payday doesn't make anyone particularly happy right now," Steve chimed in, wagging his finger at her. "Assuming anything closes at all, given what you've done. You have put all of our livelihoods in jeopardy."

Leonard now held up his hand to Steve like he was the patriarch trying to get his unruly children to fall in line.

"Ami, as you know, there's the morality clause," Leonard said.

Her eyes met his.

"Pursuant to that provision, the fabrications about your university degree in Singapore and the manner in which you attended LBS mean that it has been violated."

She gulped. Knowing this was the inevitable outcome didn't make it easier.

"Given that, the Board has no choice but to relieve you of your duties as CEO of Amala effective immediately. Divya will step into the role, which as you know, she was going to be doing on Monday anyway after the deal with Propelle closed."

Monica exchanged a look with Divya and saw that she took no pleasure in this turn of events. She regretted ever thinking Divya could be the person who was trying to take her down.

"If that deal even closes," Chad spat. "Thanks to you, everything we worked toward is in jeopardy."

Monica was about to ask what exactly Chad had worked toward beyond transferring some money and getting overly familiar with the women in the company, but Leonard shot her a look that made her back down.

"Given that you'll be removed prior to the close of the deal, the CEO payout will not apply to you, and frankly our legal team is looking at any additional ramifications that could come from this."

Monica had known it would happen but hearing the words was different. She was losing Amala. Not selling it for a lot of money as she would have been doing on Monday, but having it taken away from her for nothing. Her life's work gone because of one article that came out forty-eight hours too soon. But the timing wasn't a coincidence.

"What will happen to that money?" Monica asked, hoping it would go to Divya.

"It will be allocated pro rata among the investors," Leonard said.

Monica looked around the room at each of the five men. "So, it goes to all of you."

Leonard gave a half shrug.

"It should go to Divya," Monica said.

Leonard cleared his throat. "Given how unprecedented this is, we had the lawyers take a careful look and this is what we've been told. Either way, it's none of your concern anymore, but rest assured that Divya will be taken care of."

She suspected that his version of taking care of himself and taking care of Divya were not the same, but he was right that she no longer had any control over it.

"We'll need to collect your company devices," Leonard said. "Your access to the server has already been disabled."

"Do you really think that I would do anything to jeopardize Amala just because I'm not a part of it?"

"It's protocol," Leonard said. "I'm sure you can understand."

Monica wanted to lash out at him even though she knew he was just parroting what the legal team had told him.

"I can help you clear out your office," Divya offered.

Monica had never brought a personal thing into her office so there was nothing to clear out. "No need. It's all yours now."

"Another thing," Leonard said, "is that you'll need to vacate the house within two weeks."

Monica felt her heart sink. She knew the house was the property of Amala, but even when they'd thought she was exiting the company on Monday, there had never been any talk of her leaving the Venice house. Obviously, the situation had changed, but this stung.

"It's the most time I could get for you," Leonard said. "It's an Amala asset so it will belong to Propelle. Before all this, I'd carved it out of the deal, but now it doesn't make much sense to do that. Walter wanted you out on Monday, assuming they go through with the deal, so consider this a blessing."

"Thanks," Monica mumbled.

"The last thing is that your work visa will be withdrawn on Monday since you are no longer with the company. Again, had things gone through as planned, you had a consultancy role on paper to keep your visa intact, but now, things have obviously changed."

Monica widened her eyes. "I need to leave the country on Monday?"

America, for all its imperfections, had become the closest thing she had to a home and she hadn't considered that she'd be forced to leave it. Sure, she had planned on going to the

Maldives until the dust settled after Naira's article, but she had always thought she could come back when she felt ready.

"I believe there is a grace period. A couple months for you to try to find another job before having to uproot yourself. That kind of thing. But I can't offer you any legal advice and you should consult your own attorney for that."

"A couple months? That's hardly enough time to start something new or secure funding. What am I supposed to do? Get a job at the grocery store? Even if I could, in that type of job they aren't going to hire someone who they need to file visa paperwork for."

Leonard shrugged. "As I said, you'll need to consult with your own attorney on those legal matters. We cannot offer you any advice on the subject."

She'd known her life would blow up. She'd known she'd lose her business. And quite a few relationships. She wouldn't blame Leonard, Divya, or Oliver if they never wanted to speak to her again. But she didn't consider that she'd lose her country. Permanently. That her life in America was permitted for as long as she fell in line, and as soon as she stepped out, even though she'd been living here for fifteen years abiding by all the rules, she'd be cast aside. She had the privilege of living in America for as long as Americans could benefit off of her, but not of being American.

Monica raced to the exit after her ousting, but Divya caught up to her in the reception area.

"I'm not happy about how all this happened," she called out.

Monica stopped and turned around. She saw the hurt on Divya's face and regretted that her actions had led to that.

"I know. I'm sorry."

"How could you do that to me? To Amala?"

"I didn't feel like I had another choice. If you'd known the truth, then you would have been in a bad position having to choose between Amala and me. This way, you're clean and can stay on and shape the company's future."

Some of the anger on Divya's face subsided.

"What you said at the Gala . . . I understand why you did what you did."

Monica offered her a wry smile. "You might have been the only person seated at one of those tables who did."

"So, this is why you were so afraid of press all these years and didn't want to put your face on marketing materials?"

Monica nodded.

"How did Naira find out?" Divya asked.

"I don't really know. At first, I thought it could have been you."

Divya's hand flew to her chest in protest.

"Don't worry, I know it wasn't. It could have been Oliver. Or maybe even someone from Singapore. I wasn't close to many people, so I really don't know."

Divya's jaw fell slack. "How would Oliver have found out?"

Monica shrugged. "Who knows? Someone like him has unlimited resources, right? Maybe he hired someone to dig up dirt on me. Maybe he encouraged Naira to do it after they met. It doesn't really matter much. The end result is the same."

"You're not livid?"

Monica sighed. "Being angry won't undo this, especially when I don't even know who to direct my anger toward."

"This is why you went to Singapore," Divya said, her expression showing she was starting to put the pieces together.

"I started getting anonymous text messages that made clear someone knew my background, so I had to go back and see if

I could figure out who. But I wasn't successful and still don't know who was behind them."

Divya shook her head as she learned about how much had been bubbling beneath the surface.

"And that's why your eczema came back."

Monica nodded. "This isn't how I wish my life would have turned out, obviously, but part of me is relieved to not be hiding in the shadows anymore."

Divya took a step closer toward her. "Is this also why we were never friends?"

Monica stared at her. "We were friends."

Divya shook her head. "No, we were colleagues. I've tried to become friends with you since LBS. But it was always so hard to get close to you. Eventually, I stopped taking it personally because I saw you were the same way with everyone. I figured that was just how you were wired."

Monica's shoulders sagged. "I was too afraid of getting exposed. Maybe my life would have been easier if I'd been found out back in business school. Then I would have had nothing to lose."

"You'd also not have left this important mark on the world. You were right. The idea for Amala was always good. You got the funding for it because you were at a prestigious business school and acted the part of someone who already had wealth and could be trusted with bringing more of it to investors. Different clothes and different confidence wouldn't have changed how good the idea was, but it wouldn't have gotten people to open their wallets and take a chance on you."

"That's why I can't regret what I did. For some years, I managed to help a lot of people, and gave myself a taste of the life I thought I always wanted."

Divya shook her head. "I wish the world were one in which

you could have become a Global Changemaker without the lies. But society just repeats past cycles, doesn't it?"

"The rules of the game were set long before either of us was born. I don't regret trying to change them and jump ahead, even if I was ultimately pushed back down."

The two women looked at each other solemnly, knowing this was the most honest conversation they'd ever had. And the first in which both were truly being themselves.

"I don't think many people could have pulled this off the way that you did. That alone is worthy of an award. I'm still so mad at how you handled this, but anger will fade, and once it does, I'd really like to be friends with *that* person." Divya extended her hand. "Should I call you Ami or Monica?"

"Ami is pretty tainted. I think it's time for me to go back to Monica."

She took Divya's hand and felt like they might finally have a true friendship. One in which they knew the other's truth, and still respected them as an equal.

"Your work mattered, you know? With Amala. You made a difference to lots of people who look like us. Maybe your name won't survive this, but I'll make sure the company does. Indian girls in North America deserve to feel comfortable in their own skin. We have enough other things to worry about as it is."

A small smile crept onto Monica's face. "Until recently, I didn't even know if I was Indian."

Divya raised an eyebrow.

"I knew I looked a certain way, but there are lots of countries where people have this skin and these features. The orphanage where I was raised recently sent me a necklace that I'd been left with." Monica pulled it out of her handbag so Divya could see. "It wasn't until I saw the Hindu Swastik that I knew."

"I can't imagine living without knowing your heritage."

"No one gets to choose their lot in life. Not entirely. That was the point I was trying to make at the Gala." She met Divya's eyes. "Now you know why Indian customs were never my thing. But I'm thinking it might be the right time to learn about my heritage."

Divya put a hand on her shoulder and for once Monica didn't inch away from the contact. "Happy to be your guide, and welcome to the club. Membership includes a lifetime of racism, but our melanin-rich skin means we get to look good while its happening, especially with Amala products." Divya brought her hands beneath her chin to frame her brown, even-toned, wrinkle-free face and cast an angelic smile.

Monica laughed. It felt good to know enough about her heritage to identify where she should belong, even if it was going to take work for her to learn enough about the customs and norms to decide if she actually did.

When she returned to her home in Venice, she saw Oliver had let himself into her front yard and was sitting on the stoop. The thick glass Global Changemakers Award was in his hand. He lifted his head as she approached.

Placing the award to the side, he said, "They're sending me one that doesn't have your name already etched onto it."

Monica stood before him with her arms crossed and jaw clenched. "Was it you?"

He looked at her wide-eyed. "What are you talking about?"

She cocked her head. "Were you Naira's source?"

He stood. "You think I did this?"

She stared at him. "It would guarantee you the Global Changemakers Award, and you have always had something to prove to your dad."

"Ami." He leaned closer and touched her elbow. "I'd never do something like this to you. Not for my dad or anyone else."

She studied his face and he looked tormented. And behind that was hurt and disappointment. There was none of the cockiness or smug satisfaction she'd expect to find if he had coordinated this. Her mind reeled. Naira had to have had a source, but who was it?

"You didn't feed Naira this information? You haven't been texting me from an anonymous number in Missouri?"

He held his arms open in surrender. "What on earth are you talking about? I'd need to have the information in the first place to be able to feed her anything. And I've never set foot in the dreadful middle of this country, and have most certainly not used a number from there. You know I'd never even trade in my 310 number for that second-rate 424 one."

He seemed genuine, and had always been strangely boastful about having secured a number with the 310 area code, so she knew that type of thing mattered to him. And there was no reason for him to lie anymore now that the secrets were out. But that meant she was still filled with questions that had no answers.

His voice caught as he looked at her and said, "You shared a bed with me, but not your real name."

Monica felt a lump in her throat. She knew he'd have felt hurt when he learned that.

She motioned for him to sit on the stoop and she sat next to him. "I'm sorry, Oli."

He shook his head. "I could never get close to you. No matter what I did. That was really the problem between us, wasn't it? You know, during that first year in London, you always had this slight twitch of your face whenever I said your name. Only ever so slightly and I wondered if it was my accent and maybe it sounded strange as I said it. Or maybe the way I said it reminded you of your dead parents. I never knew what it was—only that there was something there when you thought no one was looking."

Monica shook her head. "I wasn't used to being called that. And I didn't much care for the person whose name I was using, so it took some getting used to for me to respond to it."

"I've always wondered what went wrong with us, but now I realize that I never had a chance, did I?"

Monica sighed. "I was too young and too scared to get involved with anyone. But you came along with your charm and self-assurance and I wanted to learn to be that way. We come from such different worlds, and had you known the truth, you would have seen just how much. You'd likely not even have given me a passing glance."

He looked wounded. "That's not really fair. I've never cared about money or pedigree."

"You've never cared, because you've never had to. It's always been there. By virtue of the family you were born into, you were only ever around other people like you. Have you ever dated anyone who didn't attend a prestigious university?"

He ran a hand through his hair as he reflected, but it was clear that the answer was no.

She continued, "People like me would only have crossed your path when cleaning your house, or serving you at a café, or putting your garments in a fitting room. I know you're kind to them, and give them extra tips and things like that, but how many of those people who have filtered in and out of your life have you formed a deep connection with? Can you even remember the name of a single one of them?"

He flinched as he absorbed her words.

"Don't beat yourself up. It's the way the world works. You've spent your entire life trying to curry your father's favor. Imagine if we'd stayed together and one day you tried to bring home a Singaporean maid. They'd have labeled me a fortune hunter or gold digger. I didn't have a family to worry about so I wasn't giving up anything, but you'd have had to choose. Once I realized there was no path forward, I did my best to make some distance between us."

"You managed that well enough." He appeared to be contemplating what would have happened if he had tried to bring home the real Monica, without the gilded facade she'd created, and seemed to register that it wouldn't have been easy. He turned to face her. "It was that day, wasn't it? When we were walking along the Thames? I'd asked you about your parents and you gave a weird answer and then shut down when I tried to follow up about it."

She managed a half smile. "It was that day. I knew then that your elephant-like memory would be my downfall, and I couldn't be close to you."

He looked pensive. "You gave me the real answer. The Monica one."

She nodded.

"Were you already so worried I wouldn't accept the real version of you? We already knew each other by then."

"I was worried about a lot of things. I was new to this life I had chosen, and I realized the best way to protect myself was to keep my story straight. That meant not getting too comfortable with anyone else and letting down my guard."

"Sounds rather lonely."

Monica stared ahead of them into the distance. "It was."

It was the first time she had ever admitted aloud the greatest downfall of the life she had chosen. And she wondered how many other of the affluent people she had sought approval from had felt the same way, because even if they weren't lying about their identity, there was still something isolating about a life like Oliver's in which he was always wondering if people were in his orbit for him or to be in closer proximity to the Dalton wealth. Maybe money and deep connection were mutually exclusive, and she hadn't given enough thought to what the wealth would actually buy her.

Oliver nudged her shoulder with his. "Perhaps we can both cut through some of the loneliness and be friends. Without the lies. You're still Am—" He paused. "What shall I call you now?"

"I'm working that out for myself, but I think Monica feels right." She met his eyes. "I'm really sorry, Oli. About everything. I don't know what else I can say."

"I still can't believe you thought I would do something this awful to you."

"I didn't know who I could trust. I guess I still don't if you weren't behind this."

"Are there more secrets you've kept locked up that someone can expose?"

She shook her head. "All the skeletons are out of my closet."

"Then maybe it doesn't matter who's behind the messages. Doesn't seem there's anything left to lose."

"That's true. I've already been fired. And who even knows if this deal with Propelle will go through now even with me ejected from my own company. I could be in for a world of legal trouble if it doesn't."

He cocked his head. "Naturally."

She gestured to the house behind her. "I'm losing my home. And on Monday, I'm losing my visa, so I'll need to figure out a plan that doesn't involve me living in this country."

Oliver shuddered. One of his many privileges was that his mother was American so Oliver grew up having both British and American citizenship. He carried two of the most powerful passports on the planet and never had to worry about eviction or deportation from a country he considered home.

"That's a rough lot to handle, Am—Monica."

"I deserve it. And in some ways, it's a weight off my shoulders." She gave him a dry smile. "You may not believe me, but lying to everyone and keeping people at arm's length wasn't exactly fun for me."

"I reckon it wouldn't be." He met her eyes. "So, you have parents then? They didn't die in an accident?"

"I don't really know. They left me when I was a baby, so I suppose they could have died in an accident or they could be alive. They were never a part of my life, so anything is possible."

"I'm sorry. You didn't deserve that."

She stared at her garden and the canal beyond it. "No one does. But every day people who probably shouldn't become parents have children and the cycle repeats itself."

"Have you ever tried to find them?"

Monica thought about the little girl who dreamed of her parents walking through the Convent Gate one day and sweeping her up and telling her it had all been a big mistake. Every child who has been abandoned fantasizes about that.

"I wouldn't even know where to start. Or what I'd find if I tried." She thought of Sister Francis and her convent friends. "I was loved. Even if it's not the kind most people expect."

She knew it was hard for him with his picture-perfect family who summered in the French Riviera and posed in matching sweaters for Christmas cards to understand that, for her, family meant something other than blood.

"I'm glad." He looked at her, his brown hair curling on his forehead. "But I do wish you'd told me."

"I had too much to lose."

"I could have avoided being angry at you for so many years."

"You still would have been angry with me."

He raised an eyebrow quizzically.

"You hated always coming in second to me." Her lips curled

into a half smile. "And that would have been the case no matter what my name was."

He laughed. "It has been that way since LBS, hasn't it?" He gestured toward the small UrbanGreen garden inside her gate. "You managed to keep the herbs alive."

She followed his gaze. "You made a good product."

He picked up the glass award he'd set aside. "Some might say, a product that is worthy of becoming a Global Changemaker. That is, if you just cover up that bit there." He pressed his finger over where her name was and they both laughed, releasing the years of secrets between them into the cool, night air.

29

Monica's story had been plastered all over the media in the way she had most feared, and the press had been camped outside of her neighborhood since the news had broken the day before. Despite Naira's best efforts to humanize her in the article and explain the systemic societal issues that led to Monica choosing that path in the first place, the American media's focus wasn't on why she'd lied and whether the barriers between social classes existed for any reason other than to keep "lower" people out. But, of course, it never would have been. The American media was generally comprised of people from elite backgrounds as well, and they'd never tell a story that could uproot their foundation. Instead, they were salivating over a lower-class scandal, calling her an "Indian Anna Delvey." She resented the comparison because her company and products were legitimate. She'd never tried to scam people out of what was rightfully theirs, whether or not they deserved it. And she wasn't sure what to make of the "Indian" qualifier. Did that somehow make her more or less likely to have ended up in this predicament and why did it matter? But she'd lived in America long enough to know that it did, and that the media cared more about shock value than anything else. Given the unwanted attention, she'd been inside her home since Oliver left on Saturday evening, not even daring to go onto her deck for fresh air.

When she heard her doorbell ring, she was worried that one of the reporters had been brazen enough to come right up to her home. When she saw Divya's face on the security monitor, she was relieved.

"It's a circus out there." Divya removed her shoes and followed Monica into the living room.

"I know. I haven't left the house since I got home yesterday."

Divya gestured toward the two half-filled suitcases and the piles of things to arrange and pack next to it. "Leaving?"

Monica shrugged. "I can't stay here, so I figured I might as well go back." She couldn't bring herself to add *home* to the end of her sentence because Singapore hadn't been home for a long time, but it was the only place she could go right now.

Packing up the Venice house hadn't been difficult. She'd done so little to personalize it, as had always been her way. It was mostly her clothing and shoes, and as she'd stared at her closet full of designer labels, she suspected that she would have very little use for those items in whatever the next phase of her life held. She would keep no more than the two suitcases that she was allowed on the flight. The one thing she made sure to take was her sewing final exam that she had clipped to her dresser.

"Why are you here?" Monica asked.

Divya dropped onto the sofa and looked around the room. "We really did come a long way with Amala."

"Why are you using the past tense?"

"Propelle pulled their offer. There's no merger."

Monica sank onto the sofa next to her. Her worst possible fear.

"What will you do?" Monica asked.

"That's why I'm here. I was hoping you still had some clever solution left in that brain of yours."

Without the money from Propelle, Amala couldn't fund the inventory it needed for the existing lines as well as the Releaf one. That had always been the reason to join forces in the first place.

"What did the Board say? Can they tap their contacts for a new investor or merger partner?"

Divya shook her head. "Given all the press around you, Amala is now persona non grata. No one is coming near us, and honestly, I'd have misgivings about anyone who would want to. The Board voted against the Releaf line. There's not enough cash to launch something new. I think they are just trying to find a way to sell Amala off for parts at this point so they can recoup some of their investment."

Monica flinched. She'd tried so hard to protect the company and the team, but she'd failed miserably. She knew that Amala only had a few months of operations left before it would need to shutter. Maybe even less if part of that money had to go to damage control in the wake of Monica being exposed.

"I'm sorry, Div. I never wanted this to happen."

"Maybe not, but it did. I might have one of the shortest CEO runs in history given how things are going."

Monica hung her head. Her heart broke at the thought of Amala no longer being there and she had so many more questions, but she was trying to approach Divya as a friend rather than a founder.

"What will you do after that?"

"I don't know. I'm going to do everything in my power to try to find funding before I give in to that type of thinking. Maybe I can tap some contacts in India and see if there are some partnership opportunities there. Maybe even build out the social good component and move more operations to Chennai with Amala hiring local women who need work."

Monica smiled. "I knew you were the right CEO. How has the team responded to everything that is happening?"

"As expected. I read them your note, and they've all read Naira's article. I'm sorry about that, by the way."

"About Naira?"

"Yeah. I pushed her onto you."

"It wasn't your fault. The truth was going to come out eventually. There was already someone else out there toying with me about that. Whoever that person was had to have been Naira's source."

"No wonder she was one of the first to reach out for the feature and then was so persistent about it. I thought it was about Indian solidarity, but clearly, she had a different agenda. I wish I'd seen through her."

"I didn't see it either, so don't be too hard on yourself."

"Still, we were so close to having it all. Off by a mere matter of days. And I can't help but shoulder some of that responsibility."

Monica shook her head. "No. This is on me. And I know that if anyone can find a way to save Amala, it's going to be you. I'm just sorry that I put you in this position."

Divya stood. "Let's hope you're right."

30

If Oliver hadn't been Naira's source, then clearly someone else was, and Monica couldn't leave America without trying to find out who, especially knowing that they had taken down not only Monica, but likely Amala as well. Fortunately, Naira had agreed to meet her.

On that Monday morning when the Propelle deal was scheduled to close and Monica was meant to have the largest sum she'd ever considered deposited into her account, she instead snuck out of the back entrance of the home she was soon to be evicted from in a large hat, oversized sunglasses, and baggy clothing that made her seem several sizes larger than her usual frame. Her anonymity was paramount right now and being among the throngs of people at Venice Beach would give her that. She made her way through the back of her neighborhood, crouching low as she crossed the bridges, to get to the meeting spot she had arranged with Naira. She surreptitiously looked around her as she sat on the bench to see if anyone had followed her, but it seemed she was in the clear. She took in the sounds of the crashing waves, boardwalk vendors, and seagulls one last time before she left this life behind her.

She watched Naira approach and take a seat beside her.

"Thank you for meeting me," Monica said.

Naira propped her sunglasses on top of her head. "I hope you know it wasn't personal."

"Everything is personal. No matter what we tell ourselves. I'm just glad you agreed to meet me."

"I wanted to apologize. You may not believe me, but it wasn't easy for me to publish that piece. I tried to tell your side of the story to lessen the blow, but we have both seen that it didn't work out that way."

Monica offered a wry laugh. "Life rarely does. Especially not for people who look like us in this country. Did you honestly think that people would focus on the social class story? No matter what words you used, or what tone you conveyed, it was always going to be about a Brown interloper trying to be somewhere she didn't belong."

Naira stared ahead at the ocean lapping against the shore.

Monica continued, "I hope you got what you wanted out of it."

Naira chewed her bottom lip, and Monica could tell she was mulling over what to say next. "I got an offer from *The New York Times* and an on-air presenter offer from CNN."

"I'll take that as a yes."

"I didn't report anything that wasn't true. And it's good for our community to see people like us on the screen and in papers doing work that we've been historically excluded from."

"You sound like Divya."

"Divya's a smart woman."

"She is." Monica watched a group of people who were approaching with a camera until she could confirm they were just tourists. When they were out of earshot, she said, "That article didn't just change my life, you know. It had a ripple effect that went far beyond it. The merger with Propelle was called off and the entire Amala team has been impacted. In the wake of this scandal the future of the company remains uncertain. You can say what you want about me, but those products are needed by so many in this country, and I don't know if the company can find a way to survive after this."

"I'm sorry, but I didn't intend that."

"I believe you. As we get older, we learn the difference between impact and intention."

"And have you learned it?"

Monica breathed in the salty air. "I'm working on it." She faced Naira. "For example, I am not going to expose you just because you exposed me."

Naira inhaled sharply. Monica suspected that was the real reason Naira had agreed to meet—to get clarification on whether she was next to fall. She wouldn't want a public spectacle after accepting one of her high-powered job offers.

Monica continued, "The impact of bringing you down with me doesn't change anything. I'm tired of the games and the lies. I do think Indian women should work together to get ourselves ahead. If that means you had to sacrifice me to promote yourself, then so be it. A younger version of me would have done exactly the same thing. But I no longer feel like revenge is the answer, and I hope you'll use the platform you will gain from this to go back to the values that I believe are truest for you: lifting up other women rather than cutting them down."

Naira shifted uncomfortably. "I don't know what to say."

"Did you know that around the time you became so eager to tell my story, I started getting threatening text messages. The person never identified themself."

Naira looked queasy. "What kinds of threats?"

"To expose me."

Naira's jaw was set, but her expression was conflicted. "I'm sorry to hear that. I didn't know."

Monica believed her. But she could also tell that, like Monica, Naira believed her source was behind them. She did seem bothered about not being able to share her suspicions, and Monica took some solace in that.

"I need to know who that is."

Naira's voice was barely above a whisper. "I can't do that. I'd never give up a source, and I need to make sure I'm always doing things by the book going forward. I really wish I could help you." She looked at Monica, fear on her face. "Are you going to change your decision about my past now?"

Monica considered whether the threat would be enough leverage to make Naira reveal her source, but then decided there had been enough threats lately. "It won't be me who reveals your past, but be careful. Your secrets may not be as safe as you think they are. I'm proof of that."

Naira exhaled sharply, visibly relieved. "I am really sorry about the way things worked out."

With that, Naira stood to leave and Monica took a few final minutes to herself to memorize the sights, smells, and sounds of the beach she'd been able to see from her house. She was now a woman without a home, a career, a family, or a country.

She gave the vast ocean a final look, trying to imprint it into her memories in case she never returned to this side of the world. Soon, she'd be in a plane crossing it. She was leaving for Singapore that evening, flying economy rather than business class, but that was the least of the many changes that were about to enter her life. She had never wanted to set foot in Singapore again, but regardless of whether she called herself Ami Shah or Monica Joseph, it was the country of her citizenship and the only place she could go right now. The ability to navigate borders and immigration was a privilege unto itself and she had just lost hers.

She stood from the bench and started walking back to her neighborhood. As she made her way off the sand, past the bike path, and through the overpriced public parking lot used mostly by surfers and tourists, she saw Naira standing next to a dark blue SUV at the far corner of the lot. She was embracing a woman, whom Monica presumed to be her girlfriend. Monica was about to discreetly walk past them, when she caught a closer look at the woman's face.

It couldn't be.

But it was.

Monica hadn't seen that face in many years, but it gave her all the information Naira couldn't. She'd asked the private investigator to look into Naira's job when she should have been asking for her to look into Naira's personal life. Because if she'd seen Naira's girlfriend's name, all the pieces would have fallen into place.

31

Her return to Singapore was different than her last visit. She could no longer afford to stay at the Raffles, but she didn't need to be there. She knew where she ultimately would end up, just as soon as she finished the task she had been stewing about on the entire flight over.

Now Monica stood outside the gate in Goodwood Hill steeling her nerves. She'd tucked her luggage off to the side under a tree, knowing it would be safe in this neighborhood. She touched the woven necklace that she had wrapped around her wrist and fastened into place while she'd been on the plane. At some point, someone had wanted this piece of jewelry to protect her and maybe it still carried that sentiment. She had clearly lingered long enough as she saw Grace approaching from the main house.

"Hello, ma'am. You're back," she said as she neared the gate.

"Yes, I'm sorry to come unannounced again, but is Ms. Ami home?"

"She is, but may I ask what this is regarding?"

Monica pleaded with her. "Grace, I need to speak with her for a few minutes. It's important."

Grace texted something on her phone and waited for a response. Finally, she opened the gate. "Ms. Ami will see you, but she said it must be brief as she has another engagement."

Monica nodded as the two of them made their way up the driveway to the main house, for what Monica knew would be her last time here. Her days as their maid felt like a lifetime ago, and they were. She didn't belong here anymore. Not as a helper and not as a resident of these estates, as she'd once hoped she could be. She had to build a life for herself somewhere between affluence and poverty, and she promised herself that she would. She didn't have the lavish payout from an entrepreneurial exit but she had some savings. Not enough to carry her for long given that most of her "wealth" had been tied to the Amala assets that were no longer hers, but it was more than the nothing she'd had when she left here. And she was willing to put in the work. Money and skills were an essential part of establishing a baseline of financial security, and she would use hers to start over.

Monica walked into the formal living room again and positioned herself on the edge of the sofa. She couldn't make herself comfortable as a guest in this home, especially not given what she now knew.

Ami breezed in and sat across from her. "What is so urgent?"

"I know it was you."

"What was?" Ami leaned forward, faux confusion on her face but the glint in her eyes belied her.

Monica pulled out her phone and showed the chain with the 573 number. "This."

"I'm not sure what you mean."

"Stop it, Ami. You've won. You always wanted to make sure I stayed in my place and you've succeeded on an epic scale. I'm sure you already know that I lost my company and my home, and my reputation in North America is completely ruined."

"Don't you mean *my* company?"

The two stared at each other hard, neither wanting to be the first to blink.

"It was never your company. And never could have been. You didn't have the work ethic or skills to bring something like that to fruition."

Ami balked. "This is a rather odd way of apologizing for stealing my identity."

Monica sighed, trying to collect herself. "I am sorry for what I did. But I didn't have another choice if I wanted to make something of myself."

"Again, these aren't the words people use to apologize. Was this what you were plotting the whole time you were working for us?"

Monica bristled at the thought that she'd been that conniving. "Of course not. After you decided to go to CEIBS, you gave me the stack of letters to send to the other schools rejecting your admission to them." Monica forced herself to make eye contact. "And I did that . . . for all except the LBS one."

"That part I've gathered, but I'm not sure how you pulled it off. Surely, they would have known it wasn't me."

They occupied such different places in society that it was impossible for Ami to conceive that she and Monica could ever be mistaken for one another.

Monica shook her head. "They were expecting an Indian girl from Singapore and they got one. Fortunately, it was before social media and everyone putting their lives online for the world to see."

Ami scoffed. "There are so many details about my life you'd have to know. It just doesn't make any sense."

In a steely voice, Monica said, "A helper in your home will know more about you than you even know about yourself. I knew the quality of your sleep based on the tangle of your sheets, whether you fully digested your meals from the previous day, and even where you were at in your menstrual cycle, all without you saying a word. I knew your moods and habits better than you probably did. I even knew how mad you were at your dad or how desperately you were trying to get him to pay attention to you based on how much you shopped in a particular week and if you left the packages in a place where he would see them and chastise you about your spending. On top of that, we went to school together. It wasn't that hard for me to piece together the information I needed. I kept fearing I'd get caught, but once I got past those initial weeks, I realized people didn't really care enough to dissect every little thing I said. They were focused on their own classes and job prospects, and, at the end of the day, people care most about themselves. As long as I kept the focus on them, they didn't ask too much about me. The world has a lot more talkers than listeners."

Ami's mouth formed a thin line. Monica noticed Grace shuffling in the background as she cleaned and pretended she wasn't listening, the same way Monica used to when she had that job.

"It's just so ridiculous. You've spent all these years pretending to be *me*?"

"I did change my name, legally, before I left, so Ami Shah is technically my name now, although I'm going to change it back immediately. But yes, I used your background and admission at LBS to propel myself forward. I was the top of my class there, just like I was at CHIJ. But you already know that, don't you?"

"You got rich off of my name." Ami was now on her feet pacing in the room and shaking her head. "I should have you arrested."

Monica laughed. "I could have, but trust me, you made sure I'd end up with nothing, and that's exactly what happened. You can give yourself a nice pat on the back for that, and for your acting skills the last time I was here. It was truly worthy of an Oscar."

Ami narrowed her eyes. "I had hoped your visit the last time was to confess and apologize. Something—literally *anything*—to try to make amends. When I saw you were just here to cover your tracks, well, it was easy to make sure you got what you deserved with maximum impact."

A part of Monica knew Ami was right. She did deserve some penance for her lies and misrepresentations. Whether she deserved as much as she got was harder to say. But she would own her part in this.

"How did you find out?" Monica asked.

Ami crossed her arms. "How did you find out it was me?"

They stared each other down again, neither wanting to give in. Monica broke the silence. "I'll tell you, if you tell me."

Ami gave a curt nod to signal her agreement.

"I really didn't think it was you after I left here the last time, especially since you were sitting in front of me without a phone when the message came in—" Monica began.

Ami had a smug smile on her face. "Technology is so easy to manipulate these days. I was so proud of myself for having timed that text delivery as well as I did. I wasn't sure exactly what I was going to do with you, but I wanted options."

"You succeeded in throwing me off. But then the reporter knew so much about me from Singapore, and that list of people is short. I couldn't figure out how she'd have any ties to here. She'd even said she'd never been to Singapore. But then I saw her girlfriend. You always made me clean in front of your friends, so once I saw your university friend Zaynab Osman, I knew what the link was."

Ami frowned. "Naira was never supposed to mention her girlfriend."

"She didn't. I saw them together, and I never forget a face. Your turn."

Ami waved in the direction of the entry table with the fresh flowers and stacks of mail. "For years, I'd been getting alumni leaflets from LBS, mostly asking for donations and things like that. Same as I'd get from CEIBS and NUS, and I've just been tossing them. Figured it was some glitch in their system. But then one day I came home and saw your face on the cover with my name. There was a whole article about you and this other bloke from there being nominated for the Global Changemakers Award. I started researching your company but couldn't find much about you. Zaynab has been in LA for years, and I knew her girlfriend was a journalist, so I asked her to look into it. I told Naira everything I knew from your time in Singapore, and she dug up what you'd been up to since, and we pieced everything together. I was shocked to learn how long it had been going on. Maybe if you hadn't been in that article, I would never have learned the truth."

Monica recalled the glossy LBS mailer with photos of her and Oliver on the cover that she'd quickly tossed into her recycling bin. She felt the irony that the very university that had started her life as Ami Shah was also the same one to take it away from her. She almost laughed at the absurdity of how much her life had changed twice due to glossy LBS leaflets, and that her downfall had been the relentless need for institutions to hound alumni for donations.

Ami continued, "I knew you were always jealous of me. I didn't think you'd take it so far though. You were always such a rules follower, never daring to step out of the Sisters' favor."

"I wasn't jealous of you," Monica said. "I was envious of the privilege you were born into. I thought it was unfair that even though I had always done better than you in school and worked harder than you, that the world kept opening door after door for you because you were already wealthy and had the pedigree that came with that. And because I hadn't been born into the right family, I couldn't even get close enough to see those doors, let alone walk through them."

"It's not my fault you're an orphan. I did so much to help you, including getting you this job with my family. I treated you like a friend."

"Help? You did everything you could to remind me of my place and that it was always beneath you. I know you always passed your hand-me-downs directly to me when we were growing up rather than donating them to the convent like everyone else, because I was doing better than you in school and you wanted to remind me that I wasn't your equal. And, because I needed them, I had no choice but to wear them and then endure your patronizing comments about how they looked on me. When you told me you were going to help me get a job after secondary school, I thought you meant for your family's business, not as your maid. You, of all people, knew I was capable of so much more than cleaning your toilet. And then when I worked here, you made a point of putting on display that I was your helper when other girls we went to school with showed up at the house. Having me fetch snacks or mop the foyer while they were here so everyone could see that the furthest I'd gotten in life was doing your floors. Would you have gotten into any of those business schools if I hadn't written the essays for your applications? The only thing we know for sure is that when left to your own devices, you didn't complete the degree at CEIBS and came running back home to let your mummy and daddy take care of you. Ask yourself if you'd really be where you are today if the world were a meritocracy. If it were, I don't think I'd ever have been your maid."

Ami seethed. "You're right. If you hadn't been an orphan, then you wouldn't have been my maid. You would have been living in squalor in that dingy apartment on Buffalo Road. But the chance I gave you to be a part of this home wasn't enough for you. You had to go and take more because you always wanted what I had."

Monica's eyes narrowed. "What apartment on Buffalo Road?"

Ami's hand flew to her mouth as if she were trying to stop the words that had already been released.

Monica leaned forward. "Ami?"

Ami rose and began pacing from her chair to the large window overlooking the impeccably manicured garden. Finally, she stopped and turned back to Monica.

"I did think we were friends. Maybe you didn't, but I did. It hurt when you left like that. I had already stuck my neck out with my family to get you a job in our home. I thought it would be a chance for us to get closer. I saw you needed a family, and well, I never had a sibling so here I was foolish enough to think we could be like sisters."

Monica took a gentle step toward her. "I cleaned your toilet. I wore a uniform. I slept in the servant's quarters. We could never have been sisters. We could have been friends, but that only works when people respect each other as equals, and I don't think you ever saw me as that."

Ami crossed her arms over her chest, but didn't bother to argue.

"Why did you bring up Buffalo Road?"

Monica had only ever been to Buffalo Road when she was picking up food for the Shahs when she worked for them. It was the Little India of Singapore, a sea of faces that looked like hers, and occasionally she'd been sent to get crispy samosas or paper dosas. They'd never included an order for her when placing their own.

Ami chewed her bottom lip as she contemplated her next words.

"When you were working here, I asked my dad to try to find your birth parents. Through our business, of course, we're well connected to the Indian laborer community." Even when it was just the two of them, Ami felt the need to assert that her family stood above others. "He employs a lot of them, and Singapore is a pretty small town at the end of the day. No offense, but we figured it was going to be a low-income family, so my dad was able to track them down by talking to the Brahmin at the temple in Little India, and then following up with his employees from the area. A woman who was pregnant and then had no baby wasn't an everyday occurrence."

Monica felt dizzy and sank to the sofa. "You know who my birth parents are?"

"Not really. My dad went to see them. He wouldn't want me around those types of people by myself. He came back and told me that there were a bunch of them living in a dingy two-bed apartment. They were nothing like the people we grew up with at CHIJ and didn't seem like people you would have wanted in your life."

Monica shook her head at how easy it had been for Mr. Shah to find her parents, and she wondered if she should have tried to search when she was a young girl. Or maybe the Sisters should have tried harder. But then she realized, it was probably easy for Mr. Shah because of who he was and the deference Singaporean Indians gave to him. Neither she nor the Sisters were likely to have had people be so forthcoming with them.

"A bunch of them? A bunch of who?" Monica asked, thinking about what Ami had just said.

"I don't know. Their other kids maybe? Or cousins? I didn't get the details, because we could tell you were better off with us."

Other kids? Did she have siblings? Or cousins? She had

envisioned countless scenarios of reuniting with her birth parents, but in none of them had she pictured other family members.

Monica shook her head as if trying to make the pieces fall into place. "Your dad met my birth parents when I was working here? And then you all decided not to tell me?"

Ami swallowed hard and then sat back in her chair. "They were really poor. It wasn't a life you would have wanted. I was sure of that. I saw how you admired my clothes and shoes, and our family vacations. I know you tried my stuff on when we would go away and pretend they were yours. There was nothing they could have offered you."

Shame was the first thing she felt, because Ami was right that Monica had tried on her things and wondered what it would have been like to own them and go somewhere important wearing them. She thought she'd always been careful to put them back exactly how they were and was surprised Ami had noticed. But then the shame gave way to anger, betrayal, and confusion as she thought about the gravity of what Ami had done. She balled her fists. "That wasn't your decision to make."

Ami hung her head like she knew Monica was right. "We really did think it was best for you to stay with us. You'd have more opportunities that way."

"What opportunities would I have had as your *maid*?" Monica spat. "Did you really think you did what was best for me or did you not want to lose your paid friend?"

Ami flinched. "It wasn't like that. With me going off to business school, I had already started talking to my dad about maybe finding you a job at our company. I knew you didn't want to clean for the rest of your life."

Monica's mind reeled, and she felt the falseness of Ami's words. "Your dad was never going to give me a different job. When he thought I wasn't listening, he said all the time that I was the best maid your family had ever had. But I was always listening, and even if you'd gone to business school, he wasn't going to make his life harder to make mine better. None of you were."

Monica fumed at the thought that Ami had interfered in her life so spectacularly and she had never even known about it.

Ami winced. "It wasn't like that. I really thought we were doing what was best for you at the time. I wanted to protect you. Some of the other orphans had such dreadful stories of their birth families and it looked like yours would be the same. Why put yourself through that?"

"Did they know about me? What did they say?"

"Once my dad saw what they were like, he didn't tell them anything. He said he was there for his business and looking for new employees or something like that. He had them fill out application forms along with some other neighbors so nothing seemed suspicious. He said they just seemed happy at the prospect of new jobs with the Shahs. We didn't hire them, obviously."

Monica felt the air leave her lungs. She thought of the times they had sent her to pick up food from Little India. She could have walked past her parents and neither would have been the wiser. She now recalled that sending her with the driver for takeaway orders had stopped at a certain point during her tenure there. She hadn't thought much about it, grateful to have the extra time to finish her chores earlier so that she could then curl up in her bed with her sewing or a book, but now she suspected this was the reason. They couldn't risk the best maid they'd ever had running into her birth parents and maybe learning after all these years that she was part of a family, one that may, in fact, have wanted her.

"I can't believe you kept this from me." It was Monica's turn to feel betrayed.

"I guess we both made decisions that hurt the other."

Monica was hardly sure if these were in the same category.

"I wonder if they are still there," Monica said.

Ami met her gaze. "They are. We had their names from the job applications. When I learned what you had done, I had someone confirm that they were still around. I considered giving Naira that information too in case she wanted to include them in her article, but then I decided she didn't need that for her piece."

Monica wasn't sure whether to thank her or strangle her. She wasn't sure how to feel about all the power Ami had wielded and continued to wield on her life. But the voice of the little girl inside her was solely focused on the fact that she had parents, they were alive, and they were mere miles away from where she sat right now.

"Why?" Monica asked, trying to understand the lines that Ami was drawing.

Ami sighed. "I don't know. I guess the part of me that still thought we'd been friends didn't want you to find out that way."

Ami rose and disappeared into the expanse of the house leaving Monica alone. Monica shook her head, as if that would settle the overload of information she had just received. She numbly sat on the couch thinking of all the times she'd dusted this furniture when the residents knew the story of her birth family and kept it from her. Why did the wealthy always think they knew what was best for other people? Was it another layer of control? A way to keep themselves at the top of the hierarchy, and ensure people like Monica could never rise above them?

Ami returned and handed Monica a piece of paper. "You can decide what to do with it."

32

She made her way down the sidewalk and paused at the entryway. The piece of paper from Ami was tucked into her handbag. This was the home she was meant to have had she stayed in Singapore. This, or the maid's quarters of a family she worked for, but this would have been the place that her heart gravitated toward because of the people in it. She wrapped her hand around the woven necklace encircling her right wrist, realizing this was the second time she was seeking refuge from the IJ Sisters while wearing it. She took a hesitant step inside the IJ House and listened for sounds coming from the rooms. She heard water running in the kitchen and made her way there.

Qi was at the stove stirring mushrooms in a sauté pan, and the smell of garlic, ginger, and soy sauce perfumed the air. Esther was meticulously removing the string from the snow peas, her tongue poking out of her mouth while she concentrated. Victoria was at the sink washing dishes. They turned toward her, surprise on their faces. Esther broke into a wide smile and clapped.

"What are you doing back here?" Victoria asked as she turned off the water. Her tone was neither warm nor cold, and she stated the question simply.

It was clear that whatever media circus had been surrounding her in LA hadn't made it past these protected walls. To the three women before her, she was the same person she had been a few weeks earlier. She didn't know how much to tell them because most of the material life she'd lost wouldn't matter to them. And maybe that realization said more than anything else about the decisions she had made while away from them. And now, despite all her efforts, she was back to where she had started from, back to where she had always been meant to be, and maybe that was the right answer all along.

"I'm sorry for the way I treated you," Monica said. "The last time I was here, and all the years before that."

The sizzle of the mushrooms against the hot skillet echoed in the room. Victoria and Qi looked at her solemnly as if they could sense that she was in need. And of course they could. They had been each other's family for so many years, and that intuition and understanding didn't disappear just because she had.

"Do you want to join us for lunch?" Qi asked.

Monica nodded, swallowing the lump that had formed in her throat. "Can I help with anything?"

"Why don't you set the table and stay away from the food," Qi said.

They all laughed. They had no reason to think that Monica's culinary skills had improved in her time away, and they were correct. Victoria pointed to where the dishes were and Monica set out to do her task. It felt like old times. It felt like the right place for her to be.

"How is Sister Francis?" Monica asked.

"She is napping right now, but we need to wake her for her medication after we eat," Victoria said.

There was much to say between them and between her and Sister Francis, but for just this moment, they could enjoy a home-cooked meal together and forget the weight of the world. It would all still be there after they finished.

Qi had only refined her cooking skills since Monica had last had one of her meals. Her balance of flavors was as satiating as dishes Monica had eaten in the finest restaurants in LA.

"Have you ever thought about becoming a chef, Qi?" Monica asked after they'd cleared their plates.

Qi shook her head. "I do some cooking for the family I work for when there's time in between my cleaning."

Monica knew that family was getting quite a deal hiring Qi at a maid's rate and then getting these gourmet meals that would be on par with those of a renowned chef. Monica was about to suggest that with a little training on presentation, Qi could aspire to more, but then she held her tongue. Aspiring to more hadn't made her particularly happy in the long run, so maybe she shouldn't be imposing her misguided beliefs on others, especially people who were clearly already happy. Her thirst for more had pushed her to limits that she hadn't known she was capable of, all in search of these opportunities that she believed the wealthy had and that she had so desperately wanted for herself. There was nothing wrong with Qi, Victoria, and Esther being content with the lives that they had, sitting around a table with their chosen family and enjoying the ritual of meals together. And that was what she wanted for herself now too. If, that is, they would have her.

Victoria left them in the kitchen to bring Sister Francis her medicine. She came back after a few minutes and encouraged Monica to go up while Sister Francis was rested and in good spirits. There was no way of knowing how long that would last.

Monica entered the room carefully. Sister Francis was propped up by pillows on the bed. The glass of cold water Victoria had brought up for her pills was already gathering condensation along its exterior. Given the previous visits, Monica expected Sister Francis to not recognize her. Spending time with her in any capacity was a precious luxury, and that was what she needed to focus on.

"Hi, Sister Francis. Do you mind if I sit with you for a little bit?"

Sister Francis didn't respond but watched her walk to the chair between the bed and the window. Cool air blasted from the unit near the ceiling, ensuring the room was a comfortable temperature, but Sister Francis still had a blanket over her withered frame and appeared to shiver.

"Is it too cold for you? Shall I ask Victoria if we can change it?"

Sister Francis gave a dismissive wave. "I'm always cold these days. It's like being back in Ireland."

Monica sat next to her. Sister Francis stared at Monica's right hand, and then reached out to touch the orange, white, and green woven necklace she had wrapped around it.

"This was Monica's," Sister Francis said, clasping Monica's wrist. "She was wearing it when I found her. But how did you . . . ?" She brought her gaze to meet Monica's now teary eyes. She searched her face as if seeing it for the first time. Monica nodded, and Sister Francis's eyes widened. "Monica? Is that you? It's been so many years."

"I know, Sister Francis. I'm so sorry." Relief flooded through her at being recognized as herself, but it was followed by the apprehension of knowing it was time to show her truest self to the most significant person in her life.

"What happened to you? We were so worried."

"I'm very sorry to have worried you. It's such a long story." A tear slid down her cheek. Monica didn't know how long she'd have this version of Sister Francis with her—the one who *knew* her—and she wanted to savor every second.

Sister Francis gave Monica a sympathetic smile. "No long faces for me. I know my mind and body aren't what they once were, but I want to hear everything." She shook her head. "I can't believe it's really you."

"First of all, I know you must be so angry with what I did. Asking you to help me get the money from CHIJ, and then disappearing." She took a deep breath. "What I told you before about how I left for London was true, but it wasn't the whole truth. I didn't get into university in London by myself." Her eyes turned toward the floor. "While I was working as a helper for Ami's family—" Monica looked up. "Do you remember her, Sister Francis?"

"Of course, I do. There weren't so many Indian faces among the girls who came to study with us."

Monica told Sister Francis about how she had taken Ami's identity in order to get to LBS, and the life she built from there.

When she finished, Sister Francis squeezed her hand. "Does she know?"

"Yes." Monica didn't see the point in telling Sister Francis about the threatening messages and games Ami had been playing with her. Their moments were precious and limited, and Monica didn't want to waste them on Ami. "We won't be friends, I suppose we never really were, but now there are no lies between us."

Sister Francis nodded solemnly. "Friends or not, we must

always hold ourselves accountable and make amends when we've wronged someone. I hope you've done that."

"I tried my best." Monica gestured toward the necklace wrapped around her wrist. "You recognized this. What can you tell me about it?"

"You were the first one I'd personally found at the Gate, so I will never forget that night. When I found you, you had this necklace on and your tiny hand was clamped around it. It was the only clue we had to your heritage."

"That's why you were always so sure I was Indian. Why didn't you give it to me, though?"

Sister Francis let out a soft sigh. "It's hard to know if these things were right at the time. We were all relatively young girls learning the ways of a country that was both foreign to us and constantly changing as it searched for its identity after the war. If anything had come with the babies left at the Gate, we stored those items in their files, but didn't give them to the girls. We didn't want to create any rivalries or bitterness or division among a group of children that had already suffered so much. And it was still relatively soon after the war, and we worried people would confuse the Hindu symbol with the Nazi one, so we thought it was best that you didn't have it."

Monica now had confirmation that her birth mother had left a token symbolizing protection when she'd dropped off her baby. An unfeeling woman wouldn't do that. Monica felt her chest constrict. She'd invented plenty of stories about the absent mother in her life and in none of them had she envisioned a woman who had cared for or protected her. It was far easier to paint the woman as a villain rather than think about all the space that existed between villain and saint. But most people lived in the space in between.

"If she cared about me, why do you think I was left at the Gate?"

"We can never know what's in the heart and mind of another, my child. Only that desperation can cause us to act in ways we could never have contemplated."

Monica knew that feeling all too well.

Emotion flooded her voice. "I don't know what I would have done without you. I might not even be alive. You're the only moth—"

With some strain, Sister Francis squeezed her hand. "I'm not your mother, dear. But I am someone who loves you. By choice and not any kind of obligation, and that's the purest kind of love there is. You are the most shining example we have ever had from the orphans. You took our teachings and learned in a way that exceeded all the girls before you. You proved that girls can have a second chance at life. Even if you lost your way for some period after that, what matters is that you found your way back home."

"I have so many regrets about who I've become. I didn't keep up with the IJ traditions the way I should have."

"No one lives a perfect life. Not even the Sisters, but I don't live with regret and neither should you." She cupped Monica's face. "I've served the Lord and helped more people than I ever thought possible. I'm a long way from that village in Ireland where I grew up and I never thought I'd see this much of the world. From a scared girl coming to Asia for the first time to now calling it home for the past sixty years . . . life truly does surprise you. How many people can say they were present for the birth of an entire nation and helped shape its identity?" She released Monica's face and again held the wrist with the necklace wrapped around it. "I have spent my life with you girls. You, Esther, Victoria, Qi, and so many others before you. That is the greatest gift that was bestowed upon me. I am so proud of all of you."

"Pride is a sin, right?" Monica said, not feeling worthy of the praise.

Sister Francis let out a small laugh. "The scriptures didn't get everything right. As long as we can find balance in our lives, that is enough. When you are my age and looking back on your life, make sure you leave this world with more than you took from it. That's the only thing we can control."

Monica swallowed the lump in her throat. She had such mixed feelings about the way she'd earned her success, and yet part of her didn't regret the lies she'd told to get there. The world acted as if people who worked hard and had good values could achieve anything. But that wasn't true. The stain of your station in life followed you wherever you went. Honesty ensured never being able to climb to higher ground, so why was it valued so much? Even though she could intellectually rationalize it, and she was a living example of how effectively those barriers worked and how quickly they could be resurrected if they'd been breached, a larger part of her felt the shame of having earned her achievements through dishonesty. She thought back to the girl who wrote the essay. She knew which was the righteous path, but not which was the *right* one. And maybe the answer changes over time.

Today, she felt like she was making strides toward the right one. And she couldn't ignore the grandiosity of the life she'd built or the pain of the fall from it, because those experiences were embedded in her and would guide her toward the next phase of her life. She looked at her wrist with Sister Francis still holding it. The woman who had raised her but was not her mother. For the first time, she allowed herself to believe that maybe her mother was worth finding. But now Monica also had to grapple with whether *she* was worthy of the woman who had abandoned her.

33

Monica softly closed the door to Sister Francis's room as she tucked in for a nap. If Monica was this emotionally spent, she could only imagine how much the conversation had drained Sister Francis. She found her friends in the kitchen, now playing cards on the cleared table.

"You were up there for a long time." Victoria placed her cards face down in front of her. "Was she okay?"

Monica nodded. "We had a conversation that was long overdue, and I'm glad she was feeling well enough to understand everything that I needed to say." Monica sat at the table. "I owed her an explanation, and I owe the same one to all of you."

Taking a deep breath, Monica told her story for the second time that day, while Victoria, Esther, and Qi listened.

"You went through all of that only to end up back here?" Qi said. "Was it worth it?"

"I've asked myself that every day since I got the first message from Ami. Earlier than that, if I'm being honest. In the choice between money or connection, I'm no longer certain money is the right one. I know it doesn't change anything, but I thought about the three of you all the time."

"That's why Ami came here, then? Wasn't it?" Victoria said.

Monica raised her eyebrow. "What do you mean she came here?"

Esther looked carefully at each of them in turn while they spoke, absorbing everything like a sponge.

"She visited Sister Francis a little over a month ago. Sister Francis hadn't been in a terribly good state that day, but they had a quick visit."

"I wonder if that's why Ami was easier for her to remember than me."

"Could be," Qi said.

Monica felt something release in her. It hadn't been that Ami had left a more lingering impression on Sister Francis than Monica when they were in school all those years ago, it was that Ami's was the most recent face she'd seen. She'd never know if that were true, but it was what she would choose to believe. Sometimes, the story we needed to believe mattered more than the truth.

"The money—it was from you, wasn't it?" Victoria said. "I helped track the donations and there was a large amount every year in the same denomination. Sister Francis seemed to understand what it was, but never told us."

"$37,850. It was the amount Sister Francis arranged for me to get as a scholarship when I said I needed money for school. I knew it had come from the inheritance she'd received after her parents passed. It was enough to get me to London and get me through my first year, and I worked on campus for what I needed after that. But once I had earned enough through my company, I anonymously donated to CHIJ every year. It doesn't excuse what I did. But I wanted to make sure all of you were looked after."

"You didn't realize that we would rather have had you than the money?" Qi asked.

Monica hung her head. "I didn't. At that point in my life, I thought money was the key to an easier life. I was surrounded by people who measured their lives according to the value of their cars, homes, and clothes, and I got caught up in that, forgetting that isn't true for everyone."

"So, the whole time we were growing up, were you miserable that we didn't have more?" Qi said.

Monica paused to reflect. "I think I was always envious of the choices the paying girls had. I equated those choices to money. But I realize it's so much more than that. Money is part of it, but it's more society's expectation of what people with certain backgrounds are capable of. I thought it wasn't fair to have our choices limited simply because of the manner in which we came into this world, when that was completely out of our control. My leaving didn't have anything to do with any of you. I've spent over twenty years looking for people who made me feel as happy and free as I did when it was just us running around the grounds of the Town Convent, and I never found that anywhere else."

Qi nodded, accepting her answer.

"Are you going to seek out your birth mother?" Victoria asked.

"I don't know if I should," Monica said. "The last time I went searching for something that wasn't really mine, things turned out rather poorly."

Victoria's expression was solemn. "It's a difficult decision. You have to be careful."

Unlike the other orphans, Victoria had grown up knowing who her birth family was and where to find them. At times when they were young, her birth family would come to bring her home for a few months or weeks at a time, but then they blamed her for the bad luck that fell upon the family while she was with them. "Tiger baby," her mother spat at her when her father lost his job or another of her siblings fell ill. She'd truly believed that Victoria's very existence was the reason for her family's misfortune. Even though Victoria always received the same rejection from her birth family when she saw them, it hadn't stopped her from trying to get them to take her back in. Memories could be short when it came to blood. But she knew better than many orphans the visceral pain of knowing just how unwanted she was. When parents and birth families were unknown, it left room for the heart and mind to make up stories they could accept. Anything other than the simple and harsh reality that they had been born to people who would rather live a life without them in it.

"I won't expect anything from her," Monica said, her decision coming into focus. "But I have to know how I came into this world."

Victoria's face registered the sadness she assumed Monica would find pursuing this path. Monica knew she was trying to protect her. But she also knew that there was no such thing as an objective opinion. People were a collection of their past experiences and those shaped every decision they made and every viewpoint they had about the world. Monica would prepare herself for the same reception from her birth family as Victoria had gotten from hers, but she had to experience that for herself.

"We can come with you if you want," Victoria said.

Upon hearing the words, the heaviness in Monica's heart lifted. Because she knew that whatever happened at the address in Little India, *this* was her family. And she'd never take that for granted again.

34

The four of them took a Grab to Buffalo Road. Monica rubbed her hand along her neck. Despite the strain of all she'd lost recently, her eczema was receding, so it seemed that releasing the secrets she'd been carrying for so long was what her body needed to find balance again and restore itself.

When they arrived at Buffalo Road, she took in the colorful assortment of shophouses with businesses on the ground floor. Grocers, restaurants, florists, spice merchants, and home goods stores lined the street. She inhaled the smells of samosas, chaat, dosa, and sambar wafting outside of Tekka Centre and knew she now could claim these smells as part of her culture. That was the one part of all this that gave her some relief. She knew her heritage and was no longer adrift. She'd have to learn so much more about it, but at least she'd spent a decent amount of time in India with Divya for Amala and could picture the country. She'd always thought of herself as an outsider there, but if she were to go again, maybe she could see parts of herself in the people around her the way Divya always had.

With the location mapped on her phone, they easily found the building next to the Tekka Centre. The address was on the second floor.

She hesitated at the stairs, her friends—no, her *family*—behind her in support. "I think I should go by myself."

"We'll be right here," Victoria said.

Monica slowly mounted the stairs. When she arrived at the second-floor landing, she saw a new side of Singapore. It was far from the opulence of Goodwood Hill and the Raffles, but still not the same as the Town Convent. Homes spilled out onto the wide covered walkways with sofas, chairs, and tables arranged outside the apartment doors. Clothing and umbrellas hung from the pipes overhead to make for an outdoor closet. Cabinets without locks were interspersed along the wall. And the homes had racks of shoes before the front doors, as was expected throughout Asia. Parts of this place reminded her of what she'd seen on the trips to India she had taken with Divya.

She saw an older man sitting on one of the sofas sipping tea and approached him, gripping her phone in her hand.

"Do you know Roshni Paraiyar?"

The man set his mug on the table next to him. "Who are you?"

"Monica," she said softly as the man looked her up and down.

He grunted, seeming to accept her answer and pointed down the corridor. "Three doors down."

She thanked him and walked in the direction he'd said. The apartments she passed had open doors and it seemed almost like communal living. Her home in Venice had always been locked. Her wealthy neighborhood was a prime target for theft. The residents here in Little India seemed to have complete trust in their neighbors. Or maybe they were confident that there wasn't anything to steal.

At the third apartment, she found a screen door that was not fully closed and the wooden interior door wide open. Inside, she could see a woman in black pants and a pink shirt stirring a pot on the stove. A TV could be heard coming from a back room. There were children's toys strewn around the living area and small clothes and shoes tossed about. This could not possibly be the right place with so many young kids' items, and it wouldn't surprise her if Ami had misdirected her out of spite. She had already shown how much she enjoyed that.

Monica rapped on the screen door, trying to get the woman's attention. She didn't turn from what she was doing, so Monica pulled open the screen and knocked harder on the wooden interior door. Still no response over the noise coming from inside the apartment.

Maybe she should leave. She could still escape to the women waiting on the ground floor and go back to the IJ House and never revisit this part of her life. It would be easier, especially given what she had seen of the home and Victoria's admonitions. But she had come this far.

She took a hesitant step in and said loudly, "Hello."

The woman turned and Monica could see her weathered face and gray hair. The front of her shirt had what looked like oil stains that had been there for quite some time and had never been properly washed out.

"Who are you?" the woman asked, before turning back to her pot and continuing to stir.

"I'm Monica."

The woman faced her again with a confused expression.

"Are you Roshni Paraiyar?"

She nodded, ladling what looked like kitchari from the pot and into a small bowl. "What do you want? My granddaughter is sick so I need to get back to her."

Granddaughter? She thought back to Ami saying there had been a bunch of kids.

Monica took a deep breath and reminded herself that this woman had played no active role in her life. She could not hurt her. It was a lie, but one she needed to believe right now. She forced her shoulders back, and pretended she was at a board meeting, in control and in command.

"Did you leave a baby at the Town Convent in 1977?"

The woman stopped moving and stared at her. She didn't blink and Monica felt her eyes boring through her.

In a soft voice, Monica said, "I'm that baby."

The woman continued to stare. In Monica's dreams of this moment, no matter how many years had passed, her biological mother would be able to sense their connection and instantly know who Monica was. Tears would spring to her eyes and she'd embrace Monica and they'd both feel an instant bond. Monica's fantasies about this reunion had been far off the mark.

Someone called for dadi from the inside room and the woman quickly grabbed a spoon and put it into the bowl and then disappeared into the back. Monica stood unsure of what to do and unsure if the woman was coming back. Her demeanor had made clear that she was the right person. Was she really going to walk out on Monica after such a revelation? It wouldn't be the first time. Monica stared at the closed door and wondered if she should knock on it. She decided to wait and took in her surroundings. The home was cluttered. What looked like it should have been the living room instead had three thin mattresses placed directly on the floor with lumpy pillows and worn blankets.

In the dining room, there was a folding table and a few mismatched chairs. The table was covered with piles of paper, toys, and clothing. She tried to picture herself here. Ami had been right about their living conditions. Would this have been better than the Town Convent? It was hard to say. The orphanage was always clean and free of clutter. The Sisters made sure of that.

There was always fresh food. They made sure of that too. She couldn't tell if those two things were always a given in this home.

The woman emerged from the room without the bowl. She stared at Monica, her eyes falling to the orange, white, and green necklace wrapped around her wrist. "How did you find me?"

Monica flinched. She'd abandoned her forty-two years ago, and those were her first words to her? Wasn't she curious about her well-being or how her life had turned out? Monica had tried to convince herself that this woman could not hurt her, but she'd been naive to think that.

"I just—I—wanted to know you. I've never known what happened. Why you . . ."

She stared at the woman and her surroundings and could not picture herself here. Who would she have been if she'd been raised in this apartment? No one. That's who. She'd never have developed Amala. Never been up for—let alone won—the Global Changemakers Award, because she would never have done anything worthy of changing the world. She'd have been one anonymous blip in society who would never have mattered. The room began to feel very claustrophobic and the humidity in the air felt oppressive.

"You want to know why I left you there?" Her tone carried none of the emotion that Monica felt this occasion called for. It was unsettling.

Monica nodded.

"It was what was best. I already had two children to feed and not enough food."

"I have siblings?" Monica asked, feeling the weight of the words. "Where are they?"

"Your elder sister and brother are in the back room. Your younger sister is at her job."

"You kept . . . other children." Monica felt like she'd been slapped.

For so many decades she had never fathomed that she could

have siblings. Not until Ami planted the thought a couple days ago. She had always pictured a mother who could not care for a child because she was too young, or too poor, or medically unable. Never had she considered that there were other children and it was only *she* who had been abandoned. And a younger sister. That meant that *after* she had been abandoned, this woman decided to have another child and keep her rather than coming back to claim Monica. She could not even begin to fathom the logic at play. Victoria was right. The truth of an orphan's origin was always more painful than anything she could have imagined.

This set of facts was something that Monica found unforgiveable, and anger swelled inside her. What possible explanation could there be that would justify her being singled out for abandonment among the other choices. And then another child came—another girl—whom this woman decided to keep instead of coming back for her? While she didn't agree with it, she knew the climate in Singapore was such that boys were favored, so she could almost make peace with this woman deciding to keep a boy and give away a girl. On the rare occasions when boys were left at the Town Convent, they'd be adopted practically before their first diaper change. But to have had two other girls and to have decided Monica was the one worthy of being discarded? She felt a physical pain shoot up her spine but was determined not to crumble before this woman.

Before Roshni could speak, a door opened and a man and woman in their forties walked out.

"This is Santosh and Lavangi," Roshni said.

"You all live here?" Monica asked, certain this home was packed beyond capacity given the mattresses in the living area.

Lavangi nodded. "And our kids."

Monica stared into faces that unmistakably looked like her own. She had the same nose as Santosh and the same lips at

Lavangi. She turned back to Roshni to see if she could identify which of her features had come from this woman. They shared the same nose. But not their eyes and lips. Maybe those were more like her biological father, whoever he was. Monica wondered if he lived here too. She tried to picture what seemed like three families living in this small space and thought of how generous the IJ House and her place in Venice were in comparison.

"Is this Rachana?" Lavangi asked.

Lavangi took a step closer to Monica, and Monica instinctively took a step back.

"Rachana?" Monica said, looking between them.

Roshni nodded.

Monica realized that this was her birth name. Rachana. She rolled it over in her mouth, tasting how foreign and unfamiliar it felt. This was her name before the Sisters had baptized her as Monica Joseph. She'd been Rachana Paraiyar.

"Where have you been all this time?" Lavangi asked.

Monica's eyes bugged out at the question as if she were a member of the family and had been missing for a night rather than over forty years. She wanted to scream, *At the orphanage where she left me!* But she couldn't get those words out, and said the first thing that came to mind because how could she explain her life from orphan to entrepreneur back to orphan in just a few sentences?

"America," Monica said.

The three pairs of eyes staring at her widened.

"You live in America now?" Roshni said.

Monica didn't feel she owed them her life story. Monica suspected that they had spent their entire lives in this apartment—a twenty-minute walk from the orphanage in which she'd been raised—but had never bothered to try to find her. It would have been so easy to come and reclaim her, but that would have required the desire to have her in their lives. Looking around, she knew her life had been better than theirs. Maybe this woman had done her a favor by selecting her to be outcast. One look at Santosh and Lavangi with their worn, outdated clothing, bad teeth, and downtrodden demeanors made clear that of the Paraiyar children, Monica was the one who had made it. Her life with her birth family would have meant the furthest she would have gotten in life was to be a cook or a maid—and not even a maid in Goodwood Hill. Ami had been right about that. She probably would have been a day maid for a middle- to lower-income family, and then come home each night and slept on a flimsy mattress on that living room floor.

"I did," Monica said.

"I can't believe you made it." Santosh's voice was astonished.

It felt to her like this group was disappointed that she hadn't died as a baby, and was now standing in their home. It was hard to believe these people who had callously abandoned her while remaining together were her flesh and blood. And after all this time, there was no warm welcome or loving reception to find out what happened to the baby who had been cast aside. The reason no longer mattered to her. Victoria had been right.

She looked at these family members—no, not family members—biological relatives to whom she had no other connection, and began to back out of the room. It felt like the air was being sucked out of her lungs and she needed to get outside. She had nothing in common with them and she'd made the wrong decision in coming here. She turned and rushed out, gripping the railing on her way down the stairs. She tried to picture herself running along them as a young girl. Children, as long as they were loved, rarely noticed the difference between poverty and wealth and could find joy in so many simple pleasures. Maybe she could have had a good life here, playing with her siblings and then being crammed into the apartment as if they were having an endless sleepover. Some parts were always going to be the same for her. At the Town Convent, she slept in a room with many other people just as she would have done in that apartment with her birth family. She was going to have hand-me-downs regardless of where she'd been brought up because neither situation had wealth at its core. But the main thing she kept coming back to was whether she could have gotten an education.

At the bottom of the stairs, Victoria, Qi, and Esther were waiting just as they'd promised. She rushed toward them and they held her. No one asked what happened, knowing it didn't matter. What mattered was that the four of them were safely in each other's arms in this moment.

While Monica shook, Victoria whispered into her ear, "Birth families are not always the family we are meant to have."

As she felt their love around her, she knew she'd gotten more than an education by being abandoned. She'd gotten her true family, and for that, she'd forever be grateful.

35

Back at the IJ House, Monica told the women what happened. For the first time in so many years, she had confidantes again and could speak freely. She hadn't realized how much she missed that after training herself to bottle everything inside. They listened with rapt attention. Esther frowned in response to the severity of the mood around her. Monica wished she could tell Sister Francis anew how much she had saved her life, but her condition was delicate today, and she didn't recognize Monica at all. She'd stared at her worried, like a stranger had entered her room. Qi told her that there were days like this and there would hopefully be better ones ahead. Monica hoped so because she would now be there for them. She'd moved into the IJ House, and had her own room next to Esther. She relished being close to people again.

That evening, Esther came into Monica's room and pointed toward the front door, pulling Monica with her. Monica allowed herself to be guided and then froze when she saw what Esther had been so anxious about. Waiting behind the screen door was a man she'd never seen before, but Roshni Paraiyar lingered behind him, waiting at the edge of the covered walkway, wringing her hands.

Monica moved like molasses as she registered who the man must be. Esther looked at her and gave her a hug and then flung open the screen door before Monica could stop her.

"Rachana," he said. His tone was far warmer than that of the other family members she'd met.

"It's Monica."

She looked at the man whom she knew had to be her father, and confirmed that she did have his eyes and lips. She'd never had a male figure in her life. Growing up in a convent had pretty much assured that. And her avoidance of relationships with men since that time solidified that she wouldn't have them in adulthood either. Her life had been about strong women like Sister Francis, Victoria, Esther, and Qi.

"Monica." He held his hand over his heart in forgiveness. He looked her up and down as if taking in each centimeter of her. "I can hardly believe I'm seeing you."

"Are you my father?"

He bowed slightly to confirm. "Haishan."

Esther was close to her, peering over her shoulder, a smile on her face. She appeared to be optimistic even though Monica didn't yet know if this was a happy occasion or not.

"This is Esther," Monica said, and Esther offered a shy wave before sinking deeper behind Monica's back.

Haishan bowed in greeting to her as well. Monica whispered to Esther to go find Victoria and she scampered off.

Haishan continued to stare at her. "I wasn't sure I would ever get the chance to see you." He gestured toward the end of the walkway. "Please, can Roshni join us too?"

Not knowing what else to do, she gave a slight nod. After Roshni got the signal and made her way up the path, the three of them went into the kitchen and sat at the dining table. Monica chose the seat furthest away from them.

He looked at her with bewilderment. "You're all grown up."

Monica sat stiffly and couldn't help but notice that Roshni's posture mirrored her own.

Roshni said, "I'm sorry for how shocked I was."

"That makes two of us." Monica crossed her arms over her chest.

Haishan said, "I thought we all owed it to each other to know the truth, if you are willing to hear it."

Monica gave a curt nod, and then Haishan gave Roshni an encouraging look.

"You were our third child," Roshni began. "We had very little money. It's still that way, as you saw. When you were born, you were covered in red rashes and the skin beneath that was a sickly yellow. One of your eyelids was so red and puffy that you couldn't even lift the lid. We—" her voice broke "—didn't think you would survive. You were so weak and wouldn't take milk and were constantly fussing. We had no money for a doctor. Others in our community had proclaimed that you were not strong enough to survive. Once the Brahmin at our temple confirmed that you were very sick, we had no choice. Everyone in Singapore knew that the nuns at the Town Convent would look after abandoned babies. I thought maybe they could make you comfortable until you . . . passed." She cast her eyes downward with the weight of the world on her shoulders.

Monica processed the information. It explained why of the

four children, she was the only one who had been abandoned, assuming her siblings had been born healthier.

"Did you ever learn why my skin was like that?" she asked.

Both shook their heads.

"I had eczema. Apparently, it's not uncommon in babies. That's what caused the inflammation, rashes, and flakiness." She pulled her hair back from her neck to show them the trace of eczema left on her skin. "I still get it from time to time, but it's very treatable. Not life threatening. The yellowed skin was jaundice, which is also rather common and easily treatable."

Their eyes were wide. "We didn't know."

Roshni leaned forward in her chair. "You were fine? Your skin is fine?"

Monica nodded. "The Sisters took me to Saint Andrews, and the doctors applied some topical ointments, and it took a few months of care, but then I was okay. As an adult, I learned it is triggered by stress, so I have to manage that, but it's a treatable condition. Unpleasant to look at and very uncomfortable to live with, but it is not life-threatening."

She studied their faces, looking for anything that would show that they already knew this but there was nothing. Their surprise seemed genuine. She could see that they had limited resources and if a Brahmin in their Tamil community had said their baby was going to die, then they had no reason not to trust that. She couldn't picture who she'd have been if she'd been raised with them. She questioned everything and her thirst for knowledge was limitless, but was that because of her genetics or because of the way the Sisters raised her? She'd never know. She couldn't fault the Paraiyars for not focusing on education. Survival was their primary motivator and anything else would have seemed superfluous when meeting basic needs took up every ounce of their energy. She could also see on their faces that they wouldn't have had the ability to offer her any treatments like the Sisters were able to do in conjunction with Saint Andrews, so whether it was life-threatening or not, she had still needed the help the Sisters could provide that her parents could not.

"We are so sorry." Haishan hung his head. "We didn't know."

"It's okay," Monica said. "I don't regret my life. It was different from a lot of people's, but it was also the same as many other little girls who were abandoned at the Gate. The Sisters took good care of us and taught us as many skills as they could. I was one of the lucky ones who built a life outside those walls, and I'll always be grateful to them for that."

The feeling she had long carried of being abandoned by her birth parents was starting to leave her body and was being replaced with the feeling of being found by Sister Francis, Esther, Victoria, Qi, and all the others who had shared the Home for Abandoned Babies with her at the Town Convent. Her biological parents felt they'd made a mistake, but they had actually set her free from the shackles that would have bound her to them.

"You were cared for?" Roshni asked.

She couldn't stop the wide smile that spread across her face. "Very much so."

Hurt flickered across their faces and Monica wondered if it was because they were disappointed that their child loved someone else more than them. They had no right to expect anything different.

"I saw her," Roshni said. "That day, I hid in the shadows to make sure someone came to collect you. I will never forget her face."

Monica sat straighter at hearing this. "She told me she called out for the mother, hoping she was nearby."

Roshni nodded. "She did. Leaving one's child is not an easy decision. When I left you at that gate, I thought it was the best thing for you, so I had to let you go."

Monica considered her words and the small glimpses into the love this woman once had for her.

"Could we meet her?" Roshni asked.

Monica was surprised, but then realized she should have expected that request. She'd have wanted the same, but she wasn't sure how she felt about sharing the woman who had raised with her with the woman who had chosen not to.

Monica reached into her purse and pulled out the tiny woven necklace. She'd removed it from her wrist after her earlier encounter at their home. She was protected by much more than a woven chain now.

"Did you make this?"

Roshni nodded. "To keep you safe as you moved into the next life."

Monica ran her thumb over the soft threads. "Maybe it helped me in this one instead." Turning back to Roshni, she said, "Is embroidery something you are good at?"

Roshni shrugged. "I'm a cook. That is what I do best. They say I make the best samosas in Singapore but who can really know that."

"I've never been much of a cook, but I've always been good with a needle. It was something the Sisters focused on when I was growing up—embroidery, needlework, sewing. I still take comfort in the simplicity of a perfect stitch."

Roshni looked like she was unsure what to say and sat awkwardly. There were so many things that Monica and her biological parents would not be able to connect on. She wasn't sure if they'd find any common ground, but at least now she knew the truth about how she'd come into the world. The sting of feeling like she'd been chosen for abandonment among the other children was beginning to dull. In their own way, these two people had been trying to save her. And they did. Not in the way they'd thought, but she'd been saved nonetheless.

"I can see if Sister Francis is up for guests," Monica said. "She has Alzheimer's so I don't know if it will be a good idea."

Roshni looked at her husband and they nodded.

Haishan cleared his throat and said, "I hope we can continue to get to know you as well. You should know your brother and sisters and their spouses. There are four grandkids too."

She didn't know what kind of relationship she could have with them, but that wasn't something she needed to decide today. She could take things one step at a time, and that started by introducing the Paraiyars to her family.

36

It was not lost on Monica that her biological parents had entered her world as Sister Francis was making her way out of it. That couldn't be a coincidence. There was something divine about this timing. She didn't think Roshni and Haishan could ever fulfill the role that Sister Francis had played in her life, but she didn't need them for that.

Victoria, Esther, and Qi poked their heads out with curiosity as Monica, Roshni, and Haishan made their way to Sister Francis's room after Sister Catherine had confirmed that it was okay. Sister Catherine stood as they entered.

"Your visitors are here," Sister Catherine said near Sister Francis's ear and her eyes fluttered open and began scanning the room.

Monica traded places with Sister Catherine, so she could hold Sister Francis's hand. "I brought some people who wanted to meet you."

Monica looked at Roshni and Haishan who took tentative steps closer to the old woman.

"We are Rachana—excuse me, Monica's—parents," Haishan said.

"She has told us how well you looked after her and we wanted to say thank you," Roshni said softly. "Leaving her was one of the hardest things I've ever faced."

"Who is Monica?" Sister Francis asked, looking between all of them.

Haishan and Roshni shifted uncomfortably, and turned to Monica and Sister Catherine for help. Monica wasn't as hurt as she'd been before. She was just grateful that she'd already had the one conversation with Sister Francis that she really needed to have.

Sister Catherine smiled apologetically at them. Turning to Sister Francis, she said, "You remember Monica, right? She's just next to you. You took care of her at the Town Convent."

Sister Francis gave her a blank stare. "There were so many babies there. We couldn't help them all."

"Yes, but you were able to help this one and her parents want to thank you." Sister Catherine motioned for Roshni to speak.

"We didn't know," Roshni said softly. "We didn't know her medical condition wasn't serious. If we had, we would never . . ."

Sister Francis said, "God always has a plan. All of our journeys are preordained." She smiled at Monica, although it wasn't clear if she recognized her or was simply stating platitudes. "Even yours, my child."

Roshni looked hesitant. Although these two women did not believe in the same God, they believed in whatever being had watched over Monica from the time of her birth until now, and both women were aligned in wanting what was best for her.

"You gave her a life that we could not have," Roshni said.

Sister Francis looked between Monica and the Paraiyars, seeming to be both confused and understanding of what was going on around her. Monica put the woven necklace in her palm. Sister Francis took it and closed her eyes, seeming to rifle through her memories. When she opened them, they had a sharpness and Monica could feel the shift in the room.

"You're her parents?" She looked from the Paraiyars to Monica.

They nodded.

Sister Francis clutched Monica's hand in her own as if she were trying to hold on to this moment.

"We are very sorry for having left her," Haishan said.

Sister Francis looked confused. "Please forgive yourselves for whatever mistakes you think you made at that time. If you were acting out of love, then there is no mistake. That love led her to being where she is today."

Haishan and Roshni bowed their heads as if receiving absolution from this woman could heal them.

"How can we thank you?" Roshni asked.

Sister Francis said, "I am happy to have been of service, but I can't look after her anymore. And I know she will take care of herself. She always has. But remember that she stopped being your child the day I found her at the Gate, so you cannot expect her to be that now. But trust that you'll find what you need in each other." She met Monica's gaze. "And that means you too, my child. You are brilliant, but you are stubborn. I encourage you to find a way to be as open with your heart as you are with your mind. That is the only way to let the light in."

Tears pricked Monica's eyes. Even in her final days, Sister Francis was trying to take care of her. The way a mother would. The way a mother *should*. Monica knew better than anyone that not everyone was blessed with that kind of parent. But she'd been blessed in so many other ways.

Haishan and Roshni thanked her again and left the room. Alone, Monica turned back to Sister Francis.

"I know you hate me thinking of you as my mother, but you were the closest thing I had."

"We don't hate, Monica."

Monica laughed as a tear slid down her face. "Dislike."

"I don't want to leave this world without at least having taught you not to use that word."

"I'm sorry I missed so many moments we could have had like this."

"Child, you were off building a life for yourself. There's nowhere else I'd rather you have been. You will find your place in this world. I've never had any doubt. I know you think the company you had was your greatest achievement, but you are just getting started. You are destined to help many, and you'll find your path."

"What will I ever do without you?"

Sister Francis gave her arm a weak pat. "You'll take care of Victoria, Esther, and Qi. You four are the last of the Gate of Hope girls and you are each other's family. They need you more than I do."

Monica nodded, knowing she'd do everything she could to fulfill that promise. She sat holding Sister Francis's hand while she closed her eyes. Monica watched her rest and enjoyed the silence around her for the first time in her life. She knew that would likely be the last lucid conversation they would ever have and she wanted to stretch out those moments for as long as she could.

She was in her room, arranging photos Victoria had printed of the four of them, and basking in the feeling of knowing she didn't have to hide parts of her life anymore. Oliver's name flashed across her screen. They hadn't talked since their heart-to-heart on her stoop. She thought they both needed time to digest what had happened.

"Divya promised I could deliver the news to you," he said.

"What news? Is everything okay?"

"Being a Global Changemaker has really increased business. I told you that would happen, right?"

"Sure," Monica said, uncertain of where this was going.

"After the merger with Propelle fell through, Amala got another offer and it just closed today."

Panic began to course through her. "Are Divya and the team okay?"

"I reckon they'll be fine."

"How do you know? New owners always want to put their people in the top positions to have more control. I should call her. I had no idea."

"The new owner is Dalton Holdings Limited."

She let the words sink in while he paused for effect.

"Your dad's company?"

"I told him it was a good investment. Not that he'd take my word for it. He had his team run the numbers and then concluded that I was, indeed, correct. Pity he can't really see how often that is true, but here we are."

"What about Leonard and the investors?"

"Those old chaps are happily counting their money in their lairs. It's just Divya and the Amala team that remains . . . and you, if you'd like to come back."

"What?" Monica wasn't sure she'd heard him correctly.

"Amala has been one hundred percent you since you came up with the idea in B-school. I told my dad your story and he rather saw it as an asset. He said anyone willing to make up an entire fake life to get ahead is exactly the kind of person he'd want leading any company."

Monica swallowed hard. She knew that was meant to be a

compliment because in corporate circles, it was. But the description didn't sit right with her anymore. That was something that would have applied to Ami, but now she was Monica again. The girl who had grown up in a convent and had learned to always mind her manners and to, above all else, be of service to others.

"What do you say?" Oliver asked. "It wasn't fair what happened to you. Even if what you did wasn't entirely right, you also weren't wrong about a lot of things. This is a chance to set things straight again. And we'd be able to get you another visa to get back to the US where you belong. Even managed to make sure we secured the fancy house in Venice as part of the portfolio if the CEO wants to resume her rightful place there. I hear it has a fantastic herb garden."

Was the US where she belonged? That fancy house in the Venice Canals? Sipping imported wine on the rooftop while staring at the Pacific Ocean? Working the daily grind with Divya and Oliver? She wasn't sure anymore. It felt like a lifetime ago even though so little time had passed. She was proud of Amala, and had done a lot with it, but she thought of Sister Francis's words and began to think that maybe she was destined for something new. Something where she could recalibrate who she was and what her values were and then, finally, be herself with all the parts she now knew of her identity. And while she understood that Oliver was looking out for her and giving her what he thought she wanted, it was also her duty to look out for Divya. Monica coming back would not be fair to her. Divya had paid her dues and bided her time and she deserved the chance to lead the company without Monica swooping in and taking it away from her.

"Thanks, Oli. Really. I know what you're doing and I appreciate it. But I think it's better if I stay in Singapore. There are some people here that I need to take care of and it's best for me to do that from here. I have a lot of things to sort out, and I'd like to do something that focuses more on meaning than money."

"Sounds like you've gone soft on me." He chuckled, before sounding serious again. "If you're sure. LA won't be the same without you."

She could hear the disappointment in his voice. "I am. And somehow, I think you'll do just fine over there without me. I hear a Global Changemaker's work is never done."

They both laughed.

Monica and Oliver promised to keep in touch despite the distance. Time would tell if either of them had meant what they said. They were connected to each other through a life that no longer felt like hers, and the only thing she was certain of was that she wanted to be moving forward with integrity. *Simple in virtue, steadfast in duty.* She wanted to return to those values. Not because she was an orphan whom they were thrust upon. But because they were who she was at her core. Whether she had money or not, she was still a CHIJ girl and that was something she could be proud of.

EPILOGUE

Sister Francis passed quietly in her sleep one night a couple months later. None of them said it, but it was almost as if she'd been holding on to find out what happened to Monica, and seeing her having returned to the IJ House safe and sound was the final thing she needed to move on. After that, Monica doubled down on her efforts to be there for Victoria, Qi, and Esther, just like she'd promised Sister Francis. She knew that whatever business venture she started next, she wanted them to be a part of it. They weren't sisters by blood, but they were a family bonded by shared experience. And that mattered more than anything else. They knew the real her and she knew the real them. She had a big idea to share with them, but before they embarked on this next chapter, she wanted them to experience something together that none of them could have even dreamed of as little girls. It had taken some work to get them passports as none had ever needed one before, but they were excited for their first plane trips.

She wasn't sure if the overstimulation of Changi would be too much for Esther since she'd never been in the chaos of an airport or set foot on a plane, but Esther seemed enamored rather than overwhelmed by the newness around her. It was as if she'd been a bird in a cage and was finally being set free. Monica wondered how high she could soar if she were given a chance.

There was nothing more rewarding than seeing their faces light up as they saw the small islands made of white sand dotted along the pristine turquoise and emerald waters of the Maldives. It was a trip that she had thought about so often in the past, but in her previous dreams, she'd always gone alone. The resort was completely outside of their grasp but Monica could think of no better way to use part of her savings. Unless she managed to strike it big somehow, this was her last luxury trip as well, and she could think of no one better to spend it with. They needed to grieve the passing of Sister Francis, and she was ready to talk to them about starting a new beginning.

The Pullman Maldives had placed them in two villas next to each other on the sunset side of the resort. The thatched roof looked like the embroidered piece she'd begun in LA and finally completed, and she smiled at the sight. It was always nice when imagination and reality came together as one. They marveled at the spacious villas and outdoor bathrooms. She roomed with Esther and watched her peer over the edge of their private deck at the ladder leading down to the clear sea below and pointing that she wanted to go into it. Monica went down first and waited at the bottom to make sure Esther also descended safely. The water felt cool swirling around her lower body and she could see the coral and fish swimming around her. Experiencing it was so much better than having seen it on Ami's blurry water camera photos all those years ago. Monica slipped on her goggles and ducked beneath the surface to take it all in. The world was so wondrous and it was hard to believe that places like this existed.

Esther timidly stepped into the water and then splashed

around with joy. The two of them walked carefully, hand in hand, among the sharp coral as they made their way to meet Victoria and Qi, who had also stepped down from their villa. She might not be able to have a place like this be an annual trip for her like the Shahs, but she was grateful to have been granted this once in a lifetime experience with the people who were most dear to her.

Later that evening after they'd showered and indulged in a decadent meal, the four of them were gathered on the deck of her villa.

Monica swept her arm toward the endless expanse of ocean before them. "I wanted to bring you here because I thought we could use a little magic in our lives."

They nodded eagerly, sipping on their mocktails while Monica held a glass of chilled Chablis.

"I am so grateful to be back in Singapore with you all. Not as the kids we were when we were growing up on Victoria Street, but as the women we became."

"We're so happy too," Victoria said. "We missed you."

"I think one way we could continue to help each other is to start a business together. We're the last of the Gate of Hope girls, and I want to make sure that we are remembered. One of the things we all learned and could do together is our sewing and embroidery."

They looked at her quizzically.

"Through my old business, I learned a lot about what wealthy people value and how to sell and market to them. I thought we could use the embroidery that we all know and, at least *most* of us, love doing." She cast a glance at Qi who looked sheepish. "I think if we made beautiful linens that are hand stitched, then I could find a market for them."

"You mean like the project you did to pass secondary school?" Victoria asked.

Monica thought of her sewing final exam, which the girls had framed for her and it now hung in the hallway at the IJ House, proudly on display.

"I was thinking more like the kitchen towels Esther did. Functional pieces that are still beautiful, but also have a rich story about how they are made. We could make decorative pillows, towels, and other household items that people would want to put on display."

Qi and Esther looked to Victoria. It was clear she had become their leader after Monica left and they'd take their cues from her.

"You think we can sell those?" Victoria asked. "Why would anyone buy from us?"

"I'm sure we could. If there's one thing I've learned, it's that a good product is nice, but branding and marketing are everything. That is an area that I excel in. And I know how good the products would be because no one does a French knot or satin stitch better than an IJ girl."

They began to nod and Monica could sense their enthusiasm. In this new venture, instead of hiding her past, she'd shine a spotlight on it. She'd highlight the abandoned girls and prove that they could be something more than maids or wives. She'd show that they were all worthy and deserving of a better life if they worked hard to get it. She was energized at the thought of finding more orphans who had perhaps fallen on hard times and who might want to join the business. In a venture like this, there was room for all of them.

Esther glanced at them before shyly pointing to herself and then looking away.

Monica placed her hand on Esther's forearm. "Of course you will be involved. No one does a feather stitch better than you. Your tea towels are what sparked this idea."

Esther beamed at the praise and Monica knew she was finally

on the right path. It was work that would make a difference. The business school side of her couldn't stop herself from fantasizing about it becoming another glorious empire like Amala had, but even if it didn't, she knew they only needed enough for the four of them to be comfortable and live a good and honest life. She no longer needed more for the sake of more, and was choosing to surround herself with people whose values aligned with hers.

She turned toward the setting sun, a fiery red orb that bathed the wispy clouds in vibrant oranges, reds, and purples as it sank beneath the horizon. She felt a warm breeze kiss her skin, now healthy and fully cleared of any blemishes, and felt that Sister Francis was there with them.

She closed her eyes and whispered into the wind, "I'm sorry it took me so long to come back home and fulfill my promise to use my education to benefit CHIJ. But I'm here now, and I'll never stray from that mission again."

Family was something that was different for everyone and changed based on circumstances. These three women were the family she was choosing. Today, and forever. The people she would support and who would support her no matter what life threw at them. She wanted to use her education to build something that would benefit them as much as herself, because that was what truly defined family. If their business did scale into something bigger, they could take the extra money and donate it to other children in need around the world so they could get the helping hand and resources that the four of them had gotten from the CHIJ Sisters. She wanted to prove that just because a girl had been abandoned, it didn't mean she had to carry that weight with her forever. She could find purpose, and through that, she could find herself.

★ ★ ★ ★ ★

AUTHOR'S NOTE

I will never forget the first time I stood at the Gate of Hope and read the placard on Victoria Street about the baby girls who had been left there throughout Singapore's history. I immediately felt chills. I couldn't stop thinking about the thousands of babies who had been abandoned simply because they were girls, and before I learned anything more about the history of this very real and very remarkable place, I knew I wanted to tell the story of a baby girl who was abandoned at the Gate of Hope. I felt it like a flash that I wanted this woman to become a successful entrepreneur who had lied about her background in order to get the opportunities that are often limited to certain classes. I knew she would be nominated for a prestigious award, which would risk the shadows of her past being forced into the light, threatening everything she had built. That premise came to me fully formed as I stood at the Gate of Hope. I've heard of this happening to other writers, but it was the first time that I had the "bolt of lightning" experience where an idea came to me so suddenly and demanded to be written.

AUTHOR'S NOTE

That night, I was in my hotel room googling everything I could about the Gate of Hope and the baby girls who had been raised there, and I was surprised by a few things. First, how little information there was about this part of history that seemed integral to Singapore. Second, that it didn't appear that anyone had written a novel yet with this iconic place at its core. And third, that the juxtaposition of what CHIJMES now was (an entertainment venue with trendy restaurants and bars) compared to its rich history wasn't being discussed more. I could not get over the fact that this religious institution that had been at the center of so much of Singapore's history was barely present and that so many people would go there for a meal and never know the history of the land on which they sat.

By the time the sun rose, I knew I had to tell this story, and that meant I would need to do a lot of research to ensure that I did justice to the place that had sparked my idea. I did not take that task lightly because the Convent of the Holy Infant Jesus is a religious order focused on the education of young girls that was founded in 1854 and exists to this day throughout the world. Its mission was and remains what I have described in my novel.

In many ways, this feels like my most ambitious novel thus far, because I am delving into a very real and iconic part of a country's past and using it to tell a story that might be unexpected. CHIJ and what is now CHIJMES are real places with storied histories, and it was important to me to honor that foundation as I told Monica's story. As a baby abandoned at the Gate of Hope, Monica's upbringing was rooted in Catholicism, so in addition to learning about the historical details of CHIJ and Singapore, I had to research a religious order that is not my own. While I focused intently on learning the actual historical details—my lawyer side has a strong need for accuracy—I must note that I made some significant changes in order to suit my narrative.

The first and most notable is that the CHIJ schools and con-

AUTHOR'S NOTE

vent were relocated from Victoria Street in 1982, which is much earlier than I described in the book. The Victoria Street location then underwent extensive refurbishment before it opened as the event and entertainment space known as CHIJMES in 1996. It became a National Monument of Singapore in 1990, so that parts like the Gate of Hope, Caldwell House, and CHIJ Chapel retained their historic structures when it reopened with its modern purpose. For my story, I kept CHIJ open until 1995, so that Monica could spend all her schooling years at the iconic Town Convent. If you are ever in Singapore, I highly suggest you take a moment to visit the original site on Victoria Street and then of course have a stellar meal at one of the CHIJMES restaurants.

The second is that while CHIJ and the IJ Sisters have an unparalleled history of rescuing baby girls, by the 1960s, the social climate in Singapore had changed and babies were no longer being left at the Gate of Hope, so babies like Monica, Victoria, Esther, and Qi would not have been abandoned during the years in which they were in my story. But the stories of my characters were inspired by baby girls who had been abandoned at the Gate during earlier time periods. There are four orphans who were originally abandoned at the Gate of Hope who do continue to reside at the IJ House, but they are much older than the characters in my book, and I did not interview or meet with any of them, so if any similarities exist between those four women and my characters, they are purely coincidence.

Third, while I would love to say that Monica's story is inspired by an actual orphan from CHIJ who defied the odds and rose to ranks beyond what was expected, in my research, I could not find evidence that any such orphan stories existed, so Monica's story is a pure work of fiction.

Any good fictional story is grounded in facts, and there were some non-fiction books that really shaped my understanding of

AUTHOR'S NOTE

the history and life of the Sisters, students, and orphans at CHIJ. This novel would not have been possible without the fastidious research contained in *Convent of the Holy Infant Jesus: 150 Years in Singapore* by Elaine Meyers (2004), *The Site of the Convent of the Holy Infant Jesus in Singapore: Entwined Histories of a Colonial Convent and a Nation, 1854–2015* by Sandra Hudd (2016), and *135 Years of CHIJ in Singapore: 1854–1989* by the National Library Board of Singapore (1990). I would recommend these books as a starting place if you would like to know more about the history. In addition, through Singapore's National Archives, I was delighted to find hours upon hours of audio interviews with IJ Sisters who had been at the Town Convent, and these interviews were invaluable for learning the small details about CHIJ and orphan life that enabled me to enrich the characters and story.

I also had the privilege of going to the current IJ School in Toa Payoh and meeting with the principal, Rachel Lee, as well as one of the longstanding teachers, Shu Quo Mathews. Mrs. Mathews was a teacher at the Victoria Street location who then made the transition to Toa Payoh and provided invaluable insights into the world I was building for this story. She took time out of her schedule to tour the historic sites at Victoria Street with me, and this novel is richer because of her dedication to helping me have as much information as possible. While I have done my best to maintain accuracy about CHIJ, its Sisters, and the orphans (with the exceptions noted above), any errors regarding CHIJ or Singaporean history within these pages are entirely my own.

I hope this novel inspires readers to learn more about the small but mighty nation of Singapore and its rich and fascinating history.

ACKNOWLEDGMENTS

This novel is especially close to my heart, because it made me feel like I had truly achieved my writer dreams. For so long I had wanted to be a full-time writer who traveled the world telling stories, and with this novel, I took a moment to appreciate that after so many years of hard work, this was finally my reality. The idea for *Saving Face* came to me in that lightning moment that I've heard other authors speak of but had never experienced myself. Once the story took hold of me, I began to research everything that I could about CHIJ and its history, including a research trip to Singapore that involved several interviews and during which the story really started to take shape. It was when I was in Singapore, coming back to my apartment after a long day of interviews and location research, that I looked in the mirror and realized I finally had the career I had always dreamed of.

First and foremost, I owe a huge thank-you to the IJ School in Singapore, headed by Rachel Lee, for welcoming me and answering my questions. I especially owe a huge debt of gratitude

ACKNOWLEDGMENTS

to Shu Quo Mathews, who took time in explaining so much of the school's history to me both at the Toa Payoh campus as well as the former Victoria Street location. Without your time and knowledge, this book would not have been possible.

I also had the pleasure of coming across Singaporean tour guide Michelle Chen, who went out of her way to help me discover the sights and locations in Singapore that I had planned for my story. Sometimes the fates are aligned, and as fortune would have it, her mother, Cecilia Lau, was a student at CHIJ on Victoria Street. I cannot thank Cecilia and Michelle enough for opening their home and hearts to me as I embarked on this journey. Cecilia was kind enough to share her sewing final examination with me (she still has it framed), and it inspired the one that Monica has kept with her all these years.

In addition, I was able to tour and view the iconic Raffles Hotel, where Monica stays, including the suite in which she would be able to look upon the current CHIJMES complex, and I have Jia Yi to thank for that opportunity.

This novel pushed me to my limits and beyond from an editorial standpoint. Jennifer Lambert of HarperCollins Canada, thank you for believing that I could rise to a higher level and for making sure I got there. You are a visionary and a trouper. I was fortunate to have begun the editorial journey with Nicole Luongo at Park Row Books, who then passed the baton to Annie Chagnot to bring the final draft home, and I thank you both for the different insights and values you brought to this story. I can safely say that this final version is unrecognizable from that first draft, but in the best way possible. Without these three talented women, the story would not be anywhere close to where it is today. This is the story I'm most proud of so far, the one in which I learned the most as a writer, and the one in which I truly feel as if I'm hitting my stride, and I could not have gotten here without each of you.

ACKNOWLEDGMENTS

Gordon Warnock of Fuse Literary, thank you for being my most zealous advocate and always supporting my work. We are just getting started, and I can't wait to see where we end up. A huge thanks to the rest of the team at Fuse as well for making sure there are always excellent social media posts with each milestone.

There are so many people that go into turning a story into a book, and I am grateful to each of these talented people: Iris Tupholme, Cory Beatty, Lauren Morocco, Peter Borcsok, Neil Wadhwa, Gareema Dhaliwal, SarahElizabeth Lee, Katie-Lynn Golakovich, Elvira Malikova, Amanda Roberts, Cari Elliott, Bonnie Lo, Tracy Wilson, and Judy Brioux.

Books are and will forever be judged by covers, and I'm so grateful to have had Elita Sidiropoulou, Marion Ben Lisa, Sean Kapitain, and Karen Becker design mine.

Soneela Nankani, you bring my stories to life, and I am grateful that you always say yes when the call comes in.

I also owe an immense debt of gratitude to Anisha Vinjamuri, CEO and mastermind behind the Ayurvedic-inspired skin care line Umm (@ummskincare). When I was researching Ayurvedic companies and asked if anyone had had experience with them, Anisha saw my post and responded with the most generous four words: How can I help? We scheduled a call and I learned her fascinating story. Not only did I get tons of great ideas for this novel, but I made a friendship that has gone so far beyond that. This generosity of spirit combined with a relentless passion for perseverance is what defines Anisha, and I hope that it also defines Monica. Monica's Amala is fictional, but fortunately, Anisha's Umm is real, and I would recommend these products to anyone looking for natural products that work and a female-led company that delivers what it promises.

Paulette Kennedy, there are not enough words to express my gratitude. You are chosen family, and this book and my life are better because of you. Nicole Chambers, you love and believe in me so much and are also chosen family. Your enthusiasm for my work often keeps me going.

Lyn Liao Butler, thank you for always offering another set of eyes and compassionate ears when I need to vent. Namrata Patel, one of these days we are going to meet in person, but until then, I'm glad to have you in my corner. And I'm glad that when both of you got the call that blurbs were needed, you were ready and willing.

Jill Girling, I didn't have you in my life for as long as I would have liked, but I'm grateful for the years we had together. You inspired me, gave me courage to become a full-time writer, and took me to places that I'd never have had the chance to experience without you. More than anything, you showed me what was possible when writing from a place of authenticity, and I hope I have done you proud. Rest in peace, my friend.

I am fortunate to have relatives in Singapore who took the time to share their personal stories with me so I could have a better understanding of what it is like to be Indian in Singapore and create more authentic characters. A huge thank-you to Ami Masi, Sanjay Masa, and Akash.

Prashanth and Tara Ranganathan, thanks for answering my questions about Tamil Nadu and Tamilians in Singapore. I can't wait to see where in the world we meet up next.

Mom, Dad, and Tejas, I would not be living my life doing what I love without your support, so thank you for always believing in me.

To my Street Team, you all have lifted me up in so many ways and I am humbled by your belief in me and my stories. The #BookTok and #Bookstagram communities do so much when it comes to highlighting authors, and I am grateful for all of the content you've created and shout-outs for my books over the years.

I am also immensely grateful to the teachers who have cho-

ACKNOWLEDGMENTS

sen to teach my work as part of your curriculum. That will always be the most "pinch me" part of my writer journey.

As we all know, none of this is possible without readers supporting the work that I do. I read every review and see every social media post I'm tagged in, so thank you for picking up my books and getting to know my characters. Once a book is published, I've always felt like it stops being mine and becomes yours, and I am humbled and honored by the space you give my words in your own lives. Channeling my best flight attendant voice, I know there are many choices when you read, and I thank you for choosing my book each time that you do.